Dear Jean -
I never would have seen York if it weren't for you.
Love you & miss you -
Abigail Drake
2-5-16

Traveller

by

Abigail Drake

Traveller

Contact Information: info@thewildrosepress.com

Cover Art by *Debbie Taylor*

The Wild Rose Press, Inc.
PO Box 708
Adams Basin, NY 14410-0708
Visit us at www.thewildrosepress.com

Publishing History
First Black Rose Edition, 2016
Print ISBN 978-1-5092-0569-1
Digital ISBN 978-1-5092-0570-7

Published in the United States of America

"What's wrong?"

Michael glared at me, threw some bills on the table and stomped out of the shop. Like an idiot, I grabbed my backpack and followed him.

He walked quickly through The Shambles, dodging pedestrians and umbrellas with ease. I wasn't quite as lucky. The rain poured down, filling the street with puddles. Michael wore combat boots and jeans. I had on a useless pair of flats and no jacket. It only took seconds for me to be soaked to the skin and miserable. In minutes, I looked like a little blonde drowned rat.

I'm pretty fast, even in slippery shoes, and I was motivated. I kept him in my sights until he reached a side street at the end of The Shambles that led down a narrow lane. I was only half a block away when he turned and looked at me, his eyes locking with mine, and disappeared.

He hadn't walked away. He hadn't moved. He'd been there one second, and gone the next. Running as fast as I could, I reached the spot where I'd last seen him and looked down the lane and on either side of the street. My ribbon flew out of my hair, blowing away in the wind as I slid on the wet cobblestones and nearly fell. I skidded to a halt, realizing I hadn't been fast enough. It was a dead end, and he was gone.

Praise for Abigail Drake

TRAVELLER won third place
in the 2014 Pennwriters Novel Beginnings Contest.

Dedication

This book is dedicated to my lovely husband,
who slays all the monsters for me
and makes everything possible.

Chapter One

"He was as nervous as a long tailed cat in a room full of rocking chairs."

~Grandma Sugar

If Michael Nightingale had been a dessert, he would have been decadent, dark, and sinful. Something high in calories and definitely unhealthy, but completely and utterly irresistible.

I met him because of a craving for pastry, but falling for him had nothing at all to do with carbohydrate addiction. I knew he would be bad for me, dangerous even, but I took one look at him and just couldn't help myself. Like a rich chocolate torte or a cake covered in ganache, I craved him.

Mrs. Betty Burke, the round little English lady who owned the teashop near our flat, tried to warn me about him. When I asked her about Michael, pretending to know him from one of my classes at the university, she saw right through me.

"You should stay away from him, Emerson," she said as she poured my tea.

"Why?"

"Because that one is trouble, and trouble is the last thing a nice lass like you needs."

I didn't listen. I never listened. That may have been part of my problem.

Mrs. Burke's shop sat on the edge of The Shambles, the historic district of York. She called everyone "pet" and "love" and made the best scones in town.

The cobblestone streets of The Shambles had spurned modernization and remained delightfully narrow and uneven, with buildings jutting out at odd angles and touristy shops sitting next to old pubs and fancy restaurants. My favorite place in a city filled with dozens of quaint little nooks and crannies

The first time Michael walked into her shop I'd been eating one of Mrs. Burke's famous scones and almost choked. His gaze had skimmed the tables, but if he saw me coughing up pastry, he certainly didn't acknowledge it. He sat down at a tiny table by the window and never even noticed my existence.

He seemed rough, with his bad attitude, piercings, and tattoos, and he should have frightened me, but he didn't. Something about him tugged at me, like he possessed the pull of a giant magnet I'd seen once at a science museum, and I was nothing but a big lump of scrap metal. I couldn't explain or understand it, but I felt an instant rush of attraction for him as soon as he walked through the door.

I should have stayed away from him, but I'd never been a person with a great deal of common sense. Grandma Sugar, the lady who'd helped raise me back home in Kentucky, often said I didn't have the good sense God gave a goose. She may have been right, because even weeks after my first Nightingale sighting, my interest had not abated even one tiny bit.

Just this morning, I'd woken up extra early to make sure I didn't miss him, rushed off to the tea shop, and parked myself at the table with the best vantage point for viewing his entrance. He'd be there in a few minutes, sit at a table next to the window, stick his nose in a book, and ignore me completely. That, sadly, was the highlight of my day.

I wore a pale brown cable knit sweater I'd bought at a store called Jumpers with a tweed mini-skirt and brown tights. It was raining, as usual, and my hair had frizzed out like crazy. The curse of a curly-headed girl. I'd pulled it back into a low ponytail and tied it with a wide, cream-colored ribbon, but there was only so much I could do.

Mrs. Burke watched as I sat still as a statue and stared at the doorway. "You've got it bad, don't you?"

"I sure do." No sense in trying to deny it.

Mrs. Burke sighed. "And you don't even know what he is."

I would have asked her what she meant, but at that moment, Michael Nightingale walked into the teashop, completely knocking every coherent thought right out of my brain. It had begun raining harder, and droplets of water rolled down the leather jacket that encased his broad shoulders. He wiped them away, and ran a hand over his shaved head before squeezing his long legs under his usual table. The table looked almost too small for his tall, muscular body. As the storm picked up in intensity, the sky grew dark and ominous. Because of the lights inside the shop, however, I could see his reflection in the window clear as day as he dug through his backpack and pulled out a giant textbook. It was almost as good as staring at him directly.

Mrs. Burke sighed again.

"I know," I said softly. "It's hopeless."

Mrs. Burke patted my arm. “Not so much hopeless as senseless. And stupid.”

“Thanks,” I said, frowning, but she’d already moved away.

I pulled out my dog-eared copy of Sun Tzu’s *The Art of War* and pretended to read as I snuck glances at Michael. The book had been a gift from my father, eminent professor and world-renowned expert on military strategy Dr. George Shaw, and it was my own personal bible. A former Junior Miss Kentucky might not seem to have much in common with a two-thousand-year-old military strategist, but I referred to Sun Tzu’s teachings almost every single day of my life. He was my hero, my teacher, and also my guide.

He’d been by my side as I dealt with the aftermath of my mother’s untimely death. He’d supported me as I became a serious student of the martial arts, in spite of my southern drawl and petite stature. And his practicality with a hint of ruthlessness was something I employed to win countless beauty pageants. Now I used it to find a way to get Michael Nightingale to notice me. I really was ten shades of pathetic at this point.

I knew for a fact boys like him weren’t interested in girls like me. He wore leather and a permanent scowl and exuded a sense of danger. I was as edgy as a cotton ball, and my looks definitely fell into the blonde, brown-eyed, wholesome, girl-next-door category. Michael existed in a different league altogether.

He shifted his book, allowing his entire face to reflect in the glass. I swallowed hard when I realized what was actually going on. He wasn’t staring at his book. At this very moment, he watched me just as stealthily and as intently as I watched him.

According to Sun Tzu, any good warrior knows to use whatever weapons are at hand, and my hair had sometimes been called my best feature. It hung well past my shoulders, and on days when I had a few extra hours to spare and decided to straighten it, it nearly hit my bottom. I'd never straightened it for pageants back in Kentucky, though. Southern judges loved nothing better than a contestant with a head full of curls.

I wondered if Michael liked my hair as much as those judges. I twirled a lock that had come loose from my ponytail around my finger to test the theory. He watched, mesmerized, and I realized Sun Tzu had been right yet again. Every opponent had a weak point, and Michael Nightingale seemed enthralled by a something so simple it almost made me laugh. A lock of hair. Who would have thought?

Finally, after weeks of being ignored, Michael Nightingale saw me. Really saw me. I took a deep breath and blew it out slowly. Now or never.

One of the most critical elements in planning a battle is timing. I could either make the first move with Michael Nightingale, or sit here every day watching him from a distance like a creeper.

I slammed my book shut, making the woman at the table next to me jump. "Sorry," I murmured, my cheeks turning pink.

Michael had stuck his nose back into his book, and ignored me once again. I walked over to the counter on the pretense of getting more sugar. On the way back, I paused at his table, and read the title of his book.

"Organic chemistry. That must be hard."

Worst pick up line ever. I should have listened to Mrs. Burke and just stayed at my table and drooled over

Michael from afar. I was about to run away when he looked up, knocking the breath right out of my lungs. From far away, his eyes looked blue, but up close they were the color of a clear turquoise sea.

Clear turquoise sea. I'd moved beyond pathetic into scary.

"Why are you talking to me?"

His voice was low and rough. I blinked at him. Several times. I'd been prepared for small talk, but his question sounded more like a confrontation.

My cheeks burned as he stared at me, waiting for me to speak. I opened and closed my mouth like a fish out of water. Not my most attractive look. Between the blinking and the gaping, Michael probably thought I had serious issues. He may have been right.

I squared my shoulders, realizing I'd almost waved the white flag of defeat before the battle had even begun. I gave myself an internal slap on the head, slid into the seat across from him, set down my cup of tea, and folded my hands on the table. He raised one eyebrow in surprise. He didn't realize I'd just made an important battle decision. The white flag had been buried in the dust. I was now on the attack.

"Your voice is deeper than I expected."

If I ever decided to make a list of the top ten most idiotic things I'd ever said, that would be on it. It might even rank in the top five. I considered giving up completely, leaving the teashop, and taking a vow of silence. There must be a group of nuns or monks somewhere eager to take in and rehabilitate a former Junior Miss Kentucky.

Michael put an abrupt end to my fantasy of running away to Tibet by speaking to me again. "Yours as well.

And you're American."

My eyes widened in surprise. "Yes, I am. You thought about how my voice might sound?"

He scowled. "I thought you must have one of those high Minnie Mouse voices. Squeaky and annoying."

"I'm *not* squeaky and annoying?" The idea made a huge grin spread across my face.

His lips twitched, almost like he was about to smile himself. "Your voice isn't, at least."

"Well, someone once told me I had a Jack Daniel's voice, smooth and rich like a good Kentucky bourbon, but Grandma Sugar insists it's just deep and husky due to overuse."

Michael looked completely perplexed. "Who are you and what do you want from me?"

I took a deep breath. It probably wouldn't be a good start to tell him he occupied my every waking thought and most of my dreams, too. I decided to go with a more conventional approach.

"You're here every morning, and I thought I'd say hello." I stuck out my hand. "Emerson Jane Shaw."

Michael stared at me like I'd just whipped off all of my clothing and danced on the table in my bra and undies. Not in a good way. In a "Jeepers, this gal is crazy, get me away from her" kind of way. It almost made me feel bad for him. Yes, he had been extremely rude, but it was also adorable how he nibbled on the small silver hoop that pierced his lower lip as he watched me. I'd seen him do it while studying, and had grown a bit obsessed with nibbling on that hoop myself.

He surprised me by reaching for my extended hand and holding it firmly. His hand, large, warm and rough, had cuts and bruises all over the knuckles. He had faint bruises on his face, too, and some small wounds still in the process of healing. He'd been in some kind of fight recently.

It didn't surprise me. He had the look of a warrior about him, the lean strength and watchful eyes of a predator, and he was lethal. Sun Tzu would have seen it, too. He would have recruited him without a moment's hesitation.

"Michael Nightingale." He stared at me with those hypnotic eyes as he continued to hold my hand, using it to pull me nearer to him.

"I know. Mrs. Burke told me." I couldn't focus on what I was saying while he touched me, not that I'd done such a great job up until now with my witty repartee.

He tilted his head to one side, studying me the way a lion studies a gazelle before he eats it. His face was only inches away from mine.

"Do you like to flirt with danger, Emerson Jane Shaw?"

"Not usually, but today I can make an exception."

The touch of his hand sent an electric current through my body that made my heart speed up and my brain slow down. He was intoxicating. I almost had to fan myself.

Abruptly, Michael let go of me and stood up, shoving his books into his backpack. I stood up, too.

"What's wrong?"

Michael glared at me, threw some bills on the table and stomped out of the shop. Like an idiot, I grabbed my backpack and followed him.

He walked quickly through The Shambles, dodging pedestrians and umbrellas with ease. I wasn't quite as lucky. The rain poured down, filling the street with puddles. Michael wore combat boots and jeans. I had on a useless pair of flats and no jacket. It only took seconds for me to be soaked to the skin and miserable. In minutes, I looked like a little blonde drowned rat.

I'm pretty fast, even in slippery shoes, and I was motivated. I kept him in my sights until he reached a side street at the end of The Shambles that led down a narrow lane. I was only half a block away when he turned and looked at me, his eyes locking with mine, and disappeared.

He hadn't walked away. He hadn't moved. He'd been there one second, and gone the next. Running as fast as I could, I reached the spot where I'd last seen him and looked down the lane and on either side of the street. My ribbon flew out of my hair, blowing away in the wind as I slid on the wet cobblestones and nearly fell. I skidded to a halt, realizing I hadn't been fast enough. It was a dead end, and he was gone.

Chapter Two

You better give your heart to Jesus because your butt is mine.

~Grandma Sugar

"What happened to you?" My roommate Lucinda greeted me at the door to our flat with a shocked expression.

"C…c..c..c..c..c..cold."

When she realized I couldn't answer because my teeth were chattering, she ran to the bathroom, got an armful of fluffy white towels, and began drying me off, berating me the entire time for my lack of common sense. I'd been hearing that a lot lately. I stood in the doorway, a cold, shivering mess, and let her take care of me.

"It's colder than a penguin's balls out there." I still shook from head to toe, but managed to get a sentence out.

"You poor thing." Lucinda bit her lip to keep from laughing. I was pretty ridiculous.

"It's colder than a well digger's butt in January."

Lucinda pursed her lips. "I think we've established it is cold. Now to get you warmed up. It's off to the bath for you, young lady."

She gave me a little push in the direction of the bathroom. I closed the door, peeled off my wet clothing, and hopped straight into the shower. My hair hung in heavy, frigid clumps around my face, making me shiver even more. I still hadn't gotten used to the cold in England. It went directly to a point somewhere deep inside my bones and made them ache.

My hands were white, and my fingertips almost blue. It took a long time standing under the steaming rain of the shower for the color to come back and for me to feel normal again. By the time I'd dried my hair and dressed in a warm sweater, yoga pants, and thick socks, Lucinda had made a pot of tea and sat on the couch waiting for me. She patted the spot next to her, wrapped me in a warm blanket, and shoved a steaming cup of tea into my hands.

"Something tells me this has to do with the mysterious Michael Nightingale."

Lucinda and I had met after I'd been assigned a place in the dorms with an American girl named Brooke, who'd despised me on sight. I tried awfully hard to be nice to her, but concluded Brooke either hated all people from Kentucky, or she was Satan's mistress. Either way, staying with her was not an option.

I'd showed up at Lucinda's apartment with a note from the student center tucked into the pocket of my cardigan and suitcases in each of my hands. Lucinda had met me at the door in a red satin robe and feathered mules. She'd given me an assessing look, from the top of my curly blonde head to the bottom of my loafer-clad feet.

"I plan to shag someone from each of the seven continents this year as part of my thesis."

Lucinda, pursuing her Master's degree in sexual

psychology, took a very hands-on approach to research. She'd watched me closely after giving her little speech, waiting for my reaction.

"Antarctica is going to be mighty tricky."

She smiled, and I knew we'd be friends. "You're right. Nothing but a bunch of bloody penguins."

We'd lived together more than a month, and Lucinda's shagging project hadn't inconvenienced me much at all. There had been the occasional stray, half naked male in the kitchen some mornings, but I'd solved that problem by going to the teashop for breakfast. Now I went there like clockwork just to catch a glimpse of Michael.

Lucinda patted my hand. "Poor little Em. This obsession of yours is worrisome. It could almost be a case study. *Wholesome, virginal foreign exchange student from the deep-south becomes fixated on a tattooed, pierced English bad boy.*" Lucinda got a sudden, hopeful gleam in her eye. I quashed it.

"No, you cannot use me as a case study." She stuck out her bottom lip in an adorable pout, a look that had worked on many a man. It had probably worked on quite a few women, too.

Lucinda was what Grandma Sugar called sex on two legs. She had flowing black hair, flashing dark eyes, and a voluptuous body usually encased in something tight and red. Today, it was a pair of pants that looked like they'd been painted on.

"Lucinda, those pants are so tight I can see Christmas," I said, trying to change the subject.

Lucinda's bright red lips curved into a smile. "Ho, ho, ho. Now back to Michael Nightingale..."

The doorbell rang, granting me a momentary

reprieve. I hoped for one of Lucinda's boyfriends who might distract her from her line of questioning, but no luck. It was Poppy, my best friend. I'd met her my first day at the University of York, and we'd been inseparable ever since.

"What happened?" Poppy kicked off her shoes, making her about six inches shorter without the giant black wedge heels.

"Michael Nightingale happened."

Lucinda sat back down on the couch, her legs curled up beneath her. Poppy took the chair opposite us. She wore an electric blue t-shirt with a Japanese manga character on it, and a mini-skirt. Her hair had been pulled into two very short pigtails on top of her head, which made her look a bit like a punk rock Shih Tzu puppy.

"Cute skirt," I said.

"Thanks. I made it last week." Poppy was a fashion design major and although her tastes ran eclectic from her dark spikey hair to her striped socks, she was adorable.

Lucinda handed her a cup of tea. "Our girl finally did it."

Poppy turned to me, her blue eyes huge. "You spoke with Michael?"

"I sort of ambushed him. He ran away. He was terrified."

"Bloody hell."

Poppy, from a little town on the North Sea coast called Red Car, grew up in a small bed and breakfast that catered mostly to truckers and mill workers. Their vocabulary had rubbed off on her.

"He ran away from you?" Lucinda raised a dark

eyebrow at me. "Because you are so intimidating?"

Poppy laughed until she snorted. I guess it did sound kind of funny. I was about as scary as a kitten, and Michael looked like a wanted felon.

"Did you catch him?" asked Poppy as soon as she managed to stop giggling.

He disappeared right in front of my eyes. In a second, Michael was gone.

I couldn't tell them the truth. They would think I was crazy, or at least crazier than usual.

"I chased him through The Shambles, in the rain, for miles."

Lucinda patted my hand. "Poor little Em."

I sighed. "It was pathetic."

"And a little creepy," chimed in Poppy.

"That, too."

I reached into my backpack and pulled out my journal. The leather was soft and smooth, a richly distressed brown. My father had given it to me as a going away present, hoping I'd record all my thoughts and memories about England. Instead, I wrote about Michael Nightingale. I *was* a little creepy.

"What did you say to him?" asked Poppy.

I cringed. "Something about organic chemistry being hard."

"Definite penile reference." Lucinda chuckled, and I glared at her.

"I've never seen a boy act like that before. We talked. He asked if I liked to flirt with danger. Then he had a dying duck fit and ran away."

"A dying duck fit?" Poppy asked.

"One step above a hissy fit is a duck fit. One step above that is a *dying* duck fit."

"So, in other words, he was upset?" Lucinda asked, taking a sip of her tea.

"And meaner than a wet pole cat."

"I'm sure he's just a little overwhelmed because you are so adorable," said Poppy. She sat next to me on the arm of the sofa, and gave me a squeeze.

"He ran away because I'm adorable?" I covered my face with my hands. "I can't believe I chased him."

"Can we do anything to help?" asked Poppy.

I shook my head, my words muffled by the pillow. "I just need to wallow a bit in my sorrow."

"Well, I guess you won't want to study with me at the library then," said Poppy.

I glanced out at the pouring rain, and shivered. I had no desire to go outside again right now.

Poppy kissed the top of my head, stepped back into her shoes, and grabbed her umbrella. "Stay home, stay warm, and stay away from Michael Nightingale. He isn't worth your time."

"Will do," I said with a sad little smile. "I couldn't catch him anyway."

Lucinda pulled on her coat. "I have to leave, too. Will you be okay?"

I nodded. "I'll be busy wallowing."

As soon as they left, I curled up in a chair by the window. The rain still fell heavily, and the sky remained gray and dark. I wrapped the blanket closer around my shoulders and watched the people hurrying up and down the street with their umbrellas.

Sun Tzu said "*He who is prudent and lies in wait for an enemy who is not, will be victorious.*" Sun Tzu would have slapped me upside the head right now. I wasn't being prudent. I was being the opposite of prudent.

I opened my journal and paused when I saw the faded photo of my mother I kept tucked between the pages. Her red hair curled softly over her shoulders, and her smile was hesitant, as if the photographer had caught her by surprise. I had her curls, but there the similarities ended.

She'd died when I was a toddler, and had done it in such a spectacular way that I'd grown up as the daughter of "that lady who done killed herself." We'd never known for sure exactly what happened, but it hung over me my whole life like a dark cloud.

Her death had nearly destroyed my father, and given him demons of his own to battle. In the dark days, right after she died, he could barely speak and spent hours alone in his study. I couldn't remember much of it, but when he emerged, he was a different man. I knew the truth. I saw it in his eyes. He couldn't forgive her for what she'd done. She was a deserter, plain and simple, and the worst kind of coward.

I didn't say a word about her to my father. I never mentioned her name or let him know I carried her picture around wherever I went. Sometimes, I'm sorry to say, I really missed her. I'd catch a whiff of perfume, or hear a song on the radio, and the faintest hint of a memory would form in my mind. It was usually gone before I could understand it completely, but those moments felt like a gift, a ghostly kiss from my dead mother. I longed to know more about her, something I doubted my proud, stern father ever realized.

This study abroad trip had been a rare chance to walk in my late mother's footsteps, although I pretended I was simply here because of the outstanding educational opportunities. My mother had been born here. She'd met my father here. When my father finally agreed to let me come on this trip, he had no idea I planned to travel around the countryside trying to find her family. He would have been furious. And if he'd known about my fascination with the tall, leather-clad, completely unsuitable Mr. Nightingale, he would have been on the next plane here from Bowling Green.

I yawned, curling up into a ball on the chair, my cheek resting on my hand. The rain had stopped, and the sun tried bravely to peek out from behind the clouds. I played the events of the morning over and over again in my head, talking with Michael, chasing him through the streets, the look on his face right before he disappeared. If obsessing about someone was the first sign of crazy, I should have been on high alert at this point.

And you don't even know what he is.

I'd almost forgotten Mrs. Burke's words in my excitement at actually conversing with him. I jumped out of my chair, pulled on my tennis shoes, and grabbed a jacket and an umbrella. There was no time to change into a skirt. I had to move quickly. Mrs. Burke knew something about Michael that I didn't, and I needed to find out what it was.

She was locking up her shop just as I barreled around the corner. "Back again, Emerson?" She looked at her watch. "I'm sorry, pet, we close at four."

"I wanted to ask you something. Do you have a minute?"

She smiled, tucking a bank bag under her arm. "I was about to go deposit this. Would you like to walk with me?"

"Are you sure you wouldn't mind?"

"Of course not, love. Now, what did you want to ask me?"

We linked arms and began strolling down the street. The rain had stopped, and everything felt clean and fresh. As much as I hated the English weather, there was beauty in it, too, and the soft sunshine after the rain felt like a kiss on my skin. I still missed the warmth of Kentucky, but not as much as before.

"It's about Michael Nightingale."

Mrs. Burke frowned. "I saw you run after him today. I told you he was trouble."

I cringed. I'd hoped no one else had witnessed that. "That was what I wanted to talk with you about. Why did you say that?"

Her face grew still. "You can tell just by looking at him, can't you?"

"There was something else. You told me I didn't know what he was."

Mrs. Burke sighed and straightened her glasses. She took a quick look around to make sure no one else was listening.

"He's a Traveller."

"A what?"

She leaned closer to me. "A Traveller. A gypsy. Good for nothing thieves and criminals."

"A gypsy?" I immediately began to imagine myself in a sexy off the shoulder blouse and a red skirt, dancing with Michael by a campfire.

Mrs. Burke shook her head, reading my expression at once. "Oh, no you don't. These gypsies aren't like the romantic notions you hear about in stories. They're hard, mean, and dangerous. The only reason I let that boy in my shop is because he hasn't been any trouble. Yet. But if I see him bothering you, lass…"

I shook my head, frowning. "I'm bothering *him*, Mrs. Burke."

Suddenly, a man pushed against her so hard she nearly fell. I steadied her, putting my hands on her shoulders. She looked down at her hands and gasped.

"He stole my bag, Emerson. He took my money."

The man ran up the street, but I knew I could catch him. I took off, dodging pedestrians.

"Wait, Emerson," Mrs. Burke called out. "He might be dangerous."

"Stop! Thief!" I shouted, pointing at the man. Several people stopped and looked, but no one did anything. I groaned in frustration. This was up to me.

Sun Tzu said "The supreme art of war is to subdue the enemy without fighting." I chose a slightly different path. The thief was not in the best of shape, and I wore tennis shoes and pants instead of my usual skirt and flats. Middle aged and pudgy, with greasy blond hair and bad skin, he proved much easier to catch than Michael Nightingale. I grabbed him by the collar of his stained Manchester United jersey and used his own momentum to yank him to the ground. He tried to get up, and I kicked him in the chest.

"*That* is for stealing money from nice old ladies."

A crowd began to form around us. Mrs. Burke scurried up as fast as her little legs could carry her. I stepped on the thief's hand and took her bag away from him. He called me a name that was not very nice, so I dug in my heel, making him squirm.

"*That* is for calling me names."

He lifted his head and tried to spit on me, so I did

what any respectable girl would have done. I kicked him in the face, right under the chin, knocking him unconscious.

A policeman showed up, and Mrs. Burke and the others told him what happened, somewhat embellishing certain details. The policeman had a wide, kind face.

"It's brave that you stepped up to help, Miss Shaw, but not very wise. This man could have been armed. Nothing is worth your life, or your safety."

After I apologized and said, "Yes, sir," a few times, he left to call for a squad car, and the thief began regaining consciousness. He let out a little whimper and made a move to get up. His chin had already turned purple, and he looked disoriented. I'd kicked him pretty hard.

I leaned over and spoke to him in a soft voice. "You make a move, mister, and I'm going to jerk your head bald. You hear me?"

The thief made the right decision and put his head back down on the pavement. I looked up to see a guy in the crowd staring at me. Beautiful, with dark hair that hung to his shoulders he possessed eyes so light brown they nearly looked golden. As soon as I glanced his way, a huge smile spread across his face, like we knew each other well and shared some kind of secret. It made me feel a little strange, but I smiled back in spite of myself. He joined me as I waited for the policeman to finish his report.

"Well done," he said, and his husky voice sent shivers up my spine.

I stared at him in surprise, realizing I felt attracted to him. Really attracted to him. Almost as much as I was to Michael Nightingale. I either had some kind of strange hormonal fluctuation going on, or I was especially drawn to English guys. This was not my normal behavior. Not by a long shot.

"I saw you run. You're really quite fast."

"Thanks." I caught a whiff of something odd, and figured it must be Mr. Manchester United and his filthy shirt. I gave him my best squinty-eye glare and poked him with my umbrella. He looked terrified, something the boy standing next to me noticed with a chuckle.

"I'm Leo, by the way."

He extended his hand and I took it, an electric tingle shooting up my spine again. "Emerson."

"It's a pleasure."

I stared down at our joined hands, still feeling a residual jolt. Something very strange was going on here.

"I've got to go. I need to check on my friend."

He let go of my hand, and stepped away, but his gaze remained locked on mine. "Until we meet again."

He turned and walked away, and I couldn't help but watch. He really was eye candy. I had more important things to worry about at the moment, though. I had a feeling this whole episode had shaken up poor Mrs. Burke more than it had me.

She'd just finished speaking with the policeman, and gave me a hug so tight I almost couldn't breathe. Tears swam in her eyes when I handed her thc bag of money.

"You're a heroine, Emerson Shaw."

I cringed, embarrassed. "It was nothing."

"You were so quick. How were you able to pull him to the ground like that? He must outweigh you by six stone."

I leaned forward to whisper in her ear, "When I did beauty pageants back home, my talent was mixed martial arts. He never saw it coming."

"Martial arts? At a beauty contest?"

"I can't sing worth a darn, trip over my own feet when I try to dance, and never had the patience to learn the piano. I had limited options, and really liked hitting people."

I looked up and thought I caught a glimpse of familiar broad shoulders encased in a leather jacket off in the distance. I craned my head, trying to see. I couldn't be certain, but somehow I knew it was Michael. As soon as he got near, I sensed it, like the very air changed with his presence. I felt it somewhere deep in my bones, the way I felt the English cold, and it hurt just as much.

Chapter Three

That girl couldn't find her bottom with both hands in her hip pockets.

~Grandma Sugar

I spent the next few weeks trying to find Michael Nightingale. He no longer came to Mrs. Burke's teashop, the big chicken, although I ran into Leo there quite a few times. I enjoyed our friendly banter, and the company of someone handsome, nice and obviously interested, but something held me back.

"We really should go out sometime," he said one morning as we sat sipping tea. He made good company; open, friendly, and uncomplicated. He was also extremely sexy, but I couldn't get Michael out of my mind.

"I can't. I'm sorry."

It wasn't fair to date Leo when I couldn't stop thinking about Michael, but I had to wonder if I'd waited too long to have sex. Maybe my virginal state was turning me into a lust crazed maniac or a psychopath. I didn't share these thoughts with Leo.

He turned his golden eye stare on me, making me feel like the only person in the whole wide world who mattered. It was extremely hot and a bit intoxicating.

"Do you have a *beau*, Emerson?"

"It's hard to explain."

Leo should have been the perfect boyfriend. He was my age, and he didn't run away from me. A huge plus these days. The fact that he looked like the cover model for an erotic novel didn't hurt either, but I couldn't do it.

Leo leaned forward in his seat, taking my hands in his. "Just think about it."

I did think about it. The problem was a certain tall, pierced and extremely antisocial person kept interrupting those thoughts. As soon as Leo left, I used my journal to vent.

I wish I could forget about Michael and go out with Leo, but I can't. It would be settling, and I am not a quitter.

My free time was spent searching in vain for Michael Nightingale. I walked through The Shambles every day, hoping to catch another glimpse of him, and also trying to convince myself he hadn't disappeared into thin air.

Once or twice, I thought I spied him, but each time he was gone before I could be certain. He'd basically disappeared off the face of the earth.

I came to the conclusion he had a girlfriend, a dark-haired gypsy with flashing eyes and big gold hoop earrings. She probably carried a knife strapped to her thigh and wouldn't hesitate to use it on the likes of me. I should have considered myself lucky.

I tromped home after another unsuccessful day hunting Michael Nightingale, and Lucinda greeted me in a red bra with curlers in her hair. She flew around the sitting room, tidying up and swearing a blue streak.

"Emerson. Thank God you're home. You need to leave."

I dropped my backpack with a *thunk* and sank into a chair. "Hello, Lucinda. How was your day? Mine was fine, thank you kindly."

Lucinda winced. "Sorry, love. Very bad of me. It's just…you won't believe this…"

"What happened?"

Lucinda knelt in front of me, her hands on my knees. Her boobs almost burst out of her push up bra, and she had a wild, frantic look in her eyes.

"I found Antarctica."

"No *way.*"

"He's actually Swedish, but he works there at a research station. He's only here for a few weeks. I finally did it, Em. My seventh continent."

We both squealed and bounced around the room. I was so happy for Lucinda it made me nearly forgot how depressed I was about Michael. Suddenly, a thought occurred to me. I stopped bouncing.

"Why do I have to leave?"

Lucinda took a deep breath. "He's…shy. I have to approach this one gently, and it may take some time. I thought I'd bring him here for dinner." She looked at her watch and started swearing again, pulling curlers out of her hair as she ran to her bedroom.

I looked around the kitchen. Lucinda was not a cook. "What are you going to feed him?"

Lucinda ran back into the kitchen, her eyes huge in her face. "Oh, bloody hell."

I giggled and took a peek in the fridge and in the cupboards. "How about pasta primavera? I bought a bunch of nice veggies this morning,"

Lucinda gave me a big kiss on the cheek. "You are a jewel. A lifesaver."

"And I can cook." I shooed her out of the kitchen and began preparing the meal. By the time Lucinda dressed in a very tiny black dress, her hair a mass of curls, I'd made the pasta and a simple salad, and thrown some brownies in the oven for dessert.

I shoveled down a bowl of pasta. As Lucinda put the finishing touches on the table, I slipped my journal into my backpack and got ready to leave. "I'll go to the library. Poppy will be there, and I need to study."

"Just a few hours, Em. That's all I ask."

I kissed her cheek. "No problem."

The library was only a couple of blocks away from our apartment. It was getting dark, but the streets were well lit, and lots of people still milled about.

I took a deep breath, enjoying the setting sun, the cool air, and the smell and feel of this place. My mother had been born in a town called Whitby on the North Sea coast, but she'd come to York for school. I wondered if she'd liked it here as much as I did.

She'd been an only child, like me, and her parents died long before I was born. I hoped to find cousins or someone who remembered her, but so far I'd come up with nothing. I was almost ready to give up, but didn't want to go home empty handed. I decided this weekend I would start looking again. Time to forget all about Michael Nightingale and focus on why I'd come here in the first place.

The library, a big stone building with leaded glass windows and high ceilings, felt like traveling back in time and studying in a castle. I walked around until I found Poppy, and then settled down to work. Poppy's boyfriend, Nigel soon joined us.

"Hello, gorgeous," he said, giving Poppy a kiss.

Tall, blond, and a horrible dresser, he was a physics major. They had nothing in common, but adored each other.

I sighed, and Poppy heard the sadness in it. "Are you thinking about Michael?"

"Who's Michael?" asked Nigel, and Poppy glared at him. "Oh, I remember now. Dark, brooding stranger. Sorry, Em."

"It's okay, Nigel. I don't expect you to follow my love life, especially when it exists only in my imagination."

Nigel frowned. "How is that possible? You are adorable."

Poppy kissed him and gave me a grin. "See why I love him so much?"

We told him all about the teashop and how Michael had run away. Nigel rubbed his chin. It was a bit stubbly, which just added to his charmingly disheveled appearance.

"I don't know, but he sounds like a real wanker," he said.

"A wanker." Poppy nodded in agreement.

"Or he might be afraid of something," said Nigel. "I know you don't seem terribly scary, but fear can be an irrational thing. Perhaps he had a traumatic episode with a curly-headed American beauty queen as a child. That could scar a person for life. It happened to me with clowns."

He winked at me, and I gave him a dirty look. "Bullocks," I said, just a little too loudly. We laughed so hard that a girl at a nearby table asked us to be quiet.

An hour later, Poppy yawned. "I have to go, Em." She was bleary eyed, her fingers smudged with ink from the drawings she'd been working on. Nigel got up and started shoving things into his bag.

I glanced at my watch, not wanting to catch Lucinda mid-coitus on the living room sofa. "I'll stay a bit longer."

They tried to protest, but I reassured them. I had my cell phone and was only a few blocks from home. As soon as they left, I pulled out my laptop and punched in *Travellers*. It wasn't the first time I'd researched the subject, but I couldn't seem to stop. I wanted answers. Immediately, piles of information popped onto the screen. I clicked on *The History of Irish Travellers* and began to read.

The origins of Travellers were very unclear, probably due to the fact they were a nomadic people and barely able to read and write. They had horrible attendance records in school, a high infant mortality rate, and a life span about twenty-five years shorter than average.

I pulled out my journal, jotted down notes, and then sat back in my chair. It sounded pretty bleak. Different sorts of Travellers went by different names. Gypsies, Pavees, Tinkers, Knackers, and derogatory ones like Pikey or Gypo. They operated on the fringes of society, shunned by respectable people. A cruel and harsh existence.

I thought about Michael, with his nose in an organic chemistry book, and swallowed hard. Most Travellers didn't get past the eighth grade, but he was studying at university. I remembered the look on his face as he watched me in the window and could finally describe his expression.

Longing. I wrote that down in my journal because

it felt important. *He looked at me with longing.*

Maybe this connected to what Nigel said, although his beauty queen idea seemed ludicrous. According to the article, Travellers kept to themselves. Mingling with non-Travellers was definitely frowned upon. Perhaps Michael couldn't date non-Travellers. Maybe it was taboo.

I rubbed my eyes and looked at my watch. It was almost midnight, and the library would close soon. Surely, Lucinda would be done by now. I stood up and stretched, looking out the window at a patch of sidewalk illuminated by a street lamp. It was very dark, and looked like it might rain again. I reached for my coat and saw him outside, walking with his head down and completely oblivious to the fact I watched him. Michael Nightingale.

Chapter Four

Well, butter my bum and call me a biscuit.
~Grandma Sugar

I threw on my coat and tossed my backpack over my shoulders. As I ran out of the library, I pulled up my hood. My hair made me easily recognizable, and I didn't want to advertise my identity at the moment.

Instead of my usual skirt, I wore yoga pants, allowing me to follow Michael more easily this time. Seeing his face in the glow of a streetlight made my silly old heart squeeze in my chest. I'd *missed* him.

Once again, he led me through The Shambles. Twice he answered his phone, and although his words were unclear, something in his voice sounded a whole lot like fear. Maybe Nigel was right about Michael being afraid of something, but at least this time it definitely wasn't me.

The Shambles looked very different after dark. There were still people about, but they seemed seedier and more dangerous, and the smell of beer and vomit permeated the air. I ignored catcalls from the occasional drunk, kept my head down, and focused only on Michael's back. I didn't want to lose him. Not again.

Soon we reached a part of York I'd never seen before, darker and poorer than the area where I lived. Garbage bins lined the streets, and lights were few and far between. I hung back as far as I dared. There weren't as many people here, making it harder to blend in. I couldn't risk being seen, or Michael would most certainly disappear again.

He turned down a dark alley, and I followed, sticking close to the buildings and moving slowly. Three young men stood in the middle of the alley, right under a streetlight, staring down at what looked like a body on the ground. I came as close as I dared and hid in a doorway.

"What happened?" Michael's voice sounded clipped, rough. He knelt down next to the object on the street. Definitely a body, and one wearing black high-top tennis shoes.

One of the boys standing next to him shifted nervously. They all had close-cropped hair like Michael, and similar taste in clothing. They looked like a motorcycle gang. I wondered if this was standard Traveller garb.

"Tad never goes out alone. He knows the rules, Mikey."

"Then what the hell happened?" Michael's voice was quiet, but filled with anger and sadness.

A noise from somewhere on the rooftops made Michael leap to his feet, his eyes scanning the buildings. The four of them turned in unison, backs to each other, protecting the body.

"Defensive positioning," I murmured to myself.

Being a military history professor, my father had introduced me to more than *The Art of War*. I'd been fed a steady diet of books like Mao Tse-tung's *On Guerilla Warfare* and General Carl von Clausewitz's *On War* my whole life. I loved *On War* so much I'd brought it to preschool for show and tell. My teacher had not been amused.

My father was a scholar, not a fighter, but because of him I knew about enough about soldiers to realize these boys weren't part of any motorcycle gang. They had military training.

Michael pulled something out of his jacket. It shone in the light of the streetlamp, a bright flash of silver.

"A *sai,*" I said under my breath, feeling a little jealous.

Oriental weapons were my passion, right after books and chocolate. The one Michael held in his hands was a thing of beauty. Shaped like a fork with one long middle blade, it was rather ineffective as an offensive weapon, but nearly perfect for defense. They were primarily used in pairs, but Michael only had one. His other hand was balled into a tight fist.

The other boys pulled out weapons, too. One held a short sword, a classic weapon dating back to Roman times. Another had a *katana*, recognizable because of its elegant curve and blood groove, the indentation on the sides of the blade that released suction and allowed the blade to slip out of the body easily. The third boy held a bearded axe, a Norse weapon designed for hacking, so powerful it could split a metal helmet in half. All combined, a pretty impressive show of weaponry for a street fight.

Something large and dark swooped down from one of the buildings. It stood a foot taller than Michael's six-foot frame, and as soon as its feet hit the ground, it lifted its face to the sky and roared. I sank deeper into the shadows. That thing wasn't human, and unlike any animal I'd ever seen. It stood almost like a man, but had several rows of teeth and cruel, yellow eyes. It smelled, too, like something left outside and rotting.

The creature had dark gray saggy skin that hung loose on its body. Long claws protruded from its front and back paws. It had a long snout and the pointy ears of a wolf, but I'd never seen a hairless wolf walking upright. And it was definitely a boy monster. Other than the obvious male appendage, it was a living, breathing gargoyle.

The beast moved toward the body. Michael blocked it very effectively with his *sai*, and then used his fist to slam the monster in the snout.

I stood watching in horrified silence as the four men fought the monster, never leaving their protective stance, working like a well-orchestrated unit. The monster seemed oblivious to their punches and the jabs of their weapons, only interested in the dead body on the ground. Wounds covered its body, gleaming with blood, but the creature didn't care. As it lunged once again, Michael, in a blur of flashing silver, shoved his *sai* deep into the beast's abdomen.

The beast clawed at him, howling, but Michael ignored the scratches on his arms and the blood dripping from his hands. With one sudden movement, he thrust his *sai* upward into the beast's chest cavity. The creature's entire body jerked in a giant spasm, and then fell limp into Michael's arms. He pulled out his *sai,* wiped it on his jeans, and shoved the carcass aside.

"That was for our Tad," he said, kicking it with his combat boots.

I stood there, trying to give my mind a chance to catch up, but it wasn't working. Michael had just performed a sort of angry evisceration on what looked like Wolfman Jack from the *Friday Night Frights* show I'd grown up watching on TV back home in Bowling Green. That show had scared the crap out of me on a weekly basis, but nothing had ever scared me quite as badly as what I'd just witnessed. I shook from head to toe.

I'd been playing with fire. Michael really was dangerous, and in ways I never expected. As soon as Michael and his friends left, I planned to run as fast as possible in the other direction and never seek him out again.

I heard a small, shuffling sound and smelled something putrid and rotting just before an iron-strong arm wrapped around my chest. One of those creatures had me, and held me so tightly I could barely breathe as it pulled me into the light of the streetlight. Michael and his friends turned with their weapons at the ready.

"Emerson," Michael whispered, his eyes full of fear. No doubt about what had scared him this time, and it wasn't clowns or beauty queens. I'd fallen into a whole heap of trouble, and knew it.

The creature pulled down my hood and pushed my hair out of the way. I heard a noise from deep in its chest that sounded suspiciously like a chuckle, and tried not to gag as it ran its nose up and down the side of my neck. Michael took a step forward and it squeezed me even harder, making me gasp.

"You want this, Traveller?" The monster's voice was a low, terrible hiss.

Michael nodded, swallowing hard.

"Throw down your weapon."

He tossed the *sai* to the ground, and his friends did

the same. The rattling of their weapons as they hit the damp cobblestone street pierced the quiet of the dark alley with a sharpness that made me flinch.

"Very good, Traveller. I will enjoy this."

The creature stuck out its tongue and licked my neck. His tongue had the same sandpapery texture as Grandma Sugar's old cat Miss Sally. I wanted to close my eyes and pretend Miss Sally licked my neck instead of some nasty wolf-monster-thing, but I couldn't. I was firmly trapped in this present nightmare situation.

A muscle worked in Michael's jaw. Apparently, this was a little hard for him to watch. I kept my eyes fixed on his, trying to find my center of calm and strength. I knew what to do, but needed the courage to act. I took a deep breath, let my body relax, and slumped in the creature's arms like an old rag doll.

This took the creature by surprise, exactly what I'd hoped for. A basic move from Self Defense 101, a class I'd taught at the senior center for Grandma Sugar and her friends, it proved very effective against both muggers and monsters, apparently.

As soon as my body went limp, the monster released his hold on me just enough that I could swing my head forward and back, slamming him right in the face. His head flew backwards from the impact, but he still gripped my arms, his claws digging into my skin. I kicked him in the knee with everything I had, happy to hear a cracking noise and a little yelp of pain. I swung around, preparing to shove my palm into his nose so hard it would smash right into his nasty little brain, but as soon as I saw him, I paused, frowning. He didn't have a nose. He had a snout. That hadn't been part of the equation.

I stopped the momentum of my attack and lost my advantage. The monster grinned, something knowing and evil in its glowing, yellow eyes. It reached over and yanked out a few strands of my hair with its clawed, hairy hands. Michael shouted, and the creature let out a howl, pushing me away so hard I stumbled and fell onto my bottom on the wet stones of the street. It limped away, and even with an injured knee it moved with the speed and agility of a monkey climbing a tree in the jungle as it scaled the building next to me and disappeared.

I stood up slowly, rubbing the spot where the beast had pulled out my hair and spitting mad. "Get back here. I'm not done with you yet."

"Quiet, Emerson."

Michael had been down the street from me, but, suddenly, he stood at my side, *sai* in hand, and shoved me against the building. He had his back to me, obviously trying to protect me. Reassuring, but I was too angry to appreciate the gesture at the moment.

"Get out of my way." I pushed against his back, but it felt like trying to move a brick wall.

"Be still, you wee idiot." Michael clenched his jaw. He was angry, which did nothing to improve my mood. I started pounding on his back, but he ignored me.

His friends appeared right next to us, and I stopped beating on Michael. I hadn't seen them approach, but at this point I wasn't exactly functioning at full capacity. They were breathing hard, but one of them managed to speak.

"He's gone, Mikey. She's safe."

Michael turned and pushed the hair out of my face. He stared deep into my eyes, his hand brushing my cheek. "Are you hurt?"

His voice, so gentle and kind, made me snap. Slapping his hand away, I shoved him hard in the chest and put my fists on my hips.

"I'm not okay. Did you see that thing? It *licked* my neck. Absolutely ten shades of nasty and y'all were about as useful as a screen door on a submarine."

When mad or scared, my southern came out, and I'd never been so mad or scared in my whole entire life. One hundred and ten pounds of frightened fury. I had to either spew some insults or sit down and cry, and I was not about to cry. Hugging my arms across my body, I willed myself to calm down, but it didn't work.

Michael approached me, more cautiously this time. "Are you a complete lunatic? You're lucky. Not many people can face a Moktar and live to tell the tale."

"Lucky? You call that lucky?"

Michael raised one arrogant eyebrow at me. "Yes, I do. He was on the hunt, and he was…aroused."

"Thank you. I noticed." I poked him in the chest, forcing him to back up. "That thing pulled my hair."

"Your *hair*?" Michael looked around at his friends, and had the audacity to grin. "She's mad. Completely bonkers."

"I don't know what happened tonight, and I sure as heck don't know what a Moktar is, *Traveller* Nightingale, but he's going to rue the day he ever tried to mess with me, and you'd better stay away from me, too."

I shoved Michael one more time and stomped away.

Chapter Five

If you don't stop your crying, I'll give you something to cry about.

~Grandma Sugar

Michael's heavy footfalls echoed on the street behind me before I'd even made it half a block, which didn't surprise me one bit. I'd known he'd come after me. I should have employed this strategy all along. Men liked the chase, whether they were after women, squirrels, or an ice cream truck.

"Emerson. Stop. Please."

The "please" got me. I stopped, but kept my back to him, my arms folded tightly across my chest. Now that the horrific ordeal had ended, I was dangerously close to crying. I squeezed my eyes shut tight, forcing myself to hold it together as I tried to forget the blood, the gore, the monster, and the dead boy on the ground.

"We need to talk."

"That's the biggest understatement of the whole dang year."

Michael didn't respond, so I turned around slowly. He stood a few feet behind me, his head down, looking at his hands as if trying to figure out what to say. I was about to start yelling at him again, but noticed his hands and arms were scraped and bleeding, and felt kind of guilty.

"Are you okay?"

He looked up at me in surprise. "You were just attacked by a Moktar, and you're asking if I'm okay?"

"I'm not the one bleeding." I reached for his hands and pulled them into the light to inspect them. "You've got some nasty scrapes here. You might want to have a doctor take a look at this one."

I ran my finger next to a long gash along the side of his wrist. If it had been an inch or so farther to the left, it might have hit a vein, and Michael could have been in real trouble.

"Why are you being kind to me?"

I gave him a level look. "You're hurt."

He raised one dark eyebrow. "A few minutes ago, you wanted to hurt me."

I pursed my lips. "A fairly typical reaction to a stressful situation. I'm calming down now."

He muttered, "That was fast," but I ignored him and went back to looking at his wounds. His leather jacket had zippers extending from his wrists up to his forearms, and I unzipped them to get a better look. It seemed like most of the damage had been done to his wrists and the backs of his hands.

"That thing didn't look like it spent a great deal of time on personal hygiene. Goodness only knows what could be on its paws…or claws…or whatever. Anyway, these could get infected." I turned his hands over to look at his palms, and checked his fingers one by one.

He watched me, his body very still. "It's fine. Nothing soap and water can't fix." I looked up at him with a scowl. He wasn't taking this seriously enough.

"Soap, water, a little disinfectant, and a surgeon, maybe."

"A surgeon?" he asked, blue eyes full of derision.

I let go of his hands, and took a step back. "I'm sure you're too tough to go to a doctor. You'll probably stitch it up yourself using a rusty needle or something. Good for you."

I was ready to turn and walk away again, but Michael stopped me. "I would at least sterilize the needle first."

His voice was soft, and when I looked at him in surprise, I saw the faintest hint of a smile pass over his lips. That moment marked the first time I'd seen him smile, and, sadly, it ended before it started. His face reverted back to its serious self almost instantly.

The smile made me foolish. I set my backpack on the ground and took out the little first aid kit inside. I found a tube of antibacterial cream, grabbed Michael's hands again, and tried to cover the worst of the cuts. It was hard to see, but I did my best.

Michael studied me in silence for a few minutes, and then cleared his throat. "We need to talk."

"You said that already." I finished up and put a bandage on the cut bleeding the worst. It had "Hello, Kitty!" on it. I had to swallow a smile at the expression on his face.

He sighed. "I don't know where to start."

I shoved the first aid kit back into my backpack. "How about at the beginning?"

He proceeded to pace back and forth, opening his mouth once and then closing it. I pursed my lips. He was doing a very poor job of talking to me. I decided to make it easier for him.

"Why don't you start by telling me what those things were?"

His eyebrows drew together. “The Moktar?”

“I’m from southern Kentucky. I’ve seen a lot of weird stuff in my life, but never anything quite like that. Is it going to come back?”

He looked over his shoulder, scanning the street and the surrounding buildings. It made me a little nervous. “Not tonight. Can we talk as I escort you back to your flat?”

We walked in silence. I was about to start pushing him again for answers when he began to speak.

“Do you know the tales about monsters and bogeymen and things that go bump in the night that frightened you when you were small? That was all of them rolled into one big furry parcel, and much, much more.”

“And you kill them. That makes you a hero.” I tried to coax another smile out of him. It didn’t work.

“It’s my job.”

“Who do you work for?”

“A higher authority.” His voice was clipped and emotionless.

I rolled my eyes. “Could you be a little vaguer, please?”

“Oh, you drive me…” The emotionless tone to his voice vanished. Now it held an edge of anger to it. He took a deep breath, calming himself. “I can’t explain everything, but I can tell you the Moktar are evil, soulless, beasts.”

“Where do they come from?” I asked. He gave me a shrug, clearly indicating he wasn’t going to answer. I wanted to smack him. “Why have I never heard of them before?”

Michael nibbled on the silver ring on his lip. “It’s

kept secret."

"I'm sure you aren't going to tell me who made that decision either." As expected, I got another shrug. I took a deep breath through my nose and exhaled slowly through my mouth. "What *can* you tell me?"

Michael frowned. "This is very difficult, Emerson. I've never told anyone these things before. Why do you have to make it even more challenging?"

I paused, trying to see his side of it. "I'm sorry. I know I have a problem with sassing people. Grandma Sugar has warned me about it a million times."

He rubbed a hand over his head. The "Hello, Kitty!" bandage looked very out of place on his tattooed, brawny body.

"There is something you must understand, but it's going to be difficult for you to accept."

We were only a block away from my apartment, and part of me wanted to run straight to my soft, warm bed, pull the covers up over my head, and pretend none of this had ever happened. Another part of me, the bigger and more idiotic part, was dying to hear what Michael tried so hard to avoid telling me.

"What is it?"

He sighed, his blue eyes sad. "You aren't going to be able to live here anymore. You'll have to come and stay with us." His voice was low and soft, and it took me a second to understand what he'd just said.

"What are you talking about?"

He put his hands on my arms. I think he wanted to shake me, but he held himself back. He took a deep breath.

"When that Moktar grabbed you, it changed everything. They're hunters, and you just became his prey. He's going to track you, Emerson."

I backed away a few feet. He let go of me, which was wise. "I'll be careful. I'll lock my door and won't go out at night again, promise. I won't go out at all, in fact."

Michael shook his head. "It's not just your own safety you must consider. You don't live alone."

Lucinda's face flashed into my mind. "Is my roommate in danger?"

"As long as you come with me, the answer is no."

I swallowed hard. "Are you threatening me?"

When he spoke, his voice sounded very old and tired. "I ran away from you. Don't you remember? But you were silly and impulsive and wanted to flirt with danger. Well, now you have your wish." Michael's mouth narrowed into a hard, angry line.

"But what about school?"

My brain felt like it moved through slush. Michael was telling me about being hunted by a monster, and all I could think of was poetry class.

He looked at me like I was an idiot, but at least he answered my question. "The Moktar have no pigment and can't come out during the day. You're safe to go to class."

"Why is he after me?" My body started to tremble as the reality of my situation began to sink in.

"I don't know." Michael kept his steady gaze on me, which helped me keep it together. "That's an important question. I meant it when I said you were lucky. I've never seen a Dweller get that close to a Moktar and live to tell the tale."

"A Dweller?"

Michael's eyes took on a shuttered look, like he'd

said something he hadn't meant to say. He looked embarrassed. "Someone who isn't a Traveller."

"I know about Travellers. After Mrs. Burke told me about you, I researched it online."

I sounded pathetic. I was grateful for the darkness so Michael couldn't see how red my cheeks had turned.

"You know all about us, eh?" He made a noise that sounded an awful lot like a snort.

My cheeks burned even hotter. "I'd never heard of Travellers before, and I was curious."

"You know that's what killed the cat, don't you?"

"Yes, I do. Thank you very much." I'd heard that expression from Grandma Sugar more times than I could count. "How did Mrs. Burke know?"

"They always seem to know. I'm not sure how it happens. It was only a matter of time before she asked me to stop patronizing her fine establishment." His voice was soft as he stared down at his boots. I wanted to tell him I didn't think less of him because he was a gypsy, but the words just wouldn't come out.

"What do the Moktar usually do…to Dwellers?"

"Kill them, and then eat them. That's what the Moktar wants to do to you, and he won't give up, Emerson. Did you see the way that Moktar went after my friend's body? And he wasn't even tracking him. It'll be one hundred times worse for you. The only way you'll be safe is if we kill him first."

I swallowed, feeling the panic settling into my chest like a rock sinking in a lake. "I'm only here for a few months. I have to go home in December."

"That's more than enough time. Trust me. I can kill him."

He pulled himself up to his full height. He was

huge. I'd known he was tall, but hadn't realized how broad until I stood right next to him.

I stared at him, blinking back tears, as my whole world crumbled around me. "So my options are: Go with you or be hunted to the ends of the earth by a hairy Moktar who wants to eat me for supper?"

Michael tried to suppress a smile as he looked at me from head to toe. "You'd barely qualify as an appetizer, but yes, those are your choices. Come with me or die."

Sun Tzu had written an entire chapter on evaluating the intentions of others. It had come in handy during my time on the pageant circuit, and now as well. I didn't like my options, but remembering the Moktar's teeth and the flash of cruelty in his yellow eyes made my decision easier. Michael might not like me, but at least he was human.

"I guess Grandma Sugar was right." He raised one dark eyebrow in question. "She always told me if you can't run with the big dogs, you should stay on the porch. I should have stayed on the porch."

"It's too late now."

"Don't I know it." My bottom lip started to tremble slightly, and I steadied myself. "Well, Michael Nightingale, I guess I'm going with you."

Sun Tzu was probably rolling in his two-thousand-year-old Chinese grave at the moment, but I was doing my best. I was twenty years old, alone in a foreign country, and scared. Surely, even a great warrior like Sun Tzu would understand those factors. He might even sympathize.

Michael made a noise a bit like a grunt. "Very wise."

"Now I don't get called *that* very often." I turned and started toward my apartment. I had to pack up for what looked like an extended stay with the Travellers. I didn't know how to explain this one to Lucinda.

He stopped me by grabbing my hand. "I'll keep you safe, Emerson. I promise."

It sounded like a vow. I looked up into his eyes, so beautifully, piercingly blue. I might be a complete fool, and Michael Nightingale was nothing but trouble, but somehow, when he told me he would keep me safe, I believed him.

Chapter Six

Oh, Toto. I don't think we're in Kentucky anymore.
~Grandma Sugar

Entering the dark, quiet apartment, I was relieved not to have to face Lucinda, who had already gone to bed. I showed Michael to the bathroom so he could wash off the worst of the blood, and went to my bedroom to pack.

"Now what does one take when on the run from a Moktar beast?" I pondered.

"Only what you need for tonight. You can come back in the morning to get anything else you require."

Michael leaned against the doorjamb, blotting his hands dry with a paper towel. The "Hello, Kitty!" bandage was gone, but blood still trickled slowly from his wound.

"You need another band aid." I pushed him out of the doorway and led him back into the bathroom. He sat on the toilet as I looked through my things.

"You have three choices." I held up a "Barbie" bandage, one with pink fairies on it, and a purple one covered in glitter. He gave me a rather hostile look, and pointed to the purple one. I put it on over his cut, trying to be as gentle as possible.

"All better," I said with a smile.

I held his hands in mine, examining his other

wounds in the bright light of the bathroom. My assessment outside had been correct. The gash on his left arm, next to his wrist, was the worst. Michael had cleaned it well, and it had stopped bleeding, but looked deep.

"You seem to know what you're doing," he said.

"My granddaddy is a country doctor. I worked in his office during the summer and sometimes after school. Not too exciting, but I learned how to take care of a few cuts and bruises."

"Is your father a doctor, too?"

"Oh, heavens no. He practically faints at the sight of blood. He's the biggest scaredy-cat ever."

"What does he do?"

"He teaches military history at Western Kentucky University. That's where I go to school." I pointed to the wound that looked the worst. "You need stitches for this one."

He studied it. "I can take care of it right now. Will you help me?"

I swallowed hard. "No, I cannot stitch your arm back together. I'm sorry. I can't. Granddaddy tried to teach me, and the results were less than spectacular."

Michael grinned, and then bit his lip in that absurdly sexy way of his. "I don't want you to stitch it. The only thread you have would probably be pink with sparkles. No, thank you. I just want you to hold it together for me so I can glue it."

"Glue it?"

Michael stood up and dug into the pocket of his jeans. He pulled out a small tube. "Medical glue. It works wonders."

I narrowed my eyes. "You carry this around in

your *pocket*? How often do you get torn up, Mr. Nightingale?"

Without answering, he sat down and showed me how to hold the wound together. "It'll take only a few moments to set, but I need an extra pair of hands. Are you ready?"

"It's so sad you know how to do this." He lifted his left arm, resting his hand on my hip. I put my fingers on either side of his wound and pressed the edges together as tightly as I could.

"Nice work," he said as he squeezed a long line of glue along the cut.

We remained very still, and every passing breath made me extremely aware of Michael's hand on my hip. A lock of hair fell onto my face. Michael reached up and tucked it behind my ear with his other hand.

The tiny bathroom felt even smaller with Michael's giant, muscular tattooed body in it. Too shy to look at his face, I took this opportunity to study his ink. He'd taken off his leather jacket and wore only a tight black short-sleeved t-shirt. A long row of block letters curved their way around his arm like a rope. Some had small hearts or symbols next to them.

"What are the hearts for? Old girlfriends?"

Michael smirked, and shook his head. "Friends. Family members, too. People killed by the Moktar."

I couldn't see all the way up his arm, but there were easily twenty sets of initials on his forearm. There was also a large flock of black birds. "And the birds?"

Michael's lips curved up into a little half smile. "Dead Moktar. I killed those myself."

"Looks like you're winning. You can get another one for the Moktar you killed tonight."

A sad shadow crossed over his eyes. "And one for Tad, too. He was only sixteen. He just started hunting a few months ago."

"I'm sorry," I said softly. That was the most Michael had ever said to me at one time, each word heavy with pain and loss. I started to think these emotions were a constant factor in his life.

"Thank you." He touched the glue gingerly with his other hand. "It's set now. You can let go."

I did so gently, but didn't move away. He still had his hand on my hip, and I stood right between his legs, my knee brushing his thigh. That position felt suddenly very intimate. I had a funny feeling deep in the pit of my stomach, and found it a little hard to breathe.

"You can let go, too," I said.

He gave me a lazy, sexy smile and slowly slid his hand off my hip. The man was a menace, a walking, talking aphrodisiac.

I gave him a steady look. "Michael Nightingale. You'd better stop flirting with me unless you mean it or I might not help you the next time you need to be glued back together."

He looked at me in astonishment and followed me back to my room. He leaned against the wall in the hallway, his bulging arms folded over his chest. "I wasn't flirting with you."

"Uh, huh. Sure." Winking, I closed the door on him, and started to pull off my shirt, but immediately gagged at the stench of Moktar spit on my skin. Shuddering, I stuck my head out into the hallway.

"Do I have time to take a super quick shower?" I gave him my most pleading look. "I smell like Moktar."

"Oh, that's very attractive." He took a deep breath

and sighed. “Fine. Just hurry.”

I grabbed a change of clothes and scooted into the bathroom. “If you’re hungry, I made pasta. It’s in the kitchen. There are some brownies, too. Just try to be quiet. My roommate is sleeping.”

I slipped into the shower and scrubbed until my skin was pink and raw, wanting every last bit of Moktar erased. I washed my hair quickly and pulled it into a tight bun at the nape of my neck. I didn’t want to take the time to dry it. I put on a pair of black stretchy pants, a white long-sleeved t-shirt, and a gray hoodie with “Western Kentucky University” emblazoned on the front. A few sizes too big, it felt like a warm hug from my daddy.

In the kitchen, Michael wolfed down a heaping bowl of pasta. For some reason, the fact he liked my cooking made me feel absurdly proud. I filled a small bowl for myself, and wrote a note for Lucinda.

“What should I tell my roommate?” I handed Michael a beer, and opened one for me, too.

“Ta,” he said, raising his bottle in thanks. “Tell her as little as possible, but keep it close to the truth.”

“So nothing about the Moktar?” He froze with a fork full of pasta halfway to his mouth, and I grinned. “Just joshing you. I’ll tell her we hooked up. She’d believe that.”

He froze again. “She would?”

“Sometimes, Mr. Nightingale, your porch light is on, but nobody is home. Let’s just say it wouldn’t come as a surprise and leave it at that.”

My cheeks went from pink to red, but I kept my head down and wrote out a quick yet reassuring note to Lucinda. I stuck it on the fridge, and then brought

Michael a brownie. He took a bite and groaned.

"Wonderful."

I smiled so wide my cheeks hurt. The first compliment Michael had ever paid me.

He rolled his eyes at the expression on my face. "We really must go."

I grabbed my passport, and made sure my journal and books were already inside my backpack as well. I was going to have a whole lot to write about before this night was through. I just knew it.

"Ready when you are," I said, pulling on a jacket. Michael took my overnight bag from my hands.

"That's what you think," he murmured, almost under his breath.

We locked up the apartment and walked down the street in silence. Michael appeared on high alert, his muscles tensing at every sound. Clearly, he was stressed, but I'd moved beyond stressed to a weird state of calm. I'd seen too much for my brain to process. Finally, we reached the spot in The Shambles where I'd watched him disappear the first day I followed him.

"I know this place."

"You should," he said. "I can't let you see the entrance, Emerson. Close your eyes."

"Are you kidding me?" My mouth dropped open. He was completely serious. "But why?"

"Some secrets aren't mine to tell."

I wasn't happy about it, but closed my eyes and began tapping my toe impatiently. "There you go, all cryptic again. Geez Louise. You'd think you'd trust me by now after I helped glue your danged arm together."

"Keep your eyes shut." Michael grabbed my hand and pulled me forward. "And keep your mouth shut, too."

A hint of laughter colored his voice. I heard a soft creak and guessed it was some kind of door. As soon as it slammed shut behind us, everything grew completely silent and still.

"You can open your eyes now."

Michael still held my hand. It took me a moment to adjust and realize we now stood in a dark hallway. Bare bulbs hung from the ceiling, but they were dim and sparsely placed.

"Where are we?"

He didn't answer. He led me through an intricate maze of doors and up and down metal staircases. The walk was so dark and confusing I started to wish I'd brought breadcrumbs.

At last, he stopped in front of a large metal door and took a deep breath. "This is it," he said softly. "The point of no return."

"That sounds ominous."

"It is. Are you sure this is what you want?" Michael gave my hand a gentle squeeze.

If circumstances had been different, I would have been really happy right now. Michael was talking to me, holding my hand, and bringing me home to meet his family. But the fact a Moktar wanted to kill me just took all the fun right out of it.

"Well, it's stay here or die, right?"

"Yes. I'm sorry for what has already happened, and for what's about to happen now."

I frowned. "I've had enough surprises for one evening. What are you trying to tell me?"

When he looked at me, the world-weary expression on his face almost broke my heart. "Just forgive me," he said, and turned the handle on the giant metal door, swinging it open.

I thought we'd enter a room, but instead we stepped into an outdoor courtyard filled with people and noise. Tall trees and grass graced the area with caravans parked in even rows. Some of the caravans were old-fashioned, made of wood and painted in bright colors. Others were very modern and looked more like the campers or RVs back home.

The similarities to Kentucky ended there. Hanging from several of the trees were the bodies of Moktar in various stages of decomposition. I wasn't keen on Moktar myself, but recoiled at the primitive gruesomeness of it. I'd imagined something a little different for my first date with Michael Nightingale. Dinner and a movie maybe. At least he still held my hand, which was a good thing.

We'd walked in as a group of men hung their latest Moktar trophy on a low branch near the doorway. People spit at the corpse, hitting it with sticks and poles. They were working themselves into a proper frenzy. I almost couldn't hear Michael when he put his lips close to my ear and told me to follow him. As he began leading me into the center of the courtyard, the noise slowly died away. People stopped in mid swing, with shocked expressions on their faces, and soon, every eye was trained on me. The crowd had grown strangely and ominously silent.

Several people sat around a large bonfire. Michael tightened his grip on my hand and led me over to them. The crowd that had been beating the Moktar now assembled around us, the hostility in the air almost palpable.

Most of the men dressed like Michael in black and leather. The women, however, were a different story. They wore animal prints, sequins, sparkling gold lame, and bright colors. Their clothing was tight, sexy, and revealing. Piles of jewelry, lots of makeup, and very high-heeled shoes completed their looks. Even the little girls had on stilettos. I looked out of place in my hoody and yoga pants, not that I would have fit in any better with one of my wool skirts. Even my pageant dresses would have seemed subdued around these women.

Michael brought me to a man sitting in a chair in front of the fire. He was older, with graying hair and the same shockingly blue eyes Michael possessed.

"Da." Michael greeted the man with a nod. I gave him a weak smile, which he ignored.

"Why have you brought her here, Mikey?"

"She's being tracked."

"Why would they bother tracking a Dweller?"

Michael shrugged. "Your guess is as good as mine. Emerson Shaw, meet my father, Sampson."

"Pleased to meet you, sir." I was so nervous, I almost curtsied.

Everyone laughed, and my cheeks burned. "A well brought up young lady, I see. You're an oddity around here for sure."

Something softened in his eyes. "She's your responsibility, Mikey. She stays with you and you alone will care for her. I mean that. You aren't passing this off on anyone else. If anything happens to her, or because of her, it's on you. Can you accept this?"

"I can." Michael's voice was firm and clear.

Some of the people assembled around us got bored with our conversation and went back to play the

Traveller version of “Whack-A-Mole” with the Moktar carcass. Michael’s father turned to me with a smile. “Well, then, Emerson Shaw. Welcome to the bowels of hell. I hope you enjoy your stay.”

Chapter Seven

Well, ain't he just the tomcat's kitten?
~Grandma Sugar

Michael took me to his caravan. It sat on the end of one of the long rows of caravans, nestled under a large oak tree. Unlike many of the others, Michael's was shiny, new, and made of a very modern-looking silver metal. We climbed some narrow steps to a small porch, then he opened the door and ushered me in.

The inside was much bigger than it looked from the outside, and very neat and tidy. The front room had a small kitchen and sitting room. I saw the back room through a door, and most of it seemed dominated by a large bed.

"It probably isn't what you're used to, but make yourself at home," he said, looking a bit uncomfortable. When he began to walk out the door, I grabbed his arm.

"Where are you going?" I asked, terrified to be left alone.

He took my hand off his arm, giving it an awkward pat meant as reassuring, but he was obviously distracted. "I have to speak with Tad's mother. I'll be back shortly."

As soon as he left, I pulled out my journal and curled up on his couch, pushing aside the curtain to glance out the window. A group of people huddled around a bonfire, holding each other and swaying. When they saw Michael, they drew him into their circle. A woman wailed, and tears pricked the backs of my eyes. Someone had lost a child tonight. I'd been so preoccupied with my own shock and horror I hadn't really absorbed that fact. And Michael had spent the night taking care of me instead of mourning the loss of his friend.

I'm a stranger in a strange land. I put down my pen, too overwhelmed to write. I was at a point somewhere just beyond exhaustion fueled purely by adrenaline.

Unable to sit any longer, I looked around the caravan, feeling very nosy and not really caring. Behind a closet door was an extremely well organized collection of knifes, swords, and several other weapons. I closed the door, turning away. Normally, I liked looking at weapons, but I'd seen enough of that side of Michael's life already.

The caravan was rather Spartan. The only photo was of Michael's father as a much younger man standing next to a beautiful and delicate-looking woman with dark hair and eyes. She held a baby and beamed with pride.

"That was my Ma."

Michael stood in the doorway, looking completely shattered, both physically and emotionally. He must have changed out of his bloodied clothes in someone else's caravan and now wore a pair of sweats and a long sleeved blue t-shirt that stretched tightly across his chest. I'd never seen him in any color but black.

"Is the baby you?" He nodded, and I smiled at him. "How sweet."

He held up the photo and stared at it like he saw something in it I couldn't. "The Moktar…they got her a few days after this photo was taken. I can't remember her at all."

"Oh. I get it. I understand." He gave me a look that told me he thought my statement highly doubtful. "Not the Moktar part, but the loss. My mama died when I was two."

"How?" Michael's voice was soft.

I swallowed hard, unable to look at him. "She committed suicide."

"I'm sorry."

"Thank you. That's part of the reason I came to England. I hoped to find her family, or someone who knew her." I yawned, swaying on my feet.

"You're exhausted, Emerson. You should go to bed."

I *was* exhausted and didn't want to talk about his mother or my mother anymore. I wanted to shut my eyes and experience a few hours of mindless oblivion.

As I climbed into his bed, he watched me from the doorway. "I'll be at my Da's. It's only a few doors down."

I shook my head, panic setting in. "Don't you dare leave me here alone, Michael."

He glanced at the narrow couch in his front room. "I'll stay, if that's what you want. I'll sleep out there."

"You can't possibly fit on that couch."

He rested his head against the wall, like it was too heavy for him to hold it up anymore, his shoulders slouching in exhaustion. "Then I'll sleep on the floor."

"That's ridiculous. Just come to bed."

I thought he would continue to argue, but common

sense won out. He nearly fell into bed next to me, on top of the covers. I reached for a blanket folded on the bottom of the bed and covered him with it.

"Thanks," he murmured. "You were brave tonight, Emerson."

I turned on my side to face him, and unrolled my hair from its bun. It was still damp, and spread over his pillow like a big curly fan. "I'm pretty good at making the best of things."

He snorted. "That's an understatement. I don't think there are many beauty queens from Kentucky who could face a Moktar without swooning, let alone fight one off."

"How did you know I was a beauty queen?"

He yawned. "Mrs. Burke, it turns out, was quite the wealth of information."

In spite of everything, in spite of the horror and the death and the fear, a little bubble of joy sprang to life in my chest. Michael had been interested enough to ask Mrs. Burke about me. Maybe this obsession hadn't been so one sided after all.

Michael's eyelids grew heavy. "You're an unusual girl, Emerson Jane Shaw."

"Are you calling me weird?" I asked, but he didn't answer. He just pulled me into the curve of his arms and held me close, like he wanted to protect me even in his sleep.

I woke up feeling completely and absolutely warm for the first time since I'd arrived in England. Michael must have climbed under the covers at some point during the night and now he spooned me, holding me close against his big warm body and covering me like a blanket. It was bliss, until I realized we'd just slept half

Michael's voice, but this wasn't funny.

"Oh, sugar beets and dates."

"Now you're just getting dirty."

I glared at him. "My friends have been trying to reach me for hours, but my phone was off. I'd better call them before they go to the police and file a missing person's report." That wasn't an exaggeration. Poppy and Lucinda were freaking out.

Michael slipped his shoes on. "Call them. I'll get some breakfast."

I sat on his couch and allowed myself a moment to drool over the way his bottom looked in low hanging sweats as he walked out the door. I'd slept with Michael Nightingale. Maybe not in the biblical sense, but I'd been in his actual bed, with him in it.

I sighed and dialed Lucinda's number. I was a pathetic excuse of a woman if forcing Michael to sleep in the same bed with me felt like an accomplishment.

Lucinda answered in the middle of the very first ring. "Emerson?"

"Hi, Luce."

I tried to inject as much cheerfulness and enthusiasm as possible into my voice, but it didn't help. She let out a string of curse words so bad a sailor would have blushed. I couldn't even understand most of them. It took her a few minutes to finish, and then Poppy took a turn. They must have been sitting together, waiting for me to call, and had me on speakerphone. I waited for Poppy's tirade to come to a close, and then jumped in and tried to talk.

"I'm really sorry. I turned off my phone, and forgot to turn it back on. I left you a note, Lucinda."

"A very vague and extremely strange note telling

me you were spending the night with *Michael Nightingale*. What the hell happened?"

Michael came back into the caravan carrying a tray of food and what looked like a carafe full of coffee. He set down the tray, and I got another glimpse of his very delectable bottom. His sweats were just right, not too loose and not too tight.

I bit my lip as I ogled him. "I'll be home soon. Can we talk then?"

An exasperated moan sounded on the other end. I couldn't tell if it was Poppy or Lucinda.

Lucinda finally spoke. "We were very worried, but as long as you're okay, that's all that matters. We will expect a full report, however."

"Yes, ma'am."

"With all of the gory details," shouted Poppy.

"I promise," I said, and then hung up the phone with a sigh. Poppy had no idea how gory the details actually were.

Michael handed me a cup of hot coffee. "I know you usually drink tea, but I thought you'd like coffee, too, since you're American."

I stared at him. "Who are you and what have you done with Michael Nightingale?"

He gave me a puzzled look. "Whatever do you mean?"

I put down my cup and folded my hands on my lap. "For weeks, you've acted like I was someone with a particularly nasty communicable disease."

Michael grabbed a plate piled high with eggs, bacon, toast, and the ever-present English staple, the grilled tomato, from the tray of food. He handed it to me, and got another plate for himself.

"As I explained already, I wanted to keep you safe."

"From what?" I asked between bites. The food was delicious.

Michael gave me a disbelieving look. "Uh, the Moktar, the Travellers, the whole bloody mess."

"Oh, that."

"Yes, that." Michael leaned back on the couch. "And when you stumbled onto our little problem last night, it was probably the worst case scenario."

I shook my head. "No. Not exactly the worst case scenario. That would have involved me being a late night snack for a hungry Moktar. I think things actually turned out rather well." I patted my mouth primly with a napkin, and Michael shook his head, smiling.

"Rather well indeed." He looked at his watch. "Shall we go? Your friends wish to speak with you, and we have to be back before sunset."

I moaned. "What am I going to tell them?"

"Do you want me to come with you?"

I wrinkled my nose at him. "Yes. No. Maybe. I don't know what would be worse."

"I'll come," he said, and I could tell by the firm set of his jaw he'd made the decision for both of us.

"Fine," I said, "but remember what you told me last night?"

Michael frowned and shook his head.

"I apologize in advance for what is about to happen."

Chapter Eight

You'll go to hell for lying just as fast as for stealing chickens.

~Grandma Sugar

In chapter seven of *The Art of War*, Sun Tzu talked about the dangers of direct conflict, and was he ever right. Facing a firing squad at dawn might have been preferable to facing Poppy and Lucinda that afternoon. Mr. Sun Tzu himself would have run away waving a white flag of surrender. They'd spent a good five or six hours sick with worry, and I deserved to be yelled at, but I felt kind of bad for Michael.

Perched next to me on the edge of the couch, he looked perfectly comfortable, but I could tell by the tight set of his jaw this wasn't easy for him. Poppy and Lucinda faced us, wearing almost identically angry expressions. Neither of them said a word, but they were definitely not happy.

"Hi, y'all."

"Don't try that southern sweetness on us this morning, Emerson Jane. It will not work."

Lucinda wore a black, loose fitting turtleneck sweater. She had no makeup on, her hair pulled back into a severe bun. I'd never seen her look so pale, or so completely unlike herself. Heck, I didn't even know she owned a turtleneck.

“Lucinda is absolutely right.” Poppy nodded her approval. She pursed her sweet little bow-shaped lips, and I knew what was coming. Poppy was about to go on a weeping rampage. Her face crumbled as she started to cry. “How could you not check your phone for twelve solid hours?”

“Was it that long? I’m sorry. Here’s what happened…” I froze, not sure where to start. I’d gonc over this in my head, but it felt completely different sitting right in front of my friends. I wasn’t a natural born liar.

“It was my fault.” Poppy and Lucinda’s heads swiveled to Michael so fast, they might have gotten whiplash. He cleared his throat. “I was trying to fix my motorbike in front of the library, and cut my hand. Emerson gave me a bandage.”

“What kind of bandage?” asked Poppy. Clearly, they weren’t buying his story.

“‘Hello, Kitty!’ and it had pink sparkles on it.”

Lucinda relaxed ever so slightly. “That sounds accurate.”

“Emerson offered to let me clean up here. We decided to meet with my mates, and I told her she could crash at my place.”

“And we didn’t want to wake you.”

I shouldn’t have spoken. Michael did quite well without me. Lucinda narrowed her eyes, studying my face carefully.

“What else happened? You’re not telling us everything.”

“Nothing.” I tried to meet Lucinda’s stare with wide-eyed innocence. Not an easy task.

“I wouldn’t go that far, Em,” said Michael. He

gave me a saucy grin, and I blushed, elbowing him hard in the ribs.

Poppy and Lucinda watched our interaction, and seemed satisfied with whatever they saw. “Emerson, you’re the worst liar in the whole wide world,” said Lucinda, and Poppy agreed. “We’ll let it go since everything turned out fine in the end, but don’t do that to us again.”

To my horror, Lucinda’s eyes filled with tears. “I won’t. I promise.”

Lucinda blinked and wiped her eyes. “Good. Let’s have some tea.” Tea was the English cure all, and Lucinda was very, very English.

The doorbell rang, and Poppy jumped up to get it. “That’s Nigel. He was coming over to beat up Michael, but I don’t think that’s necessary now.”

I started to giggle at the look on Michael’s face. “It’s funny. Trust me.”

Nigel gave Poppy a kiss then walked over to us. Michael stood to greet him. Nearly as tall as Michael, Nigel would have been at a serious disadvantage if it came to blows. The only exercise he’d ever gotten was from lifting textbooks.

Michael grinned when he saw Nigel and shook his hand. “Nigel.”

“Michael?” Nigel gave Poppy an incredulous look. “This is the bloke you wanted me to beat up? Bloody hell. I’m glad you worked it all out. I wouldn’t want to hurt this man.” He gave Michael a little wink, and slapped his shoulder. Michael laughed.

“You two know each other?” I asked.

“Of course, we know each other. We tried to get Michael to come over to the physics department, but he refused. He wanted to stay in chemistry. Bloody waste of a great mind for physics, if you ask me."

"Physics?" I asked. Michael shrugged, apparently embarrassed by the praise.

"It's good to see you again, Nigel."

"You, too. Did you hear about Fred?"

Michael and Nigel started talking about a colleague from the physics department. Lucinda and Poppy handed them each a cup of tea, and then dragged me into my room. I sat down on my bed.

"What the hell happened?" Lucinda was never one to beat about the bush. I didn't know how to respond.

"Did you sleep with him?" Poppy sat down next to me.

"We slept in the same bed, but we didn't…you know…"

"Oh, God. She is still a virgin." Lucinda said those words a bit louder perhaps than she intended. I heard a slight lull in the Nigel and Michael's conversation in the next room, and was fairly certain they'd heard her, too.

"Lucinda," I hissed. "Must you?"

"Yes, I must." Her face softened. "Be careful. I don't want you to get hurt."

"Nigel likes him," said Poppy. Since the sun rose and set on Nigel's opinion in Poppy-land, that was a huge point in his favor. Lucinda agreed.

"He does seem to care for you, but he could trample your heart if you aren't careful."

I looked at her in surprise. "I'll be careful, but Michael isn't what he seems. He's actually a pretty good guy." They both looked unconvinced, so I changed the subject. "How was Antarctica?"

Lucinda groaned, and Poppy shook her head. "You shouldn't have asked," she whispered.

"What happened?"

"Nothing," said Lucinda. "I chased him all around the bloody apartment, and nothing happened."

Poppy cringed. "Antarctica has yet to be conquered," she said softly.

Lucinda covered her face with her hands. "It was awful. I tried everything. I showed him my cleavage. I brushed against him. I filled every sentence with sexual innuendo. I did everything short of jumping on him and ripping off his clothes."

"She came close," Poppy murmured. "He lost a button."

Lucinda made a noise that sounded like a wail. "I am one continent away from completing my thesis, but Antarctica refuses to cooperate. I'm a failure."

"You said he's shy. Give him some time."

Lucinda peeked out from between her fingers. "I'll see him again tonight. I'm forcing him to take me to the cinema."

"Be gentle."

"Gentle?" Lucinda thought about it and sighed. "That would be new for me. Oh, Em. I think actually might *like* him."

Lucinda had never used that word before. The only nice things she ever said about her other lovers were adjectives to describe their skill in bed, or their size, things like, "I had a lovely time exploring Brazil last night," or "That was quite the safari in Africa." Lucinda saw them more as case studies than actual people, but this time seemed different.

"I'm sure he likes you, too, Lucinda. All men like

you. You're like a walking, talking sex dream."

She smiled. "That is the nicest thing anyone has ever said to me. Thank you, Emerson."

I stood up and stretched. "I have to pack. I'm staying with Michael for a few days."

"What?" Lucinda asked. They both folded their arms across their chests and literally blocked the door with their bodies.

I rolled my eyes. They weren't going to budge until they got answers. "Michael usually works nights, but he's off right now. It's a chance for us to spend a bit of time together."

They still looked unconvinced, so I played my ace in the hole. "Do you really want me to go back to Kentucky a virgin?"

Lucinda and Poppy locked eyes, and then Lucinda winked at me. "If that's the case, I have something for you." She slipped out of the room, and came back with a tiny scrap of black lace hidden under her shirt. She waved it at me triumphantly.

"What in tarnation is this?" I took it tentatively from her hands and held it up against my body. It was a very tiny, very sexy black lace teddy. "Oh, my. If I wear this, I could catch old *and* new-monia."

Lucinda grabbed it out of my hands and shoved it into my bag. "If you wear this, you'll catch Michael Nightingale, and it's about damned time."

Chapter Nine

If "ifs" and "buts" were candies and nuts, then every day would be Christmas.

~Grandma Sugar

Michael and I left the apartment and walked down the street. "I can't believe you know Nigel. That made this whole situation a lot better."

"He's a good man." Michael went to shove his hands into his pockets, seemed to remember his cuts at the last moment, and linked his fingers through his belt loops instead. He'd dressed all in black again, looking like a dark, avenging angel. I'd fallen asleep with my hair wet, and still wore the clothes I'd slept in, so I looked like a weird cross between a ragamuffin and the bride of Frankenstein. We were quite the pair.

"How long have you known Nigel?" he asked.

"As long as I've known Poppy. They've been together forever."

Michael thought about this. "Has she met his parents?"

"Not yet. Why?"

Michael nibbled on the silver ring on his lip. "I met them once. They were proper snobs. You know they're titled, right?"

"The whole Nigel is really Lord Nigel or something? Yeah, I know. What difference does it make?"

"It can make quite a difference." Michael sighed. "This isn't America, Emerson. Poppy isn't in the same social class as Nigel. I could tell as soon as she opened her mouth to speak." I heard the pain in his voice and knew it came from personal experience.

I measured my words carefully. "Well, Nigel doesn't think like that. A lot of people don't think like that. He loves Poppy and won't let his parents come between them."

"I hope you're right." He looked at his watch. "Is there anything else you need to do before we go back?"

"Can I stop at Mrs. Burke's?"

"You two are rather close, aren't you? Especially after you beat up that thief for her." Michael looked at me with a smile, but it froze on his face when I glared at him.

"You *were* watching me. I knew it."

"Someone had to keep an eye on you. You're completely mad, you know." He clenched his jaw in irritation, two bright spots of color appearing on his cheeks.

"And you elected yourself to be that person?"

I didn't think he would answer me, but he surprised me once again. "Something about you made me want to protect you. Against my better judgment, I might add. The least you could do is to make it a bit easier for me by not doing the most idiotic things possible all the time."

That hurt. "Okay. Sorry."

Michael gave me a curt nod and then looked at his watch. Mrs. Burke's shop was only a few doors down. "You have half an hour."

Mrs. Burke greeted me at the door to her shop. As soon as she saw me, her face filled with concern.

"What's wrong, Emerson?"

I opened my mouth and then shut it again, not knowing where to start. "I might not be here the next few days. I just wanted to let you know."

"Is this about that Traveller?" Mrs. Burke's normally sweet, soft face turned hard. She grabbed a pot of tea and some shortbread biscuits, and pulled me over to a table in a quiet corner of the shop. "It's time we had a little talk."

Mrs. Burke went to get some teacups just as Leo walked into the shop. His eyes scanned the room, looking for me. I wanted to crawl away and hide, but he saw me and made a beeline for my table. He looked pale.

"Where were you this morning?"

My cheeks burned. "I slept in. How are you? You look tired."

"I'm fine. I had one pint too many last night, I suppose." He pointed to the empty seat in front of me. "May I join you?"

"No." I shook my head, perhaps a little too vehemently, and he looked hurt. "I'm sorry. I'm having a cup of tea with Mrs. Burke."

He shifted back and forth on his feet. "Can we talk later?"

I nodded as Mrs. Burke came bustling up with the teacups, but I couldn't quite look at his face. He hesitated only for a moment, and then left the teashop without saying goodbye. Hearing the door slam behind him, I swallowed hard. He turned and stared at me through the window, desire mixing with anger in his

Chapter Ten

She could start an argument in an empty house.
~Grandma Sugar

"What did she say to you?" It took Michael all of five seconds to get to the point.I looked around the busy street. "Nothing we need to discuss right here."

He nodded, glancing at the crowds of people walking in The Shambles. The place was filled with tourists on a beautiful Saturday afternoon. We walked to the alley where the secret entrance to the gypsy camp was located. Michael made me close my eyes again. I nearly stamped my foot in frustration.

"Really?"

He folded his arms across his chest. I gave him one more look of extreme irritation and shut my eyes.

"You and me are going to mix. You realize that, don't you?"

"Aye," he said as he grabbed my hand and yanked me through the secret door. When I opened my eyes, Michael's face was inches from mine.

"Some secrets aren't mine to share," he whispered, his voice husky.

A group of Travellers yelled at us from farther down the hallway. "Margaret demanded a council meeting about your friend. You need to come right now, Michael."

He swore under his breath, still holding my hand, and began leading me down the dark hallway. The overnight bag clutched in his hand, hot pink and covered with daisies, completely ruined his whole leather-clad, tough guy, badass persona.

"Who's Margaret?"

"She's married to my brother, Patrick." He gave me an odd look. "She could be trouble."

"Oh, great. That's what we need, more trouble."

Michael paused. "Just try to be quiet. Can you manage that?"

When we entered the courtyard, the sun had just begun to set and an angry crowd of gypsies awaited us. I wanted to cower behind Michael like a big old scaredy-cat, but I wouldn't give them the satisfaction.

"What's going on?" His voice rang loud and strong.

A tall woman with long, dark hair approached. She wore shoes so high she wobbled, a teeny tiny skirt, and big, flashy earrings. Her eyes were the palest shade of blue, contrasting sharply with her dark hair. Beautiful, but the cold hostility in her eyes made a shiver snake up my spine.

"Hello, Margaret. Lovely to see you. I don't think you've had the pleasure of meeting Emerson yet."

Margaret spat on the ground. "I saw her in a dream."

The crowd gasped. "Dreams seen in autumn always come true," whispered an older lady standing not far from us.

Michael didn't look impressed. "And that is the basis for calling a council meeting?"

Margaret folded her arms over her ample breasts.

"She stood on new grass, with lightning all around."

Another collective gasp came from the crowd. "What the Sam Hill is that supposed to mean?"

"It means death…and a funeral. And you are the cause of it." Margaret refused to look at me when she spoke. It took me a second to realize she was the scaredy-cat, not me. She'd even scared herself.

"Don't you think that could be Tad's death and funeral?" Michael asked.

Margaret and several of the other people in the crowd cowered and covered their ears. "Do not say his name. Let him rest in peace." Margaret's voice was a hiss.

"Oh, my. She is one fry short of a Happy Meal," I muttered, low enough so only Michael could hear.

"Truer words were never spoken," he said back to me, just as softly.

Michael's father worked his way through the crowd. "Enough of this, Margaret, you've called the council meeting. You have the right. They'll be here tomorrow anyway for the funeral. There's no need to get into this now."

The people in the crowd didn't look happy about it, but they slowly began to disperse. Only Margaret remained, one hip jutted out and a rather pissed off expression on her pretty face.

"Da…" she began, but Sampson held up a hand to stop her.

"You heard my words, and you'll heed them, Margaret."

A tall man with a shaved head who looked like a slightly older and heavier version of Michael took Margaret's arm. "Sorry, Da," he said. He nodded at

Michael. "Mikey."

Michael gave him an understanding look. "Pat."

Margaret wanted to argue, but Patrick gave her arm a hard tug and pulled her away. "You've done enough, Maggie."

Sampson rubbed his jaw as he watched them walk away. "It was bound to happen, Mikey. And you know this isn't just about the lass."

"I know, Da. Thanks."

Sampson shrugged. "Don't thank me yet, boy-o." A group of young men gathered, checking their weapons and chatting amongst themselves as they prepared to leave. They had identical shaved heads, black leather jackets, and dark clothing. "You won't hunt tonight, Mikey. Stay in and rest up for tomorrow."

Sampson walked away, and I scowled at Michael. "Well, that was fun. Y'all are just a barrel of laughs."

He didn't say anything. He led me back to his caravan, and then went out to pick up dinner. When he got back, he started a small fire in a pit near his front porch, pulled up a couple of chairs, and handed me a tray.

The food was delicious, a beef stew, crusty bread, and a slice of cake for dessert. He handed me a glass of hot mulled wine, and I took a long, grateful sip.

"Who does the cooking?"

The stars began to pop out in the dark, cloudless sky as we ate. It felt warmer and drier here in the compound than it did anywhere else in York. I'd slipped into a clean pair of sweats and a light jacket, and, with the heat from the fire, that was enough to keep me toasty.

"We have a communal cooking area. They make

meals for everyone."

Most of the people seemed to congregate in the center of the compound, so Michael and I sat alone. I was thankful. I wasn't in the mood to deal with Margaret or any other gypsies at the moment.

One thing I'd learned on the pageant circuit was women, in general, can be much meaner than men, and southern women, as a rule, could be downright vicious. I hadn't been here long, but if Margaret was any indication, gypsy women took that a whole step further. Keeping my distance would be the best, and safest, policy.

The compound, located in a completely enclosed courtyard formed by brick windowless buildings and imposing walls, proved to be a private oasis in the middle of the city. I had to wonder if the people working and living in those buildings, and just beyond those walls, had any idea a herd of gypsies camped out right behind them. Somehow I doubted it.

Movement in a tree across the compound caught my eye, and I realized it was the most recently killed Moktar. Children whacked it with a stick, like some kind of macabre piñata.

"Now that looks like fun. If they hit it real hard, does candy fall out?"

Michael looked over at the children playing. "That one killed the boy who died yesterday. Not long ago, he was one of those children, and tomorrow we'll hold his funeral."

I jabbed at my plate, but suddenly didn't feel as hungry anymore. "I'm sorry about your friend."

He nodded, keeping his eyes on his food.

"Mrs. Burke was attacked by a Moktar once."

Michael's head shot up. "She said that?"

"She didn't call it a Moktar, and has been trying to convince herself it was a hallucination for the last thirty years."

The fire crackled in front of us, I was filled with good food and warm wine, and a heavy sort of relaxation descended on me. I'd been so hyped up for so long, I hadn't realized how much I needed to just sit and chill.

I tried to keep my voice neutral as I told him Mrs. Burke's story, but faltered when talking about Joan's death. That particular element was hard for me, but I refused to take sides.

"When she talked about Andy being different, I understood what she meant." I took another sip of wine. It tasted like cinnamon, nutmeg and allspice, and was the perfect drink for a cool fall evening. I just wished I'd been on a hayride instead of at a gypsy camp with a bunch of people who hated me.

"She said he was so fast, she sometimes thought she couldn't see him for a second when he was running. He seemed to see things that weren't there, to sense things that others didn't. What was he, Michael? What are you?"

"I'm a Traveller."

I swirled my wine around in my glass. "You were half a block away when the Moktar grabbed me, and at my side in a second. That's a little faster than normal."

Michael stared into the fire. "We call it leaping. We look at a spot, and, without moving a muscle, we're there. In physics, it might be known as quantum teleportation, but it can't be explained scientifically because it's a paradox. It's also dangerous."

“Dangerous?” The amount of wine in my system made me very open to new ideas, even crazy ones, and much more willing to hear Michael out.

“If we aren’t careful, we can get hit by a car, or stuck in a house. I’ve even seen a person accidentally leap into another person. Both were killed instantly.”

“What else can you do?”

“Travellers are better fighters, faster than the average person and faster than the average Moktar, too. We have quicker reflexes, and heightened awareness. A Traveller can smell danger coming, hear things far away. Some of us have a certain level of psychic ability, although it varies from person to person.”

“You can’t read my mind, can you? Because that might be a problem.”

“No.”His lips twitched. If he found me amusing now, he would have really enjoyed taking a peek inside my thoughts. My mind was a scary place. “Sometimes it’s just a feeling we have, a sense of unease.”

“So you are kind of like super people?”

“Not exactly. Don’t try to make us into heroes. Have you ever heard of the burakumin of Japan?”

I frowned, feeling fuzzy from the wine. “You’re Japanese?”

He gave me the signature Michael Nightingale glare. “No. Originally, we all came from Ireland, but that’s beside the point. The burakumin are the outcasts of Japanese society. When Japan was a closed country, they did the dirty, thankless jobs and their reward was to live in squalor, like lepers.”

He poured some more wine into both of our glasses. I had a feeling I might need it.

“Even today, burakumin aren’t given good jobs or

allowed to marry outside of their caste, simply because of the work their ancestors performed hundreds of years ago."

"How does that relate to Travellers?"

He looked up at the stars. "We're an ancient race of nomads. People don't trust those who wander. They are even less fond of those who are different."

"And you are very different, aren't you? But I still don't understand why."

He sighed. "If you know anything about Travellers, you know most can't read or write. The only history we have is oral, handed down through stories. Those stories tell of a time when darkness invaded the earth, and monsters roamed freely. Rom was the gypsy name for heaven, and the gods of Rom took pity on the poor humans and came to help them in chariots made of fire and lightning. They killed the monsters and rewarded the faithful with a gift."

"What was the gift?"

"Powers given from the gods to protect their people if the monsters ever came again. There is a little more to it than that, a lot of prophecy and other such nonsense, but that's the main idea."

"Okay."

Michael blinked. "That's all you are going to say? 'Okay'?"

"Well, yes. What else do you want me to say? I got up close and personal with a Moktar the other day, and sure as shoot never saw one of those before. And I saw you and your men fight. Y'all are a little west of normal, Michael." The more I drank, the thicker my accent became. I started to sound very southern now.

"I've studied the data carefully, and I've done my

own research. There are only a few small differences between Travellers and Dwellers, most of them physiological."

"Huh?" I squinted at him. "Please don't tell me you have an extra ding dong."

Michael laughed, throwing back his head. An unexpected pleasure. I'd never heard him laugh before.

"No. The difference is just a tiny tweak in our DNA. It's both a blessing and a curse. In ancient times, people thought we were either gods or demons. We were hunted and killed and blamed for everything from crop failures to lunar eclipses. Like the burakumin, we were outcasts, but we chose our path. We decided to avoid contact with Dwellers, and it worked for hundreds of years."

"What happened to change that?"

"The monsters returned. And whatever it is in our DNA that makes us stronger and faster, it also makes us more desirable to the Moktar. The hypothalamus in our brains contains a substance that is extremely addictive to them. It's sort of like crack for Moktar, but a million times more pleasurable. They call it HT. They crave it with an intensity that borders on insanity."

A log snapped on the fire, the flames warming my face as the wine warmed my stomach. I held out my glass, and Michael poured more in. He didn't comment on how much I drank, which was wise.

"Do they like to eat our brains, too?"

"Unfortunately, yes. They prefer to dine on Travellers because the effects last much longer, but a Dweller will do in a pinch. It's sort of the difference between steak and a beef burger."

"I'm hamburger. How nice."

Michael swirled the wine in his glass, a faraway expression in his eyes. "We formed a secret alliance with governments all over the world. We take care of the Moktar, and they take care of us, providing us with a place to live and a salary. We've managed to isolate the Moktar to a few island countries, mainly the UK, Japan, and the continent of Australia. The Moktar have nests and are good at hiding, but they hate crossing water. The problem is now contained, and we spend our nights hunting them and hunting them until we die."

"Do the women hunt, too?"

Michael shook his head. "They can't. It's forbidden because the risk is too great. The Moktar discovered if they impregnate Traveller women, the resulting babies would have a touch of our powers. Our women don't leave the compound unless it's during the day and only with an escort. If the Moktar got them, they would be gang raped. If no child resulted, they'd have their heads cracked open and the Moktar would fight to the death over their hypothalamus."

I took a shaky breath. "Lovely."

Michael watched me closely. "You're handling this extremely well."

I yawned. "I have a low tolerance for alcohol and a high tolerance for weirdness. Also, I spent years in the southern pageant circuit. Brain eating Moktars are only slightly worse than some of the stage mothers I've had the pleasure to meet. So Andy was fast because he was half Traveller?"

"He's an anomaly. Usually, only babies born to Traveller women have these powers."

"Are there many mixed marriages?"

"It happens, but it's frowned upon."

"Why?" Suddenly, I was very interested in examining the remaining contents of my wine glass.

"Some people feel babies born of mixed blood are...wrong. It's the same sort of nonsense that keeps us from going to school and turns our women into nothing but housewives and breeding machines."

"Speaking of Traveller women, why did Margaret call the council?"

He frowned. "She thinks you're a threat because of her dream."

"What if the council agrees with her?"

He reached for my hand. "It's not going to happen. I won't allow it." He started to stroke the back of my hand with his thumb, which almost made me forgot what we were talking about.

"Your dad said this council thing wasn't just about me. What did he mean?"

Michael stood and pulled me to my feet. I wobbled a bit, so he held my shoulders a moment to steady me.

"You've heard enough for the night, little Dweller."

"I've *had* enough for the night, too. I'm three sheets to the wind." I swayed, giving him a loopy smile.

He took me into his caravan and helped me slip out of my jacket and shoes. I changed into my pajamas in his bathroom and insisted on brushing my teeth and washing my face before he tucked me into bed. Being a little sloshed didn't mean forgetting about basic hygiene.

"Thank you for telling me the truth," I murmured as I laid my head down on his pillow.

"We'll see if you still thank me in the morning," he said with a wry little smile.

I heard him take off his jacket and boots, and then felt the weight of his body as he climbed into bed. I sighed contently, just knowing he was close.

"It's wrong, you know."

"What's wrong?" Michael's voice was a soft rumble.

"What they did to the burakamin. What they do to you."

"Sweet dreams, Emerson," he said, and I felt his lips brush my forehead as I closed my eyes and fell fast asleep.

Chapter Eleven

This is a dog eat dog world, and you just came in wearing pork chop underwear.

~Grandma Sugar

I woke up kissing Michael Nightingale. We'd been asleep, and somehow our lips brushed and clung together, causing a sweet quickening of my heart. A very pleasant way to start the morning. When I pulled back and opened my eyes, his face was inches from mine.

"What about everything I told you last evening?"

His voice sounded scratchy and deep, heavy from sleep, but we were both completely awake now. That single chaste kiss had worked better than any alarm clock. I reached up and touched his cheek. He needed a shave, his skin prickly under my fingers, and I noticed a little bruise near his eye that hadn't quite healed yet, but to me he was perfect. He was also worried, his blue eyes filled with caution and doubt.

"It doesn't change anything," I said.

Everyone had a weak point, something that made them open to attack. I'd become a master at seeing these vulnerable spots, the reason I had won a bunch of martial arts medals and a few beauty pageant titles as well. Michael might be big and strong and arrogant, but he had a weakness. He fully expected rejection.

“How can you be so calm?” He pushed a strand of hair out of my eyes, gently caressing the curve of my ear.

“Would you rather I freak out?”

“That would be the normal response,” he murmured.

“I’m not exactly normal. At least we have that in common.”

“You believe me?” Pain and doubt hid under his words.

“Of course I do.” I took a shaky breath. “You’re keeping me safe from the monsters. You might prefer wearing black, but you’re one of the good guys.”

He stared at me a moment, stunned, and then leaned forward to kiss me again, in earnest this time. A flood of emotions rushed over me as his tongue met mine. Hesitant at first but soon demanding and hungry, he ignited a frantic need inside me. I couldn’t help myself. I stuck my hands under his shirt, stroking his smooth, warm skin and running my fingers up and down his back, but it still wasn’t enough. I wanted to caress every inch of him. I wanted his naked body touching my naked body, and I wanted that now.

When he pulled his shirt off, I gasped. His torso, covered in tattoos, formed a complex maze of Celtic symbols. That wasn’t the only thing I found interesting.

“Oh, lordy. Nipple rings. I knew it.”

Small, silver, and very erotic, when I stroked them he made a noise like a growl deep in his throat that sent shivers of pleasure through my entire body. I got even happier when his big, calloused hands went under my shirt, caressing the delicate skin of my stomach and sliding up my rib cage.

"Mmmmm…Michael."

As soon as his hands reached my breasts and slid under my bra, common sense should have clicked in, but it didn't. I arched against him wantonly. I didn't even notice he had taken my shirt and bra off until I felt his lips on my body. His mouth, delightfully warm, and the air so cool, made my entire body react.

When he brought his head up, he was breathing hard. His eyes met mine as his hand found the waistband of my pants, and then he froze, turning his head to one side and listening.

"Is that your phone?" he asked his voice, rough.

The faint sounds of "Thank God I'm a Country Boy" came from my backpack. I squealed and fell off the bed, pulling my shirt back on as I reached for it. My shirt was both backwards and inside out, but it didn't matter. I waved my hands at Michael frantically.

"Put your shirt on," I hissed, holding the phone in my hands. "It's my daddy." Michael gave me an absolutely incredulous look, but he complied.

"Hi, Daddy." My voice seemed louder than usual, and I was afraid my father might somehow know I'd almost been doing the horizontal mambo with Michael Nightingale.

"Did I wake you up, lazy bones?"

"Oh, no. I was studying. Anatomy." Michael had gone into the bathroom, but he stuck out his head when he heard that. I winced, and he gave me a sexy little grin.

My father paused. "You're taking an anatomy class?"

"Ha, ha." I tried to make it sound like a natural laugh, but I was buying time. "I meant, anatomy of…a poem."

Michael came out of the bathroom, flopped back on the bed, and pretended to applaud. Silently, of course. I waved a hand at him in irritation. "Sorry, I was distracted. How is Grandma Sugar?"

My father caught me up on all of the news, and it pulled at my heart just to hear his voice. His normal Sunday morning call and everything seemed the same back in Kentucky, but for me everything had changed. I now lived in a world where monsters, gypsies, and chariots of fire and lightning existed.

I hung up the phone and turned to Michael. "I have to go back in December whether that thing is dead or not."

"I'll get you home to him, Emerson. Promise."

I nodded, trying to convince myself it was true. "I know you will."

I went into the bathroom to brush my teeth and freshen up. My face glowed pink from rubbing against Michael's stubbly cheeks, and my lips felt warm and a little swollen. I touched my mouth. Thinking about his kisses did funny things to my insides.

Splashing my cheeks with cold water, and patting them dry with Michael's towel, I realized two important things. First of all, Michael's towels were fluffy and white and his bathroom absolutely pristine, odd for a guy his age. Secondly, I'd been completely wrong about what I wanted from him. Maybe hanging around Lucinda and her revolving door of sexual partners had made me think I could have a casual fling and go home none the worse for wear, but now I knew the truth. I wasn't that kind of girl and nothing with Michael would ever be easy or casual.

"Pleased to meet you." She gave Michael a wink, and he blushed. "Nice work, Mikey."

Ryan grinned. Shorter than Michael and Patrick, his eyes were brown instead of blue. He wore a suit very similar to his brother's, and when he and Michael started talking, Leah pulled me away, linking her arm through mine.

"These aren't the best of circumstances, but I have to tell you, I'm so glad you're here." She spoke very quietly. Obviously, she didn't want Michael to hear.

I blinked at her in surprise. "You are?"

Leah nodded. "I've never seen him like this around a girl before. He looks so…happy."

We glanced back to see Michael scowling at us, and giggled. "Trust me. He's happy," she said, and I knew I'd found a friend.

"If you say so."

"Give him a chance," she said. I planned to do more than that. What I had in mind was more like a military siege that would end only in absolute and total surrender.

"He's not that bad," she continued. "He's rather brilliant, actually. He's the first Traveller I've ever heard of to attend university."

"I'm sure you're all very proud of him."

"Not all of us." Leah bit her lip. "I feel like I should warn you. There are people who want to force him to quit school, and they could use your presence here as a reason."

"But how does my being here have anything to do with Michael going to school?"

She smiled a sad little smile. "Would he have ever met you otherwise? I hope I'm wrong, but I thought you should know."

"You are awfully nice, Leah."

She grinned at me. "So I've been told."

Ryan and Michael came up behind us. "What have you been told?" asked Ryan.

"That I'm nice," she said.

Ryan and Michael both started to laugh. Ryan pulled Leah into his arms. "Don't listen to a word, Emerson, unless she says kind things about her loving husband or her wonderful brother-in-law."

Patrick and Margaret stood across the courtyard from us. Patrick's jaw was clenched, and Margaret seemed ready to cry. Leah noticed, too.

"Poor Margaret," she said, and Ryan echoed her words.

"Poor Margaret." He shook his head. "Looking to cause trouble again. I think we should say 'Poor Patrick' here, or maybe 'Poor Ryan.' It's isn't easy being married to the likes of you, you know."

Leah gave him a kiss on the cheek. "It's a daily struggle, I'm sure."

"Come on," said Ryan. "Let's greet our guests."

Michael took my hand, pulling me closer and being adorably protective. I had to work very hard to suppress a smile of victory. I'd been wrong comparing him to my feral kitten. Next to that kitten, Michael was going to be a piece of cake.

"The council will meet shortly. Margaret will tell them about her dreams, we'll give them the logical explanation, and all will be well." Michael gave me a little smile that didn't quite meet his eyes. "And then we'll go to the funeral."

"Are you sure I should come?" I remembered the

sound of Tad's mother weeping, and it made my heart ache.

"It's better if we all pay our respects." A bell tolled from somewhere deep within the compound, and Michael sighed. "It's time."

Chapter Twelve

These people are nuttier than a squirrel turd.
~Grandma Sugar

The sky darkened as we walked toward the council meeting. I looked up and realized a huge plastic dome covered the entire complex. Rain pelted the roof, but inside it remained dry and warm.

Michael noticed my interest. "That dome makes living outside in northern England ever so much more enjoyable."

Leah and Ryan walked just ahead of us, and overheard our conversation. "Michael designed it. He's a genius," said Leah.

Michael actually blushed, and I gave his hand a squeeze. "Is there anything you can't do?"

"I can't cook," he said, rubbing his chin, "and I'm a terrible dancer."

"Well, I can cook."

"I know. I sampled your brownies."

"Sample them anytime, big boy," I said with a wink, enjoying his befuddled reaction to my teasing. "I can't dance either. That's why I chose mixed martial arts as my talent for pageants."

Michael came to a dead stop."You beat people up at a beauty pageant?" He bit his lip to keep from laughing.

"Well, I didn't beat up the other girls, although I kind of wanted to at times. Some of them were awfully mean, but it didn't seem right to mess up their hair when they'd spent so much time and effort on it. I usually asked for volunteers from the audience instead."

The council area, just ahead of us, consisted of a large stage set with a long black table, chairs, and microphones. A bunch of unmatched benches and stools had been arranged for the audience. Michael found a place for us to sit in the back, not far from Ryan and Leah.

"How did you learn to fight?" he asked.

"I signed myself up for karate lessons at age four. I was precocious. I brought the permission form home from preschool and made Daddy fill it out for me. I competed nationally until last year when I started college."

"Did you ever win?"

I leaned forward to whisper in his ear. "Darlin', I *always* win."

The expression on his face made me laugh. "I'll consider that a warning," he said softly.

I sat back in my seat, folding my hands primly in my lap. "I studied judo, taekwondo, kendo, and stick fighting, too. The only thing I didn't try was sumo."

Michael snorted. "Why ever not?"

I answered him seriously even though he thought I'd made a joke. "Grandma Sugar wouldn't let me. At around eleven, she said enough was enough, and insisted I start doing pageants, too."

"Did you like it?"

I shrugged. "To tell you the truth, once I learned the rules, it wasn't that different from karate. A battle is a battle, no matter what the field looks like, and beauty pageants are a battle. Trust me. I just planned out a strategy and did what was necessary to win. I learned to walk the way they walked, and talk the way they talked. The rest came pretty naturally due to a bit of a competitive streak in my nature."

"What was your biggest win?"

"Junior Miss Kentucky was huge. And I came in first for the talent portion of Junior Miss America."

"How did you end up in York?"

"They have a fabulous literature program, and I want to be a professor someday, but I had a bit of an ulterior motive. Since my mom is from this area, I hoped to find her family, but I've had no luck at all."

"Maybe I can help, once we solve our little Moktar problem."

I gave him a grateful smile. "That would be wonderful, but I don't know much. My middle name, Jane, was her mother's name, but I don't have a clue about her dad's name."

"Where did the Emerson come from?"

"Ralph Waldo Emerson. She was also a lit major," I said, rolling my eyes. "Just like me. I'm lucky I wasn't a boy. She might have gone for Waldo."

Michael smiled. "You're definitely better as an Emerson."

The council, twelve older men and women wearing long black robes and acting very serious, approached the stage and everyone got quiet. Their cloaks made them look like a row of crows on a telephone wire. My heart began to pound in my chest as they sat down on stiff, high-back chairs and stared out at the crowd. I slipped my hand nervously into Michael's.

A tall man with a shock of white hair and a wooden gavel chose the place at the center of the table. Michael's father sat next to him.

Michael whispered in my ear, "The council members represent all of the Traveller communities in northern England. The man in the middle is Monroe Spinner, the leader. He's a good bloke. I've known him my whole life."

Monroe rapped his gavel on the table four times. "Please come to order. Today, we are here first and foremost to mourn the death of one of our own. I'd like to start with a moment of silence."

The gypsies grew still, the men a sea of somber dark suits and shaved heads. The women were a very different story. Their dresses were so wild and bright it looked more like they were going to a club than a wake.

Bowing my head, I thought about the boy who died and his poor mother. She would live forever with a hole in her heart. I didn't know her, but I knew what that felt like.

Monroe cleared his thought. "Now let us begin. I understand Margaret Nightingale would like to speak."

Margaret stood, wobbling a little on her high heels as she walked to the stage. She looked as nervous as I felt, maybe even more so. A microphone stood at one corner of the stage. Patrick sat in the audience, his arms crossed over his chest, a dark scowl on his face.

"I had a dream about the Dweller." Her voice sounded unsteady, hesitant.

"Go on, Margaret," said Monroe.

"I saw her in a field of new grass. She wore white, and lightning filled the sky above her. Candles lit her way. As the wind picked up and it started to storm, the candles were extinguished one by one."

Margaret backed away from the microphone and made her way through the silent crowd to her husband. He turned away from her when she sat down. She looked like she might cry.

The group of girls who'd given me dirty looks sat a few rows away. One of them stared at me with a nasty smirk on her face. Exactly the sort of gypsy girl I'd imagined Michael cavorting with in my imagination. She had long black hair, dark come-hither eyes, and big gold hoops in her ears. Voluptuous and sexy, she exuded confidence. Her eyes kept finding their way back to Michael, lingering on his face, but she was pretty darned interested in me, too. If looks could have killed, I'd have been dead by now.

One of the women on the council, a bony little thing with gray hair and hard eyes spoke directly to Monroe. "Dreams in autumn always come true."

"That's Mavin," said Michael. "She's very old school."

"She looks like a witch with a 'b' to me."

He nodded. "That, too."

He put an arm around my shoulders. A casual gesture, but I shot the group of gypsy girls a triumphant look anyway. They all seemed less than happy, especially the busty one.

I leaned close to whisper in his ear. "Who is that girl over there with the sizable bosom?"

He glanced at the group of girls. "That would be Nella."

"She doesn't like me."

"She doesn't like anyone."

Michael turned his attention back to the stage. I

stared at his profile. He might not be aware of it, but he was wrong about Nella. She definitely liked the tall, blue-eyed, wall of muscle in the seat right next to me.

There obviously wasn't a huge selection amongst the gypsy community. Once they weeded out their first cousins and close relatives, slimmer pickings remained than in a small town in rural Kentucky. Michael was probably a rather hot commodity, and I could understand their resentment as an outsider tried to pluck their juiciest peach. But even if I understood why they disliked me, it didn't make me inclined to change my ways. I wanted Michael just as much as they did, maybe even more.

Monroe pursed his lips. "That's what is said Mavin, but dreams can be interpreted different ways."

Another council member, a woman with soft curls and bright blue eyes spoke. Her hair looked like it had once been red, but had faded to a silvery gray. There was something kind about her, and I liked her immediately. I liked Monroe, too.

"Perhaps what our Margaret saw was the untimely death of one of our own, and the reason for our sadness today."

"Thank you, Anselina. That could very well be the case," said Monroe.

"But the dream happened after the death." Even Mavin's voice was annoying, like nails on a chalkboard.

Anselina gave Mavin a hard stare. "Sometimes dreams work that way. I, for one, am more interested in hearing about what occurred the night our boy died."

Monroe nodded. "So am I. Would Michael, Sean, Quinn and Anthony please come here? And bring the

Dweller, too."

My heart stopped in my chest. I did not want to get up in front of these people, especially the group of nasty girls. Michael took my hand and whispered in my ear. "Imagine it's a pageant, and you're going to win."

His word helped to propel me forward. I'd dealt with jealous girls my whole life. Southern pageant girls took catty to a whole new level, although these gypsy girls may have had them beat. I took a deep breath, which also made me feel calmer, and we walked to the stage. The boys who were with us the night Tad died joined us.

"Let's start with Sean."

Sean approached the microphone. Smaller than Michael, he looked very young, so young a bit of acne still dotted his forehead. He had dark eyes and a big dimple in one cheek.

"I was supposed to hunt with the one we lost that night. We planned to meet at sunset in front of York Minster. That's what we always did if we couldn't leave together."

Sean clenched his hands. "He didn't show up. I waited for an hour and called his cell phone. He never answered."

"What did you do?" Monroe folded his hands in front of him on the table.

"I couldn't hunt alone, of course. As I walked back to the compound, I got a call from Anthony and Quinn. They said they'd found him."

"Anthony and Quinn, please tell us what happened. Which one is Anthony and which is Quinn?"

I hadn't noticed it before, but they were twins. Their different tattoos and piercings were the only things that set them apart.

One of the boys stepped forward. “I’m Anthony, sir.” Anthony had a spider web tattoo on his neck and gages in his ears. Quinn had a small tattoo of a knife at the base of his skull.

“Quinn and I were on our patrol when we smelled one of them. It stood over a body. We assumed it was a Dweller. We chased it away, but our boy was already dead.”

“Did the Moktar get his hypothalamus?” Monroe’s voice sounded hollow and sad. I wondered how many deaths the council had investigated and imagined it happened quite often.

Quinn shook his head. “We called Michael as soon as we found the body and stayed with it until he came.”

Monroe looked over at Michael. “Please tell us what you saw.”

He walked to the microphone. “He died from blunt force trauma to the head. We protected his body when the Moktar attacked again.”

One of the other council members, an older man with glasses and a kind face leaned forward. “Which one of you made the kill?”

Michael’s face remained expressionless. “I did, Councilman Jones.”

That earned a small round of applause from everyone. “And that is why you are the Ceannfort,” said Councilman Jones with a smile.

Apparently, Sean noticed my confusion. “The Ceannfort is our best fighter,” he whispered, his eyes glowing with admiration and pride.

“What happened next?” Monroe asked.

“Emerson was about half a block away. Another

Moktar grabbed her and held her."

Anselina looked at me. "I think we'd like to hear this part from Emerson."

My cheeks got hot, and my heart slammed against my ribcage. I thought about what Leah had told me, and felt terrified because there was a great deal at stake here. Michael might not be allowed to go back to school if I messed up.

"Tell us your name, child." Anselina must have seen the fear on my face. Her voice was kind.

I took a deep breath and tried to pretend this was just another pageant. I squared my shoulders, held my head high, and made eye contact with the people in the audience, even the nasty girls. "Emerson Jane Shaw, ma'am."

This earned a few titters. They probably weren't used to hearing "ma'am" and "sir," but I'd been raised right, and would never think of addressing an older lady or gentleman any other way.

"And how did you end up where the boy was killed?" Anselina asked.

I kept my gaze squarely set ahead, refusing to look at Michael. I couldn't lie, but telling the truth wasn't easy. "I followed Michael there."

"Why?" Anselina wasn't going to let me off the hook easily.

"I'm not sure, ma'am. He did his very best to avoid me, but when I saw him that night, I followed him. It wasn't his fault."

This earned a few laughs from Nella and her posse. I swallowed hard, not knowing if I'd hurt Michael's case or helped it, but telling the truth was my only option. "They killed the first Moktar, just as they said.

The second one grabbed me from behind."

"Did it try to kill you?" asked Monroe.

I shook my head. "It just sniffed me and licked my neck." I shuddered. "Michael and the other boys were too far away to help, so I did my best to fight it off."

This earned a huge reaction from the crowd. Everyone started talking at once. Monroe had to pound his gavel on the table several times to regain order. Nella and her friends stared at me with open-mouthed disbelief.

"She's lying," Mavin screeched.

Sean took the microphone. "She speaks the truth. She's a wee little thing, but she fought like a champion."

I beamed. "Thank you."

Sampson finally spoke. "Where did you learn to fight like that, lass?"

"I've taken martial arts classes since I was small, sir."

Monroe watched me, scratching his chin. "You don't know the rules here, Miss Shaw, but there's something important you need to understand. It's fine to defend yourself against the Moktar. That's your right. But only the men do the fighting. Any woman who hunts will be shunned for life."

"I'm not a Traveller."

"We do what we must to keep as many people as possible safe. If you stay here, the same rules apply to you, too. Are you in agreement?"

I nodded. I had no desire to seek out those monsters anyway.

Mavin destroyed my little moment of happiness. "Now a Dweller knows about the Moktar, and, more importantly about us. None of this would have ever happened if you hadn't let your son go to university, Sampson Nightingale. Your arrogance has put us in danger." She shot Sampson a nasty look.

"Stop your yammering, Mavin. No one is in danger, except this lass right here. And that's what bothers me," he said. "This isn't normal Moktar behavior."

"It bothers me as well, Sampson." Anselina gave me a steady look. "The Moktar is tracking you, Emerson. He wants to hunt you down and kill you. The question is…why?"

"I don't know, ma'am."

"Moktar don't usually hunt Dwellers. They simply kill them on the spot, but he let you live. It doesn't make sense." Anselina shook her head.

Michael stepped forward, his shoulders tight with tension. "There is something else. I've seen this Moktar before. He's a tricky one. Always hanging back, and letting others do his dirty work."

"Do you think he's the Alpha?" asked Monroe.

Michael paused for only a second. "Aye."

I felt the fear coming off the crowd in waves. "Is the Alpha the leader of the Moktar?" I whispered to Quinn.

He nodded. "The biggest and the baddest."

Mavin looked terrified. "She'll lead him right here. He'll kill us all."

Her words made the already frightened crowd slip one step further into panic mode. Monroe did his best to calm them down. "Mavin, you know quite well there is no danger inside these walls. Only a Traveller can open our doors."

Anselina agreed. “We are safer here than anywhere else in England.”

Michael squared his shoulders. “I vow to kill the Alpha. Once he’s dead, the danger will be gone.”

This caused the unrest in the crowd to shift into excitement, almost a palpable thing. Monroe looked at the other council members. “We’ll vote on it now.”

The council stood up and moved to the back of the stage. They argued quietly amongst themselves for a few minutes. Mavin looked really angry, so I hoped that meant things were going well for us. When Monroe spoke, he was short and right to the point.

“She’s in great danger, and so we’ll allow her to stay with us…” Mavin began to protest, but Monroe raised a hand to quiet her. “For exactly two weeks, and then she must leave whether the Alpha is dead or alive. That is our final ruling.”

Michael protested. “Two weeks? That won’t be enough time.”

Monroe ignored him. He looked at the crowd, lifted his hand, and slammed his gavel one last time.

“Meeting adjourned.”

Chapter Thirteen

This idea is like letting a monkey with a blowtorch into a room full of dynamite.

~Grandma Sugar

After the council meeting, Michael and I met Ryan and Leah under a shady tree. I still reeled from what had just happened.

"I don't know about y'all, but I'm sweating like a whore in church on Sunday." I fanned myself with my hand, and Leah and Ryan burst out laughing.

"Does she always talk like that?" Ryan asked Michael.

"It gets worse when she's nervous. Or angry."

I had to agree with him. "Or drunk. I get very southern when drinking."

"Well, I think it's charming." Leah took my arm as Sampson approached. His black councilman's robe hung over his arm, and he looked very serious. "Let's go and get something cold to drink. The boys will want to talk with their father."

We went to Leah's caravan. She poured two glasses of lemonade, and we sat outside on wooden rocking chairs. Leah and Ryan had a modern-looking caravan like Michael, but the rocking chairs and the lemonade made it seem like I was back in Bowling Green.

I leaned back with a contented sigh. "This feels like home."

"Tell me about Kentucky."

"It's different from York. My daddy's a professor, and we live in town, close to the university. Bowling Green is the biggest city for miles, so we have lots of restaurants and things to do. Nashville is only an hour away, and that's fun."

"Nashville? I'd love to go there. I adore country music."

I looked at her in surprise. "Really?"

"I even have my own cowboy hat," Leah said with a giggle.

"You'll have to come and visit sometime." As soon as the words left my mouth, I wished I could take them back. Leah wasn't leaving the compound, let alone England. It was almost cruel of me to bring it up.

Leah seemed to sense my thoughts. "It's not that bad, really. I'm happy with Ryan and the life we've built here." She put a hand protectively over her belly. "And we haven't told many people yet, but we're expecting our first child."

"Oh, that's wonderful news. Congratulations."

Leah nodded, but there was a shadow in her eyes. "We're excited, but it can be hard for Traveller women. Margaret lost three babies. They all died before they were born."

"I'm sorry for her."

I meant what I said. Margaret may have been mean to me, and tried to get the council to kick me out, but I wouldn't wish that sort of thing on anyone.

"Just be glad you aren't a Traveller," said Leah, and then she gave me a wry grin. "And not just for the baby thing, although that's reason enough."

"What do you mean?"

Leah took a long swallow of her lemonade. "You'd be trapped here like all the other women. Michael would never let you leave."

I felt a chill go over me in spite of the warmth of the day. "Well, it's a good thing I'm not then."

"I'll drink to that," said Leah, and we tapped our glasses together.

Ryan and Michael brought us lunch. After we ate, we walked to Tad's caravan for the funeral. Everyone in the compound waited to pay their respects. We stood for a long time in line before we reached the coffin, which was closed. I was happy about that. I had no desire to the see the face of a dead sixteen year old.

Michael seemed to understand my thoughts. "It's closed because we had to remove his hypothalamus before we buried him, otherwise the Moktar would dig him up."

He whispered the words into my ear and caught me when I stumbled. The idea of having to protect a dead body like that was a reality these people lived with on a daily basis.

Tad's caravan was wooden and not very big. White sheets draped over the entire structure and also on all the furniture in the yard, reminding me of the sad-looking dust covers used to protect things in long deserted or abandoned homes. The coffin was white and shiny, with silver handles. Fresh flowers surrounded both the coffin and caravan, some shaped into large, ornate arrangements and others just single stems placed reverently on the ground. The air smelled strongly of lilies, roses, and carnations. For a moment, I had a flashback to my mother's funeral, a memory so intense and painful tears stung the backs of my eyes. Tad's mother stood alone next to the coffin, wearing a wine-colored evening gown.

"His father passed away a few years ago. He was her only child," Michael murmured in my ear. "And don't say his name. It's very bad luck."

I nodded, glad he'd told me. When we reached the coffin, Michael placed his hand on it, a muscle working in his cheek as he struggled to compose himself. He embraced Tad's mother, and held her as silent sobs wracked her body. When he let go, he turned to me.

"Emerson, this is Mary."

I reached out to shake her hand. She was so small the top of her head barely reached my shoulder.

"I'm so sorry for your loss."

She pulled out a tissue and dabbed her eyes. "Thank you. He was a good boy. You didn't know him, of course. It's kind of you to come."

I followed Michael off to a quiet spot on the other side of the caravan. He was pale and looked so shaken I instinctively wrapped my arms around him. He held me tightly, his lips on my hair.

"This should not have happened."

His voice was raw and rough. I patted his back and made soothing noises, but nothing I could do or say would make this better.

Tad's funeral began after the long line of mourners had said their condolences. I didn't know how Tad's mother got through it. She had a kind word for everyone, and sometimes it seemed like she was the comforter, more than the person being comforted.

Eventually, everyone had paid their respects, and

the crowd formed into a solemn circle around Mary and the coffin. Glasses of whiskey were poured, including one for Tad. I learned very quickly gypsy funerals were composed of three things, weeping, wailing, and lots and lots of whiskey.

Sampson stood to make the first toast. “Do not cry or thy tears will sear the heart of the one we lost. Let him rest in peace. Do not use his name, or eat his favorite food. Do not use his things. Everything he owned must be destroyed. There should be nothing left now to bind his soul to Earth. He is free now, to fly to Rom, and live in fields of green in never-ending sunshine.”

Everyone took a deep drink. The whiskey burned its way down my throat, and left a mellow warmth in my middle. I had to agree with this aspect of a gypsy funeral. The whiskey definitely helped make things just a little more bearable.

Michael, Patrick, and Ryan joined a group of Tad’s friends. I waited with Leah. Margaret stood alone, not far from us. A small fire had been built near Tad’s caravan, and we watched in silence as the men carried all of Tad’s belongings and tossed them into the fire, one by one.

“Will they cremate him?” I really did not want to see his body added to the funeral pyre and was relieved when Leah shook her head.

“Never. Gypsies are always buried. Dust to dust and all that.”

After all of Tad’s belongings had been burnt, the women lit tall white candles that lined the way from Tad’s coffin to a horse drawn hearse waiting near two large metal doors. Everyone was completely silent until the last candle was lit and the procession began.

"It's good he was outside when he died," murmured Leah, as we joined the line of mourners behind Tad's coffin. "A gypsy shouldn't die cooped up. It's just wrong."

Tad's friends, including Michael and his brothers, carried the coffin slowly down the path. When they got to the end, they lifted it onto the hearse. The horses were black, with braided manes. The coffin was huge and looked heavy.

"Why is the coffin so big?" It was almost twice as wide as any coffin I'd ever seen.

"He'll be buried with things he might need in his next life, like money and food." Leah's lower lip trembled. "Anything to make the journey a little easier for him."

"That sounds very Egyptian."

Leah gave me a little smile. "Gypsy comes from the word 'Egyptian.' We've been around a long time. Some people say we bear the mark of Cain, doomed to wander the earth endlessly. Those people are just bigots who hate us and want to think we're inherently evil. Not all who wander are lost."

The horses started moving, and we joined the sad parade of gypsies that followed. We exited the compound through the metal doors, large enough to accommodate the hearse, and wound our way through the back alleys of York. The streets were completely empty and quiet, like the whole city mourned, too. We walked in silence until we came to a small cemetery. Pretty typical to others I'd seen, except empty bottles of whiskey and glasses stood at each grave, as well as small trinkets that looked like good luck charms. There was no one else around.

"Where is everyone?" I whispered to Leah.

"We placed a charm to make Dwellers stay away. It's an old gypsy trick. It'll disappear as soon as we're done."

"Why doesn't it affect me?"

Leah shrugged. "I don't know, maybe because you're here with us."

Sampson stood next to Mary and held her as the coffin was lowered into the ground. A man began playing the bagpipes. The sad, soulful sound echoed across the barren cemetery. After the last note died away, Mary took the first handful of dirt and threw it on her son's coffin. She wept, clinging to Sampson's jacket. Tears rolled down Leah's cheeks, and I swallowed hard, blinking my own away. Another round of whiskey was poured and Sampson raised his glass.

"Gone, but not forgotten," he said.

We raised our glasses and repeated his words. "Gone, but not forgotten."

Some of the men pulled out instruments and began to play. There was a fiddle, a flute, and oboe, and a rather banged up trumpet. Several people had tambourines. They gathered together and played a lively tune that reminded me of a New Orleans' funeral parade. As they played, we headed slowly back to the compound, our hearts feeling a little bit lighter. Some of the gypsies began to dance, and others started to sing.

"It's over now. We can stop the crying and celebrate his life." Leah blew out a sigh, and pulled me out of the parade to wait for Michael and Ryan. They came last, after Mary and Sampson, making sure everyone was safe and accounted for.

Michael grabbed my hand, and we walked back to the compound together. He looked worn out.

"Are you all right?" I asked.

"This was a hard one, but now you'll see what a real gypsy party is like."

"Geez Louise. I'm half-drunk already."

Michael bit his lip and gave me a sexy little grin. "Are you going to start talking all southern again?"

"I sure might. We consumed quite a bit of whiskey today."

He snorted. "As someone from Kentucky might say, honey, you ain't seen nothin' yet."

I laughed, squeezing his hand as I studied the people in the procession. "I've heard stories about gypsies my whole life, but those gypsies weren't like all of you. Are you the same or different?"

"Both." He pulled me closer so we could talk quietly. "Before the Moktar, people could marry Dwellers and start new compounds. We were vagabonds, and naturally we spread out and split apart at times. The gypsies you know about are sort of our very distant cousins. They mixed with Dwellers so much that only a bit of real Traveller blood remains. Unfortunately, it's just enough to make them excellent con artist, liars, and thieves, which gets all of us in trouble."

As we entered the compound, I looked around, noticing the gardens and old trees around the caravans. "But I think you've been here a long time. That doesn't really fit the vagabond description."

"We're forced to live here by the alliance. They like to keep tabs on us because we're an unpredictable element. But wandering is in our blood. It makes us crazy to be tied down like this."

Leah came up to us, laughing and pulling Ryan along with her. "Come, you two. The party has begun."

The rest of the day flew by in a haze of drinking, dancing, feasting, and singing. The women were extremely good dancers. The men mostly stayed on the sidelines and watched. Michael kept me close by his side. Every once in a while, one of the younger men pulled a girl away from the other dancers. She would resist, dragging her feet, but laughing the whole time.

"What are they doing?" I had to get very close to Michael's ear so he could hear me.

"That's called 'grabbing.' It's an old gypsy courting ritual, a way to steal a kiss. It's completely barbaric, and yet most find it somehow romantic. Too bad it stems from our fear of the Moktar taking our women."

Bitterness tainted his voice. I stroked his cheek. "Well, you don't need to bother with that because I'll kiss you any ole time you want."

I stood on my tiptoes and gave him a long, sweet kiss. He tasted like whiskey and smelled faintly of smoke from the campfire. I leaned against him with a soft sigh.

Patrick cleared his throat. He stood behind us, dressed in full battle gear. "Time to head out, Mikey."

The sun began to set as the men readied themselves, even the older ones. They'd drunk a lot of whiskey, and a few weren't quite steady on their feet.

When Michael nodded and slipped away, I looked at Leah in concern. "Are they seriously going out like this?"

Leah pursed her lips. "They must. The council only gave Michael two weeks to kill the Alpha. Every minute counts, Emerson."

I shook my head, the panic rising in my chest. "If anything happens to him…"

Leah took my arm and gave me a steady look. "He'll go whether you want it or not because he must. Don't make it harder for him. Just put a smile on your face, give him a kiss, and send him off."

She kept her eyes locked on mine until I calmed down. I knew she was right, but when Michael came back, dressed in all black, I couldn't hide the worry in my eyes.

He pulled me to a quiet spot under a large oak tree. "Don't fret. I'm not drunk."

"You had an awful lot of whiskey today, mister."

He playfully tugged a strand of my hair. "I've been drinking whiskey since before I could walk. I'm fine. Trust me."

I pulled him close, my hands on his leather jacket. "Be safe."

He nodded seriously. "I'm always safe."

"Be careful."

"I'm always careful."

I gave him a very stern look. "Be serious."

He grinned and kissed me so hard my knees almost gave out. "I'm never serious," he joked, his words a sweet murmur against my lips.

I had to smile back. I couldn't help it. He'd finally initiated another kiss. I held his face in my hands and kissed him over and over again, wanting him to stay so badly it hurt.

When the others yelled for him, he leaned close

and whispered in my ear, “Don’t worry. I’ll kill the monster, and you’ll be able to go home to your Da.”

I had promised not to cry, but couldn’t stop myself. “Just come back, Michael Nightingale. I mean it.”

He put a finger under my chin and tilted it up to peer into my eyes. He gave me one last heartbreakingly tender kiss, and then whispered, “I will. For the first time, there is something I want to come back to.”

Chapter Fourteen

It happened faster than a knife fight in a phone booth.

~Grandma Sugar

Sun Tzu knew a lot about war, but he didn't know how it felt to be left behind while others fought. I wasn't accustomed to it myself. The Traveller women, however, had become experts. As soon as the men left, they took their places around the fire to wait. We formed a sad little group. The women still wore their fancy dresses and sequins. They looked like a band of strippers who'd gotten lost in the woods. I sat down on a log next to Leah, and tried to study the women without being obvious.

Tad's mother, Mary, began to sing, breaking the silence with her mournful melody. The song, a sad, sweet lullaby, sounded hauntingly familiar.

"I've heard this before," I whispered to Leah.

"It's a Traveller song. You couldn't have."

When the song ended, the bottle of whiskey got passed around again. I tried to refuse it, since I'd had more whiskey in one day than I'd had my whole life, but the ladies insisted. Soon I was buzzed, along with everyone else.

"Oy. Dweller."

One of the girls called to me from the other side of

the fire pit. She wore a silver sequin dress about as big as the piece of aluminum foil a decent person would use to wrap a ham sandwich. She had long, black, silky hair and eyes so dark blue they looked nearly purple. A pretty girl, but obviously no one had ever taught her to keep her knees together when wearing a micro-mini dress.

"What do you want, Audrey?" Leah, the only one not toasted at this point, narrowed her eyes at the girl. She sipped water instead of whiskey. Although she didn't seem aware of it, sometimes her hand would cover her belly protectively. It wouldn't be long before everyone knew she was expecting.

Audrey scowled. "I have a question for the Dweller. Is it true you fought off a Moktar?"

"Yes, it is."

Audrey took another swallow of whiskey and then slammed down her glass on a small table next to her seat. "How?"

Audrey's question hung in the air, and the women all turned and looked at me. Even Nella seemed curious.

"Basic self-defense. I could teach you a few moves, if you'd like."

An older woman nearby shifted in her seat. "It's forbidden."

Audrey rolled her eyes. "It's forbidden to hunt. We have the right to know how to defend ourselves. Teach us what you know, Dweller."

A few minutes later, I showed them some basic moves. Nella and her group watched, but refused to join in. Their loss. I taught the others how to stun an attacker, how to get away when grabbed, and where to hit someone to cause the most damage. They kicked off their shoes and copied everything I showed them. Even the older ladies seemed eager to learn. Margaret stood way in the back, but she joined in, too.

After I promised to teach them more later, they decided they wanted to play a new game called "Let's Dress Emerson." Audrey and a few of the younger girls pulled me into her caravan and made me try on several dresses, laughing the whole time. They finally settled on a very short and sparkly gold tank dress with a pair of ridiculously high-heeled shoes. They played with my hair and makeup, and when they were satisfied, let me look in a mirror.

I was shocked, mostly because I loved it. The tight dress clung to my curves and made my skin glow. It showed enough cleavage Grandma Sugar would have had the vapors, and it barely covered my underpants, but it was stunning, and I loved the way my hair brushed against my naked back. My makeup looked surprisingly pretty as well. The gold in the dress and in my eye shadow brought out little flecks of gold in my eyes. They wanted to put false eyelashes on me, but I refused. I'd done that in my pageant days and vowed to never to it again. Instead, they added loads and loads of mascara, making my eyes huge in my face. They brushed my cheekbones with something that glittered, added a bit of color to my lips, and stood back to admire their handiwork.

"Nice job, ladies." I put one hand on my waist and jutted out my hip, a pageant pose.

Audrey's gaze went from the top of my head to the toes of my feet, and then a slow smile spread across her face. "I can't wait to see Mikey's reaction."

I bit my lip. “Do you think he’ll like it?”

She laughed. “He won’t know what hit him. He’s always so serious and proper. I can’t wait to see him with his tongue hanging out, panting over you.”

Thanks to years on the pageant circuit, I had plenty of experience with heels. These heels were the highest I’d ever put on, but I managed. When I walked back to the fire pit, the other ladies clapped. Nella and her friends looked less than pleased. They started whispering among themselves, and I ignored them. I did a little turn for the others and gave them a sexy pout. Leah laughed.

“Emerson, you look smashing.”

“Thank you.” I blew a kiss to the girls who’d dressed me. They waved and giggled, and Leah and I sat back down by the fire. Because Leah had accepted me, most of the other women had, too.

Margaret slid into the seat next to me and handed me a bottle of whiskey, her expression serious. I accepted it and took a deep swallow, keeping my eyes on her the whole time. Leah got up discreetly to leave us alone.

“I’m sorry,” she said, her voice soft.

I almost choked on the whiskey. “What did you say?”

“None of this is your fault. You didn’t ask for any of this to happen, and you weren’t the cause. I still feel I had to report my dream to the council, but it wasn’t anything personal.”

In the light of the fire, her pale eyes were almost colorless. It took courage for her to speak with me like this.

“Thank you. Now drink.” I handed the whiskey

back to her.

She smiled and took a swig. "You aren't bad for a Dweller, you know."

"I do my best."

Margaret gave the bottle back to me. I took another tiny sip, barely able to focus on her face, and she laughed. "But you're no Traveller, either. Whiskey is mother's milk to us."

We sat in silence for a moment. I could tell Margaret had something else she wanted to say to me, and I waited for her to get to it. Finally, she took a deep breath and started. "I liked what you did tonight, teaching us how to defend ourselves. It felt good."

"It was fun."

"More than fun." Margaret's hands, in her lap, balled into fists. "For the first time, I felt like I might not be completely powerless. That's a gift, Emerson. Thank you."

She patted my arm a little awkwardly, and then got up and walked away. As soon as she left, Anselina took the seat she'd just vacated. It made me nervous that the councilwoman wanted to sit next to me. I'd had quite a bit to drink, and wasn't up for an interrogation at the moment.

"I'm more popular than the last jar of barbeque sauce at a pork roast this evening."

Anselina smiled. "Don't worry, child. I just want to talk to you."

I stared at her. "About what?"

"About many things, but mostly I'm curious. Where are you from, and how did you end up here?"

I reached for the bottle Margaret had set down and took another swallow. I handed it to Anselina, and she had a drink, too. I told her about Bowling Green, Daddy, Grandma Sugar, and Pappy George. Several of the other ladies listened in, including Leah who resumed her old seat next to me.

"How did you end up in York?" asked Anselina. She wasn't wearing her council robes anymore; instead, she had on a bright blue dress that matched her eyes. In the firelight, I saw streaks of red in her graying hair.

"I'm here for a semester on a study abroad trip."

"I can't imagine having that sort of freedom." Leah's voice was barely a whisper. She stared into the fire, and her hand automatically came to rest on her belly again. "Not that I'd want to leave, mind you, but it would have been nice to travel."

"It's too dangerous," said an older lady sitting next to Tad's mother. "You're a Dweller, so it makes no difference if you come or go, but don't fill their heads with nonsense."

My cheeks reddened. "You're right. It's not the same for me."

"How did you meet Michael?" asked Anselina. I narrowed my eyes, and she laughed. "This doesn't have anything to do with the council. I'm just curious."

Leah patted my hand. "You can trust Anselina. She's a good old bird, but she'll drive you mad with her questions."

The whiskey helped me open up. I let out a sigh remembering the first time I caught of glimpse of Michael in all his grumpy glory. "I saw him at a tea shop. When I tried to talk to him, he ran away from me."

"What a wanker." Audrey rolled her eyes.

"He was trying to protect me. I get that now." I

first."

His yellow eyes locked on the knife, widening in fear. "I will not betray my people."

Michael scowled at him. "You aren't 'people,' you're beasts."

"Some of us are more like you than you think."

"What does he mean?" I asked Leah, who stood next to me. She shook her head.

"I have no idea." She wrinkled her nose in disgust. "But he smells bloody awful."

Chakba scanned the crowd, and once again, his eyes met mine. He smiled, showing rows of sharp, yellowing teeth. "There she is."

Michael followed Chakba's gaze. As soon as he realized Chakba had singled me out, the color rose in his cheeks. He hit Chakba again with his stick, harder this time, but Chakba kept his eyes on mine.

"She is the one."

"What are you talking about?" Michael's face was only inches away from Chakba's. I wanted to haul him back with my own two hands. He stood too close to that monster.

Chakba just laughed. "She is the one he wants. Our alpha is tracking her right now. He will catch her, too. He will have her over and over again and make her beg for more. Then, after she has borne him a few sons, he will rip her apart and eat her."

Michael took the knife and shoved it up to Chakba's neck. A thin line of blood trickled down from where the knife pricked his skin. "What is his name?"

Chakba's eyes were filled with pure malice. "He is Melo, and you should already know him."

"Why? He's nothing to me." Michael kept his knife

at Chakba's throat.

Chakba laughed. "He is the son of your delightful mother, sweet like a summer bloom, Roseanne."

Sampson howled like an animal in agony, and then slumped into Patrick's arms. At first, I thought he might have passed out, but he was simply overcome with pain and grief. Michael breathed hard, trying to control himself.

"My mother is alive?"

Chakba's lips twisted cruelly. "She was fun while she lasted, and delicious when she died." He looked right at me, his expression pure evil. "And your brother will enjoy this one, too. He's been looking forward to it. All he talks about is finding her and making her his."

Michael took the knife and began cutting a shallow line down Chakba's abdomen. He paused just above his belly button. Chakba wasn't laughing anymore. "She isn't a Traveller. Why would he want her?"

Chakba looked at Michael in surprise, and then laughed. "You Roms are completely hopeless. You can't see what it right in front of your ugly faces. Look at that golden, pretty, girl. You have no idea what she is, do you? She's a gem in a box filled with nothing but glass."

Michael put the knife to his throat once again. "What is she?"

Chakba shook his head. "I won't tell you. I'll save that for Melo." He licked his lips again, looking at me longingly. "Although I wish I could taste her first…"

Michael shoved the knife deep into Chakba's belly and then backed away, leaving it there. Chakba gasped. "I answered your questions. Kill me now, Traveller. Kill me quick."

Michael's body trembled with rage. "You allowed my mother no such courtesy. Die slowly, beast."

The gypsies, led by Sampson, approached with murder in their eyes. Chakba pleaded for mercy, but Michael ignored him. He grabbed my hand and pulled me away, but not before I saw them tear Chakba apart piece by piece. His screams sounded very human at first, but turned into the howls of a dying animal before they stopped completely.

Michael led me to a copse of tall trees and pulled me roughly into his arms. My face fit into his neck, and he smelled like sweat and blood, but he was wonderfully and miraculously alive. I felt like I could walk on air. Michael quickly brought me back to Earth. He put his hands on my shoulders and held me away from him.

"Who are you, Emerson?"

I looked up at him, perplexed. "You know who I am."

Michael's eyes scanned my body, his eyes narrowing. "Why are dressed like a whore? Did you *want* to draw attention to yourself? Are you a complete idiot?"

I blinked away tears. "The girls dressed me up. I thought you'd like it."

He let go of my shoulders and looked at me like I was lower than a cockroach. "Bringing you here was a mistake. I've put everyone in greater danger. Go back and change into your own clothes. I have to speak with my family."

"Michael, I'm sorry."

"It's too late, Emerson."

His eyes were cold and cruel. He rubbed a hand

over his head and walked away. I watched him go, my heart shattering into a thousand pieces.

Back at his caravan, I put the pretty golden dress on a hanger. I'd give it back to Audrey tomorrow. I couldn't face anyone right now. I pulled on my yoga pants and a soft, pink shirt, scrubbed my face until it was raw, and sat down on Michael's couch. I waited for the tears to come, but nothing happened. I felt numb.

I pulled my journal out of my backpack and began to write, pouring all of my pain out onto the pages. Hours later, my hand cramping and my eyes heavy with fatigue, I finally put my pen down.

Surely, my daddy had never imagined my journal would be filled with gypsies and monsters and bad boys who made me fall in love with them and then broke my heart. I picked up my cell phone to check the time. He would still be awake, but I couldn't call him. He would hear the sadness in my voice and worry.

I sighed looking at Michael's bed. He'd been cruel, and needed to be taught a lesson, but all I could think about was how much I wanted to climb into his warm bed and wake up wrapped in his strong arms once again.

I needed slapped in the face with a dose of reality. Michael had protected me, but as the Ceannfort, that was sort of his job. He'd kissed me, but that didn't mean anything either. I curled up on his couch, and as my eyes closed a depressing realization hit me. I was simply a burden to him, just like so many things in his life. I thought I was punishing him by sleeping on the couch, but the sad truth was Michael might not even care if I was in his bed or not.

Chapter Sixteen

He was as bad off as a rubber-nosed woodpecker in a petrified forest.

~Grandma Sugar

I woke up to sunshine streaming in through the windows, and Michael hovering over me. I had a dull headache from the amount of whiskey I'd drunk, and a dull heartache from the way he'd treated me. A crick in my neck from sleeping on the couch was the final insult. I wasn't in the mood for any nonsense today.

Evidently, neither was Michael. "Wake up. I'll walk you to your apartment." He was dressed and ready to go. I wondered if he'd slept at all.

I didn't ask if there was time to take a shower. I wanted to get out of his caravan as soon as possible. I brushed my teeth, yanked my hair into a ponytail, pulled on a jacket, and grabbed my backpack.

"Would you like some breakfast?"

I shook my head. "Don't bother."

We walked in tense silence through the streets of York. My phone had died completely, so I had no idea of the time, but it seemed really early. My internal clock was thrown off after so many late nights with the gypsies.

When we reached my apartment, I turned to him, unable to meet his eyes. "Are you going to class?"

Michael shook his head. "There's another council meeting tonight. I probably won't go to school anymore."

I reached for his arm. "That isn't fair."

He shook his arm out of my grasp. "Life isn't fair. Do you think it's been easy for me, hunting all night, and then trying to stay awake for chem labs? I've been doing it for more than three years, Emerson. I'm done. I'll be here to collect you at four."

He stomped away, and I slowly pulled myself up the stairs to my apartment. I had a few hours before my first class, and needed every minute of it. I was behind on all of my classwork, and wanted to immerse myself in my books and forget about Michael Nightingale for just a little while. Lucinda still slept, so I took a quick shower, made a pot of coffee, ate a bowl of cereal, and set to work on my laptop.

I finished my assignment in record time, and had to admit it was pretty darned good. The best thing about it was I had not thought about Michael Nightingale for nearly an hour.

"You came home."

Lucinda stood in the doorway of her bedroom, rubbing her eyes. Only Lucinda could roll out of bed and look like a fashion model. She ran over and gave me a big hug.

"I'm so glad you're back. It's been dreadful around here without you. It sucks, in fact. It sucks big, hairy bollocks."

I poured Lucinda a mug of coffee and stuck a piece of bread in the toaster for her. She kissed me on the cheek. "Thank you. This is splendid. We missed you so much."

"I missed you, too." I took a long sip of my coffee. My hangover had faded away, and I didn't feel tired anymore, but my heart remained like block of ice lodged in my chest. "How is Antarctica?"

She groaned, resting her forehead on one hand. "We went to the cinema, and I forced him to sit way in the back. As soon as the lights went out, I decided to go for it, and I went bold."

"Oh, no."

"Oh, yes. I tried to touch his gentleman sausage, and it was a disaster. He nearly jumped out of his seat. He thought I was trying to get the popcorn."

I bit my lip. "His gentleman sausage?"

Lucinda planted her face on the table. "It's ridiculous. I can't even call it by its proper name anymore. I don't know what's wrong with me."

I patted her back. "Grandma Sugar calls it a ding-a-ling."

Lucinda looked up at me. "My grandmother called it a toodle-pip. That's awful, too."

"Please don't start calling it that," I said with a laugh.

Lucinda sighed. "He goes back in less than two weeks, and I don't want him to leave."

The doorbell rang, and Poppy came in dressed entirely in black, her eyes red and swollen. She looked completely miserable.

"I met Nigel's parents, and they hated me."

I pulled her into a hug, and she cried softly on my shoulder. "Poor Pops."

She shook her head. "I wore my most conservative clothes. I was quiet and respectful and good. And they bloody hated me at first sight. What did I do wrong?"

"Michael warned me they were snobs. What does Nigel say?"

This brought a fresh flood of tears. "That he loves me. That it doesn't matter. But I can tell it does. I don't want him to suffer."

Lucinda leaned forward in her seat. "The only thing that will make him suffer is losing you. Now stop crying, put on an electric blue mini skirt and your craziest socks, and let him know how much you care about him."

Poppy gave her a tremulous smile. "Thank you, Lucinda." She turned to me. "How is Michael?"

I had promised myself I wouldn't cry, but as soon as she looked at me with those big, blue eyes, tears began rolling down my cheeks. I wiped them away with the back of my hand, struggling to compose myself. I'd cried enough over Michael.

"He had some terrible news last night, and he pushed me away. I just wanted to comfort him, but he wouldn't let me."

"Well, that's understandable." Lucinda filled up everyone's cup with fresh coffee. "If he opens up, it'll make him vulnerable, and Michael Nightingale does not seem the sort of man who likes being vulnerable."

"What was your first clue?" I glanced at my phone. "Shoot. I have to run, or I'll be late for class."

We agreed to meet, and commiserate, later. I rushed to my room, feeling better after I changed into my wool skirt and soft, cashmere sweater; more like myself again, and less like the strange girl in the gold dress. I had to use a lot of makeup to cover up my dark circles, but at least I was somewhat presentable.

My class on the works of William Shakespeare was

my favorite, except for the fact Brooke attended, too, and always sat in the front row. Usually, I plonked myself down as far away from her as possible, but not today. I stomped right up to the front of the room and slid into the desk next to her.

Both blonde, southern, English Lit majors, we should have been friends, but she'd hated me on sight. I had to wonder if she thought she was superior simply because she came from North Carolina, and today I intended to find out.

"Excuse me," she hissed. "That seat is taken."

"I know. By me."

She huffed and sat back in her seat. I glanced at my phone to check the time."You have exactly four minutes to tell me what your problem with me is, or I will whip you good."

Brooke's delicate little bow-shaped mouth opened in surprise. "Now that is Kentucky blue grass trash talking right there."

I leaned closer so she knew I meant business. "Keep it up and I'll cancel your birth certificate, girl."

I don't know where my new attitude came from, but could only guess I had the gypsies to thank for it. They loved confrontations. They seemed to almost thrive on fighting and bickering. I normally wasn't like that, but I had to admit today I kind of enjoyed it.

Our professor stumbled into the classroom, dropping a few papers on the way. He was adorable, with a shock of white hair, a tweed jacket, and a bow tie. I whispered in Brooke's ear as he organized his materials for class.

"After class, either you tell me what your problem is, or you and I are going to mix. Got it?" She nodded, her lips a tight, white line.

I sat back and enjoyed the class, feeling better than I had in a while. We talked about Shakespearean sonnets, and listened to our professor read them in his deep, melodic voice. As soon as class ended, we turned in our work and walked outside. Brooke looked like she wanted to run away, but I will give her credit. She stood her ground.

"You don't remember me, do you?"

I narrowed my eyes at her. "What the Sam Hill are you talking about?"

"Miss Southern Belle. Miss Peach Princess. Miss Southern Glamour. Miss Southern Beauty USA." I had no idea what she was talking about, and she rolled her eyes. "You were at each and every one, you and your daddy. We were on the same circuit."

"I've been to a lot of pageants. I'm sorry I don't remember you, but is that really a reason to hate me?"

She scowled at me. "The only pageant my daddy ever made it to was Junior Miss America. My one chance to let him see me shine, and you stole it."

"I did what?"

"I should have won talent. I always win talent. But the crowd cheered so loud after you did your kung fu side show I couldn't hear the music and missed my cue. My song was ruined."

My patience was quickly eroding. "How is any of this my fault?"

"I didn't even place because of you. Do you have any idea how humiliating that was? My mama was a former Miss North Carolina, and went onto Miss America. I bet your mama can't say that, now can she?"

"No, she can't say anything. She killed herself

when I was two."

Brooke gasped, putting a hand over her bosom. "Oh, bless your heart. I had no idea. You should have used that in your intro speech. The judges would have eaten it up."

I took a very controlled breath, and managed not to roll my eyes. Patience was not a virtue that came easily to me.

"The pageant was a million years ago. Can we just forget about it? Let's go have a coffee and talk about how awful the other girls were."

Brooke folded her arms across her chest and tapped her toe on the sidewalk. Obviously, she still wasn't sure about me, but I may have made a little dent in her armor.

"Okay then. Fine. A lady might forgive, but she never forgets. Remember that, Emerson Jane."

"Got it." I resisted the urge to roll my eyes again, but it took a lot of effort.

We went to Mrs. Burke's teashop, and I actually enjoyed talking with her, which was a pleasant surprise. I ordered a scone piled high with fresh cream and a little bowl of jam on the side. Brooke glared at me as she sipped straight black tea.

"If I hadn't hated you because of Junior Miss, I would have hated you once I saw you eat. You're one of those freaks who never has to diet, aren't you?"

I licked a glob of cream off the corner of my mouth. "I think it's because I'm so hyper. Grandma Sugar says I have ants in my pants."

Brooke laughed, and then froze when Leo strolled in, looking all hot and sexy. His muscles positively rippled as he walked, and Brooke fanned her face.

"Oh, lordy be," she said, grabbing my arm. "He looks even tastier than that cream you're gorging on."

I snorted. "I'll introduce you."

Leo's eyes met mine, and I waved him over to our table. He seemed a little hesitant at first, but then walked slowly over to us. He wore a tight, black t-shirt, and his silky hair just barely caressed his shoulders. His skin was the color of caramel, and Brooke was right. He did look good enough to eat.

I introduced him to Brooke, and he sat down. A bit tense at first, eventually, he relaxed. We had a nice time chatting, and I had to admit, I flirted with him more than I should have. Part of it was a bit of residual competitiveness with Brooke, the other part because Michael had hurt me. Badly. It felt good to enjoy a few minutes of time with an attentive male who seemed to actually like my company.

Of course, Leo read too much into it. When I had to leave for class, he wanted to walk me there. I insisted he stay with Brooke, but he looked less than pleased. When Brooke got up to wash her hands, Leo pulled me aside.

"I want to spend time with you, not her." His hand was on my arm, and he stood very close. I stepped away.

"I'm sorry, Leo. I didn't mean to give you the wrong idea. I like you a lot."

"I sense a 'but' in that sentence."

I nodded. "A big 'but.' There's sort of someone else."

Leo's reaction surprised me as his face darkened with fury. "Who is he, and more importantly, *where* is he?"

“Well, he’s certain not here, and it’s none of your concern anyway.” I reached for my coat, surprised that my hands shook.

Brooke came back from the restroom just in time. She looped her arm through Leo’s and smiled up at him. “Come on, Leo. Let’s sit down.”

He allowed her to lead him to the table, but I saw something in his expression I didn’t like. I almost hesitated leaving Brooke with him, even though I knew she was perfectly safe in a busy teashop. As I walked out onto the street, I felt his eyes on me, watching. I picked up my pace, wanting to get away from him. I didn’t know what was going on with Leo, but I knew it wasn’t over yet.

Chapter Seventeen

She was the spittin' image of her mama.
~Grandma Sugar

I walked slowly home to my apartment, nervous about seeing Michael again. Part of me wanted to lock my door and refuse to go back with him, but I'd die if I stayed outside of the compound. A Moktar named Melo wanted to kill me, but only after raping me repeatedly for years and years. A fact I couldn't ignore.

I tried to imagine what Michael's life must have been like. Losing his mother when he was just a baby, he had no memories of her. Pushed into a leadership position in which everyone he knew depended on him for survival, but wanting to go to school. Knowing all of his choices and options had been taken from him.

I stopped in the middle of the sidewalk, almost tripping an old lady walking behind me. Michael was going to marry a Traveller girl, give her lots of Traveller babies, and continue fighting Moktar until the day he died, which would probably be fairly soon. Maybe the way he acted last night had nothing to do with me personally. Maybe I was just the icing on the cake. The last straw. His last opportunity to do something for himself. His final act of rebellion.

It made my heart break for him. I'd go back to Kentucky and resume my normal life, but Michael had no chance of ever following his dreams or doing what he really wanted.

He leaned heavily against the brick wall of my building, already there and waiting for me, when I arrived. People passing on the sidewalk, scared of him, gave him a wide berth, but he no longer frightened me. He turned and his gaze met mine, nothing but pain and a sense of hopeless desperation in his blue eyes. He'd seen too much, and suffered too much, for someone so young.

I didn't say anything. I just walked up to him and wrapped my arms around his waist, my face in his chest. He hesitated only for a second before putting his arms around me.

"I expected an argument." His voice was rough and raw. "Aren't you angry with me?"

I looked up at his beautiful face. I barely noticed the scars, tattoos, and piercings anymore.

"I was hurt, not angry. I made it about me, but it should have been about you. I'm sorry."

Michael's jaw clenched as he tried to control his emotions. "I was out of line. I should be the one apologizing."

I lifted myself up on my tiptoes and gave him a soft kiss. "It's over. No more apologies, okay?"

He slipped his hand into mine. "Do you need anything?" He looked up at my apartment.

"I have everything I need," I said, resting my cheek against his shoulder.

He swallowed hard and nodded. "Let's be off then."

The peace between us was a beautiful thing, but we needed to talk. "I can't believe you live like this,

Michael. Going to school during the day and staying up all night. I've only done it for a few days, and I'm exhausted."

Michael looked embarrassed. "I exaggerated. We don't work every night. We do have some time off."

"But it's a very tough schedule, and yet still you managed to haul your very attractive butt to Mrs. Burke's every morning." I was desperate to see him smile, and he rewarded me with a sexy grin.

"It was worth it," he said, giving me a wink. "She makes some very tasty scones."

I gave him a playful punch in the arm. There was a lot about Michael I still had to figure out, but at least he'd stopped pushing me away. He'd opened the door to his heart just a crack and I did my best to squeeze through.

When we got back to Michael's caravan, we immediately crawled into his bed and slept for hours. I sighed contently, still wrapped in his arms as the sun began to sink low in the sky. I knew we had to go to the council meeting, but I didn't want to leave his bed.

Michael stirred next to me and kissed my neck. "We need to wake up," he said, his words soft and slurred.

"I know."

He stared at me in the growing darkness. He opened his mouth to speak, but was interrupted by a sharp rap on his door.

"Time for council, Michael." Sampson sounded tired as well.

Michael lifted up on his elbows. "Coming, Da." He looked down at me. "No one would think less of you if you stayed away."

I shook my head. "I want to go."

I couldn't let Michael go through this alone. He kissed me softly on my forehead, and climbed out of bed. He paused when he noticed the gold dress on the hanger.

"I have to give that back to Audrey," I said. "I just haven't had a chance."

He touched it almost reverently. "It looked lovely on you, Emerson." He turned and his eyes met mine. "Really lovely."

"Thank you."

My voice was soft. He hadn't exactly surrendered, but somehow I felt like I'd won an important strategic battle.

We joined the others at the meeting just as the council members climbed onto the stage in their black robes. It felt very familiar, right down to the nervous feeling in the pit of my stomach.

Mavin began the meeting. "The Dweller, Emerson Shaw, is a danger to our people. Because of her, even our Ceannfort can no longer be trusted to protect us. He brought a Moktar into our midst last night."

Michael paled visibly, but I almost felt relieved. At least this wasn't about his schooling.

Mavin continued. "And it has come to our attention, Mary's boy was meeting a Dweller girl when he got ambushed. This is what happens when we don't stick with our own kind."

Mary sat in the front, her face as still as a statue. "I found some notes from a Dweller in his things, but it has nothing to do with Emerson."

Mavin scowled at her. "He died because of a Dweller. That's connection enough."

Monroe scratched his chin. “Perhaps Mavin has a point. We may have been too hasty allowing a Dweller into our midst. We don’t owe her our protection.”

Several of the other council members nodded in agreement. Michael’s body tensed next to mine. This didn’t look good.

Anselina’s eyes searched the crowd for me. She leaned forward and spoke into the microphone. “Emerson deserves to have the right to defend herself. Come here, child.”

I stood and had to steady myself before walking to the stage. Michael got up to follow me, but I shook my head. The less the Travellers associated me with Michael, the better it would be for him in the long run.

Anselina led me to a chair next to a microphone.

“Tell us your name, please.”

“Emerson Jane Shaw.”

“Your middle name is Jane?”

“It was my maternal grandmother’s name.”

“Did you know her?” Anselina asked. I shook my head, not understanding her line of questioning. She continued, “And where is your mother now?”

“She died when I was little.”

“How?” she asked, her voice hollow and strange.

“What are you doing, Anselina? This is a bloody waste of time.” Monroe didn’t look pleased.

She shot him a silencing look. “I have my reasons, Monroe Spinner. Let me do this my way.”

She turned back to me. “How did your mother die?”

I looked at her in confusion. “Why do you want to know?”

“Just answer the question.”

My cheeks burned in shame, but I enunciated each word slowly and carefully. “She killed herself.”

Anselina sucked in a breath. Something strange was happening here. I folded my hands on my lap to hide their trembling. When she asked me the next question, her face looked pale and pinched.

“What was her name?”

“Jillian Catherine Parker.”

Several people gasped. Anselina’s gaze was glued to my face, and although I didn’t want to admit it, I saw the truth staring back at me through her eyes.

“And Catherine was her grandmother’s name,” she said softly. “It’s a family tradition, you see. We give all our daughters their grandmothers’ names.”

“I don’t understand.”

“You will soon, darling.” She turned to a burly man in the audience with snowy white hair. “She has the look of our Jillie, doesn’t she, Matthew?”

The old man squinted at her. He had ruddy cheeks and broad shoulders. He looked more like a farmer than a gypsy. “What are you trying to say, Anselina?”

Tears swam in her eyes. “She has Jillie’s laugh. I heard it last night. Matthew, Emerson is our granddaughter.”

Matthew walked slowly toward the stage. “Our Jillie had a child?” When Anselina nodded, he almost devoured me with his eyes.

“Your name isn’t Jane,” I said, still trying to completely absorb Anselina’s words.

She smiled. “Yes, it is. I’m Jane Anselina, but everyone has always called me by my middle name. I had an auntie Jane and it became confusing.”

I couldn’t speak, but Michael walked up to the

stage, shaking his head. "She's *not* a Traveller."

Anselina pursed her lips. "Are you so sure?"

Sampson narrowed his eyes. "It could explain why the Moktar is tracking her."

One of the older councilmen nodded. "They can smell Traveller blood a mile away. That's how they catch our women and do such dastardly things to them."

Sampson flinched, most probably thinking about his wife. He looked like he'd aged ten years since he'd heard the news about her. I wasn't the only one who noticed. Mavin stared at him, and she didn't seem pleased.

"She can't prove it." Mavin's thin lips narrowed, and the gypsies started to argue amongst themselves.

"Maybe I can." Everyone turned to me, and I cleared my throat nervously. "I have a photo of my mother. It's in Michael's caravan."

The meeting adjourned, and we walked to Michael's caravan together. Anselina and Matthew kept shooting furtive glances at me, like they were trying to see remnants of their daughter on my face. Sampson and the other council members stayed back, awaiting the outcome.

I went into the caravan by myself, dug through my backpack, and pulled out the journal with my mother's photo tucked inside. She was a stranger to me, and there was a definite possibility the strangers outside might be my grandparents. My body shook by the time I opened the door.

As soon as Anselina saw the photo, she began to weep. She gave me a large envelope with trembling hands.

"I brought these to the meeting with me. I planned

to show them to you afterwards, in private, but I had to act when the tide started turning against you. I couldn't let them cast you out of the compound like that, and face the Moktar on your own. It would have been a death sentence."

Inside were a bunch of old photographs. I looked at them one by one. My mother as a little girl with scraped knees and a gap-toothed grin. My mother as a skinny teenager, hands on hips and pouting for the camera. My mother as a young woman dressed in flamboyant gypsy clothing. I covered my mouth with my hand and sat down.

"It's true." I looked up at Michael, but he seemed at a loss.

"Can I get you some tea?" he asked.

I chuckled, dabbing away my tears. "The English remedy for everything."

"Make it whiskey, my boy," Matthew said, eyes meeting mine. "That's the gypsy remedy, and you are now a gypsy, sweet child."

Matthew opened his arms to me, and I flew into them, crying all over his pristine white shirt. He smelled like mint and tobacco, and I realized this was my first memory of my grandfather, a monumental event. Grandma Sugar and Pappy George had always been permanent fixtures in my life. Now Matthew and Anselina were there, too, and it felt so right.

Other gypsies walked past, trying to catch a peek of the newest Traveller, but we ignored them. Michael brought the whiskey, and sat down with us, but he seemed quiet and pensive. The news I was a Traveller had shocked him, perhaps even more than it had shocked me.

"Her name was Jillian, but we called her Jillie. Our Jillie. She didn't want to live the Traveller life, but we refused to listen." Anselina swirled her whiskey around in her glass.

Matthew patted her leg. "It was my fault. I thought I knew best. I wanted her to marry young and marry a Traveller, but she begged us to allow her to go to university first. I thought she'd get bored and drop it, but she didn't."

Matthew gave me a wry smile. "I got worried as her friends married and had children of their own. I decided the time had come to arrange a marriage for Jillie, and I was a little pig headed about it. I chose a nice bloke, one I thought she'd be happy with, but she was furious. I refused to listen. She ran away, and we never heard from her again."

Anselina bit her lip. "Why did she kill herself?"

I traced my finger along the edge of my glass. "I was very small when it happened, and my father doesn't talk about it. It almost destroyed him. He never really got the hang of living without her."

Anselina closed her eyes, her hand fluttering to her chest like she was trying to hold her heart in place. "I understand how he feels. All those years, we hoped she was still alive, but we knew the truth."

Matthew reached over and clutched her hand. "Everything will be all right. We have Jillie's girl here with us now."

I looked at Michael, and saw a flash of sadness in his eyes. My time here was limited, only one semester, and we both knew it.

"Did she have problems with depression when she lived here? Did she ever need to see a therapist?" I asked as I handed Anselina back the photographs. She looked through them one by one, a puzzled frown forming on her face.

"Our Jillie was always such a happy little soul," she said, and Matthew agreed.

"She never knew a cloudy day. Always full of sunshine." He had to wipe his eyes again. There was nothing like seeing the big, tough Traveller get weepy at the thought of his daughter. Anselina held it together far better than Matthew.

She tilted her head to one side. "Were they happily married?"

I nodded. "Very."

"Did something happen before she died?"

"Grandma Sugar told me they had absolutely no clue she might do something like that, which was why it came as such a terrible shock."

"A happily married, perfectly healthy, perfectly stable young woman killed herself for no good reason at all?" Anselina's eyes met mine. "Something is off here. I feel it right to the core of my old Traveller bones. I can't imagine my Jillie taking her own life."

Suddenly, I found it a little hard to breathe. "Then what happened?"

Anselina tapped her chin with one finger, her gaze directed at some unseen point far off in the distance. "We need to find out, Emerson, and I think I know how."

Chapter Eighteen

Just hold your horses. I can explain it to you, but I can't understand it for you.

~Grandma Sugar

My grandparents took me to a caravan owned by someone named Veronique. Michael went to tell the council my identity had been confirmed. I was officially a Traveller, a gypsy, and a former Junior Miss Kentucky. The first two were more than I bargained for, and the last one was only because I had a pushy southern grandmother who had tried to make me into a lady.

Grandma Sugar said, "It's like trying to make a silk purse from a sow's ear," an accurate assessment. Still no silk purse, I wasn't exactly a sow's ear anymore, either. I was mostly confused, and after today, it had grown even worse.

Veronique lived in a small wooden caravan painted with a colorful array of cheerful flowers. She embodied everything I'd ever imagined a gypsy would be, with long dark hair, large hoop earrings, and white blouse that slipped off her shoulders and exposed silky, dark skin. She looked around thirty, but it was hard to tell. On her head, she wore a scarf to hold back her hair, and her bright skirt billowed out around her, a patchwork of colors and patterns.

pushed my hands away. Then she grabbed my favorite teddy bear, one that was almost as big as me, covered it with my blanket, and ran to the car."

I swallowed hard. "Pappy George tried to stop her, but she screamed for him to get away. It had started to rain. We watched her buckle the teddy bear into my car seat, still covered in a blanket. As she drove away, I stayed by the window. I was so small I had to stand on my tip toes, and even then I could barely peek through the crack in the curtains."

"What did you see?"

My lips began to tremble. "A dark shadow came out of the woods and started running after my mother's car. I thought it was a wolf."

"A Moktar," said Anselina softly.

She was right. There was no mistaking the dark, saggy skin and ferocious face. I'd seen a Moktar at two years old and never even realized it.

Matthew shook his head. "She went all the way to America, and they still found her."

Anselina frowned. "They crossed the ocean. We thought we had the problem contained. We'll have to notify the alliance," she said. "But you haven't finished telling us what happened to our Jillie."

With no gentle way to tell her, I decided to be as direct and emotionless as possible. "She drove off a cliff. She was killed instantly." Too sad to weep, I sat in horrified silence as the truth sank in.

"She did it to save you," said Anselina. "She put your bear on the car seat so the Moktar would think you died, too."

"There must have been another way."

Anselina touched my cheek gently. "If there was,

she didn't see it."

Anselina and Matthew stood to leave, and I got up, too. I felt exhausted, emotionally and physically. We thanked Veronique and began walking back to Michael's caravan. When we got there, Matthew gave me a long look.

"Pack up your things, lass," he said. "You'll stay with us now."

I opened my mouth to protest, but he held up a hand to stop me. "No Traveller girl can stay with a man unsupervised. You're a Traveller now."

"I'm nearly twenty-one, Matthew." Not quite sure what to call him, I sort of stuttered on his name.

"Yes, you are very old and wise, but I'm older and probably a bit wiser, too. We Travellers stick to our traditions and our rules, even if they are outdated."

I tried not to roll my eyes. "Fine. I'll do as you ask, but…"

"I am your granddad." He gave me a wobbly little smile that nearly broke my heart. "You could start calling me that, if you'd like."

The wobbly smile made me reconsider my plans to force the issue. I'd stay with my grandparents tonight, and sort everything out tomorrow. I gathered my things and met Anselina and Matthew outside.

"All right, lead the way, Granddad…and Grandmother." Their faces lit up, making it that much easier to give into whatever they wanted. I'd known them one day, and already I was putty in their hands.

Anselina wrapped an arm around my shoulders. "It won't be that bad. We'll have fun."

I wondered if Sun Tzu had a bossy little Chinese grandmother who told him what to do, and was fairly certain he must have. There is no stronger power than a grandma on a mission. It was better just to give in gracefully.

"I am yours to command."

Chapter Nineteen

He's got a burr in his saddle over something.
~Grandma Sugar

The blankets on my bed in the spare bedroom of my grandparents' caravan smelled like lavender, a scent that reminded me of my mother. She'd kept dried lavender tied together with a purple satin ribbon in her dresser back in Bowling Green. I found it years after she died because Daddy had never been able to touch any of her things. Lavender smelled like home to me, and she'd probably felt the same way. I wondered if she'd thought about her parents every time she smelled it, too. Sadly, we were two generations of women who'd spent our lives missing our mothers.

Dressing for school, I slipped into a gray plaid jumper dress with a white blouse underneath, and put on charcoal-colored tights and shoes. It looked a bit like a school uniform, but it was easy, comfortable, warm, and the short skirt showed off my legs. Also, the jumper covered the wrinkles in my blouse; I had no idea where my grandparents kept their iron.

When I stepped into the main room of the caravan, my grandparents were nowhere to be seen. They'd left a pot of coffee for me, and a variety of breakfast foods. I ate a scone and drank my coffee quickly, not wanting to be late for class. I thought about wearing a sweater, but a crisp chill in the air made me shiver, so I grabbed my wool coat instead. I scribbled a note telling them where I was going, and then wrote one out for Michael, too, sticking it on the door of his caravan on my way out. I didn't want to wake him. He needed to sleep. I asked him to meet me at my apartment again at four.

The gypsy compound felt subdued early in the day. Most people stayed up all night, so they slept in every morning. No one was around when I slipped out the door and onto the streets of York. I turned around as soon as the door shut behind me, but it had disappeared.

"Gypsy tricks," I muttered under my breath.

Brooke already sat in the front row of class when I arrived. She looked polished, as always, with her smooth blonde hair, rosy lips, and a perfectly pressed blouse and skirt. The epitome of a southern lady, a skill I'd never quite mastered. The sleeves of my blouse were more wrinkled than I'd realized and makeup had not been anywhere on my agenda this morning. Grandma Sugar would have yanked me out of the classroom by my ear.

Brooke greeted me with a sunny smile, her eyes taking in my less than stellar appearance. "Look what the cat dragged in. Hi, stranger."

I tried to pat my hair down. It looked a little like I'd stuck my finger into an electrical outlet.

"Aren't you rather chipper today, Miss Brooke?"

Brooke winked, and handed me a stick of gum. Juicy Fruit, my personal favorite.

"Leo asked me out. I'll say yes. Eventually."

Something about the idea of Leo and Brooke together set off a vague sense of unease somewhere deep inside my belly, but I pushed my feelings aside. It was none of my beeswax.

"He's a nice guy. Don't play games with him, okay?"

Brooke gave me a saucy grin. "Sugar, he'll enjoy the kind of games I want to play."

She wasn't talking about Monopoly, but I was saved from further innuendo by our Shakespeare professor stumbling into the room. Always lost in thought and a little befuddled, he reminded me a bit of my own father. Daddy spent most of his waking hours thinking about soldiers who died long ago in wars people barely remembered. What may have seemed dull and dry to others was his passion.

My mother had been his other passion, and when she died, he'd slipped a little farther into his own world. Eventually, I'd have to tell him the truth about her death, and about the Moktar and the Travellers and my grandparents, but I couldn't do so over the phone. He would have been on the next plane to England to have me seen by a head doctor, and I wouldn't blame him.

Before I knew it, class ended and everyone put away their books. The professor seemed perplexed, like he'd lost track of time, too. He scratched his head and mumbled as I helped him gather his things together before walking out with Brooke. As soon as we got outside, her phone rang.

She squealed. "Leo's calling. Got to go."

Her voice turned sexy and sultry as soon as she answered the phone. I didn't understand how girls could change from one second to the next if a man was involved. It was a complete mystery to me.

She waved goodbye, but her attention already centered on Leo and nothing else. I waved back halfheartedly. She wasn't even looking.

Walking back to my apartment, I couldn't quite understand my feelings. I had no right to be jealous about Brooke and Leo, but that was the only reasonable explanation for the odd tightening in my chest at the thought of them going out together.

For a second, I imagined Leo gloriously naked, his golden eyes filled with desire. Then I imagined myself naked, too. I stopped dead in my tracks and almost dropped my backpack.

"Ew, ew, ew. Dirty thoughts, dirty thoughts."

"I hate to interrupt you. It looks like an interesting conversation you're having with yourself."

Lucinda smiled at me, and Poppy stood right next to her. I grabbed them both into a huge hug.

"Oh, girls. If you could only know where my mind just was…"

"Tell us," said Lucinda, "over lunch."

We went to our favorite café, but the cold and wind prevented us from sitting outside. The cozy interior was dark and warm, with wooden walls and a low ceiling. We slid into a booth with leather seats. I ordered a beef pie, which Lucinda and Poppy both looked at longingly. They ordered salads.

"It really isn't fair you can eat like a longshoreman and look like a Barbie doll, you know." Poppy picked at her salad and gave me a dirty look.

"Sorry, Pops." I tried to give her a bite of my lunch, but she shook her head.

"No, thanks. I love salad," she said with such a completely false smile plastered on her face I had to giggle. She looked maniacal. "So, what have you been up to?"

I had to be discreet. That meant no mention of Moktars, Travellers, or any of the other weirdness.

"I have some news," I said, and took another bite of beef pie.

Poppy's eyes lit up. "You slept with Michael."

I shook my head, almost choking. I grabbed my glass of water and swallowed some down.

Lucinda took a stab at it. "You slept with Michael and Leo. Together. Ménage à trois. I love it."

A good thing my mouth was covered with my napkin otherwise water would have spurted all over the table. Lucinda and Poppy knew all about the very handsome and sexy Leo, but it was kind of funny Lucinda mentioned him only minutes after I'd pictured him naked. Now she'd added Michael to the mix inside my head, and I pictured that, too.

"Oh, my goody gumdrops."

Lucinda rolled her eyes and then looked at Poppy. "She's still a virgin."

"How do you know that?" I asked.

"Only virgins can use that phrase. It's illegal otherwise." Lucinda went back to eating her salad.

"Don't you want to hear my news?" I asked with a frown.

"Of course we do, darling," said Poppy.

I cleared my throat. "I found my grandparents."

"How?" asked Lucinda.

I pretended to be really interested in something on my plate. "Michael helped me."

"I'm so happy for you, Em," said Poppy. "What are they like?"

"I love them already." I gushed about them for a few minutes, and then thought about my mother and how she'd died. I swallowed hard, and changed the subject. "How is Nigel?"

Poppy's face lit up. "He's spectacular. He told his parents he loved me, and either they'd respect that and treat me well, or he'd have nothing more to do with them. They are being quite bearable to me now."

"I'm so glad." I reached out and grabbed her hand. Then I looked at Lucinda. "And Antarctica?"

Lucinda's cheeks actually turned pink. "Sven asked me to come with him on his research mission in the spring."

"You're going to live on the tundra?" I stared at her in shock.

She bit her lip. "For a few weeks. I've already talked to my professors. They gave their permission. And you'll be back in Kentucky anyway. I'll be lonely."

My eyes filled with tears. "I'll miss you, roomie."

Lucinda looked a bit teary, too. "Which is why we have to make really spectacular plans for Friday."

I looked at them in confusion. "What are you talking about?"

"Your birthday, silly." Poppy pretended to pop me on the head. "You're finally turning twenty-one."

I had to think fast. "I'll plan the whole thing, okay? Nigel and Sven can come, too."

I needed to clear this with Michael and Matthew and probably the whole gypsy council. They would never let me go out at night. I had to hope they would let my friends come in somehow.

"That's fine," said Lucinda. "Our only real plan is to get you completely wasted since you are finally legal to drink in Kentucky."

"And since you are incredibly funny and southern when you drink," Poppy chimed in.

"Thank you, ladies. Friday will be interesting."

I went to my afternoon class, but barely paid attention while trying to come up with a solution for my birthday. My friends had been very forgiving regarding the time I'd been spending with Michael, but they would not understand missing my birthday. I almost groaned out loud. The last thing I wanted to do was add to Michael's problems. He already had enough on his plate.

Since Michael had learned the news about his mother's death and his new half sibling, I sensed anger simmering inside him, bubbling just below the surface. I saw it in the tightness in his jaw and in the coldly calculating look in his eyes. He wanted to stop Melo from hunting me, but he wanted revenge for his mother, too. I almost pitied the first Moktar who might cross his path.

"Hello, beautiful." Leo interrupted my thoughts, making me nearly jump out of my shoes. I hadn't even heard him approach.

The wind had picked up, and my hair blew around my face. I pushed it out of the way, glad I'd had the good sense to throw on a coat this morning.

"Hi, Leo. Where are you off to?"

Leo leaned in and wiggled his eyebrows suggestively. "Where would you like me to take you?"

I backed away a step. He made me uncomfortable. I would have thought he was drunk, but he didn't smell like alcohol. I glanced around. Enough people milled about I didn't think I was in any danger, but I felt oddly on edge.

"What's the matter, Emerson? You don't want to play with me today?"

He stuck out his lower lip in a pout. He wore a tight black t-shirt and no coat, and yet I could almost feel the heat radiating from his body. I had on four layers of clothing and still shivered.

I gave him a playful little shove to make him back off, but the look on his face wasn't playful at all. It was dark.

"Where's Brooke?" I asked and began walking back to my apartment as quickly as possible. Something felt very off. Leo seemed hyper, like he was high or using steroids or something. He also looked even more muscular than usual.

"Who cares?" He tried to put his arm around my shoulders, and I shrugged him off. He made a noise deep in his throat that sounded like a growl.

"You asked her out."

Only a block left until I reached my apartment, and I hoped Michael would be waiting outside. Leo was beginning to scare me, but I chatted with him as I walked in an effort to buy time.

I turned the corner, and exhaled a sigh of relief. I couldn't see Michael, but I saw the steps to my apartment. Running would get me there in about ten seconds. I felt around in my backpack for my keys and pulled them out. Leo grabbed my arm, gripping it so hard it hurt.

"Ow." I tried to yank it away, but he wouldn't let me. He pushed me into a dark, narrow alley, slamming me against a brick wall next to some trash bins. No one on the main street could see me now. "What are you doing, Leo?"

He was furious, positively seething with rage. His eyes looked bloodshot and glassy, and his face had turned an angry shade of red.

"Why are you playing games with me?" he asked, his voice a low hiss. He tried to pull me deeper into the alley and away from my apartment, but I dug my heels in.

"Leo, stop it. You're my friend."

He didn't answer. He twisted my arm until I screamed in pain. I swung my backpack with my free arm, hitting him on the side of his head. It wasn't enough to get him to let go of my arm, but it made him stop wringing it like a wet sponge.

"I don't want to be your *friend*."

He was so mad he spit. I wondered how I ever could have thought he was handsome. He looked like a monster now.

I started kicking him and pushing him with all my might, but he stopped me with one hand to my throat, my head pushed against the wall. He began to squeeze so hard I started seeing black spots float in front of my eyes.

For once, I was grateful for the English weather. A big fat raindrop fell on his face, distracting him. He looked up, loosening his grip on my throat just enough for me to take a deep breath. At that moment, I dealt the deathblow, kicking him as hard as I possibly could right in the crotch.

Sun Tzu had taught me even the strongest opponent has a weak spot. In the case of muscle-bound Leo, his weak spot was right between his legs. He released me immediately, his hands protectively covering his injured area, and he fell over like a tree in the forest. *Timber*.

He moaned in pain, but he'd be up again soon. I let out a yelp when he tried to grab my foot, and sprinted as fast as I could back to my apartment. Rain fell in earnest now, soaking through my clothes. Michael walked toward me, coming down the street from the opposite direction. When he looked up and saw my face he broke into a run.

"What happened?"

I started to babble, pointing back to the alley, but when Michael got there Leo had already gone. I looked around in a panic, sure he would jump out at any minute and attack me again. Michael took the keys out of my hand and pulled me into my flat.

I stared at the keys. "I could have used my keys. Why didn't I use the keys? I could have stuck one in his eye. I know that. I know that."

Michael stroked my hair and whispered in my ear, trying to calm me. As soon as I'd settled down, he pulled back to look at my face. His expression grew hostile when he saw my neck.

"What happened?"

I touched my neck gingerly and winced as I swallowed. "He tried to kill me. He really wanted to kill me."

I'd practiced martial arts for many years. I'd beaten up people, and been beaten up, on almost a weekly basis. This was something very different.

"Who?"

"Leo. He's a guy. I know him. He likes Brooke." My eyes flew open wide. "I need to call Brooke. She can't go out with him. He is crazy. He's on drugs or something."

Michael shushed me. "How do you know him?"

I told him about Leo, but didn't add the part about flirting with him on occasion. The fact I'd even talked to him was enough to put a flash of jealousy in Michael's eyes.

"Are there any other men I should know about?"

I didn't know if he was serious or not. I shook my head and opened my mouth to speak, but nothing came out. Instead, my body began to shake so hard my teeth chattered. I was wet and cold and scared.

Michael pulled me into a hug. "I'm sorry," he murmured against my hair. "It's not your fault. I was being a prize idiot."

"You're good at that." I barely managed to get the words out, but Michael laughed.

"I want to find Leo and kill him with my bare hands."

He was serious. "Can we go home now, Michael? I want to go home."

I picked up my backpack, and then realized the zipper was open. I sank to the floor, frantically searching through it.

"It's gone." My heart began to race, and I couldn't disguise the note of panic in my voice.

"What's gone?" Michael stood very still, the way he got when he was worried, but he had no idea how bad this situation had actually become.

I covered my face with my hands. "My journal. It must have fallen out when I hit him with my backpack."

Michael looked visibly relieved. "I'll get you another journal."

I shook my head. "You don't understand. I wrote

down everything in my journal. I wrote about you, the Moktar, and even about the Travellers."

Michael's face paled. "You put our secrets in a book?"

My stomach clenched. "I didn't realize it could be dangerous. I've always kept a journal, but nothing interesting has ever happened to me before."

I saw a war being waged on Michael's face. He was furious, but as soon as his eyes went to the marks on my neck, they softened.

"I doubt Leo is a danger to us, but we need to retrace your steps and make sure it isn't lying on the street somewhere. If someone finds it, they'll probably think it's a made up story."

I nodded, even though I had a very bad feeling about this. It sickened me to think Leo probably had it in his hands right now. Maybe my fears were unfounded, but one thing seemed very obvious to me; Michael was wrong about Leo. He was dangerous.

Chapter Twenty

You can't get this wad of toothpaste back in the tube.

~Grandma Sugar

We left as soon as I changed into dry clothing. My stockings were torn, so I tossed them into the trash. I pulled on heavy tights, a black skirt, and a warm sweater. My coat still felt damp, so I wore a jacket instead.

The storm had already passed, but the sky remained cloudy and gray. After checking the alley and retracing my steps, we gave up. Leo had the journal. Michael harbored some doubts, but I was sure of it. We just needed to deal with it.

"What should we tell the council?"

We walked toward the compound, hand in hand. His eyes scanned the street, making sure it was safe.

"Nothing," he said.

"Are you sure?"

His face was hard when he looked at me. "No, but I don't want to make things worse. We're already in enough trouble. It seems to follow you around everywhere you go. The little stunt you pulled today, running off by yourself, just made things worse."

I winced. "I'm sorry."

"I know," he said, his face softening. "You have so

much to learn. It's not your fault."

The rain had stopped, and the sun bravely tried to peek out through the clouds, so the street was more crowded, but people parted and made way whenever Michael approached. A man walked out of a shop and stepped right in front of us. All Michael had to do was narrow his eyes and the man scurried away. It wasn't a gypsy trick, and it wasn't just his size and obvious strength. Michael had an aura about him that made normal humans a bit nervous. He walked like a predator, head forward, graceful and silent. King of the jungle. He looked dangerous because he was dangerous, and that made me very happy. I needed dangerous right now.

When we reached the secret door, he noticed my gaze on him. He raised one dark eyebrow at me, and my cheeks burned.

"What are you thinking, Emerson Jane?"

"That you're a beautiful man, Michael Nightingale."

He frowned, so obviously confused it almost made me laugh. "You did notice the tattoos and the scars and everything else about me that screams 'get away,' didn't you?" he asked.

I reached up and touched his face. "I don't see any of it. Not anymore, at least. I just see you."

Truly flustered, he cleared his throat. "Ah. Well. Do you want to learn how to open the door?"

I squealed. It meant so much that he trusted me even after I'd been an idiot about the journal.

"Really? You aren't going to blindfold me?"

"You're a Traveller now. It'll open for you."

"I was always a Traveller. We just didn't know it."

He grinned, and when Michael grinned it did something to my body that started in my chest and went straight to my lady parts. I almost drooled, but he seemed completely unaware of the effect he had on me.

"Come. I'll teach you." He brought me close to the wall and showed me a hole in one brick, slightly larger than the width of my thumb. "Stick your finger in there."

I folded my arms across my chest. "Is this a joke? Is something going to bite my finger?"

Michael growled. "Don't be silly. Do you want me to do it first?"

I shook my head, giving him a dirty look. "I'll do it." I lifted my pointer finger, and then glared at him. "But if something bites me, I'll bite you. Just so you know."

"Promise?" Michael's voice was low and husky. He stood right behind me, hands on my hips. His breath tickled my neck.

"Stop distracting me with your manly charms. I need to concentrate."

He blew out an exasperated sigh. "You need to stick your finger in the hole. It isn't complicated."

"That's what *she* said," I muttered, but I got up the courage and put my finger in. The doorway slid open, and I stood there pointing my finger into thin air.

I laughed. "Can we do that again?"

Michael rolled his eyes. "Certainly. Every single time we come back to the compound."

He grabbed my hand and pulled me inside. Immediately, the door reappeared, and we were in the dark hallway. Michael stood very close, his hands on my shoulders. I wrapped my arms around his waist and leaned into him, my face in his chest. His voice rumbled against my cheek.

"I failed you, Emerson. I thought you were only in danger at night. I didn't take Dwellers like Leo into consideration. They weren't part of the equation."

"It isn't math. You couldn't have known, Michael."

I stretched up on my toes to kiss him softly on the lips. The added bonus was my breasts brushed his chest on the way up. A delightful sensation that almost made me purr.

Michael gave me gentle little kisses, and in between them he spoke. "It's my duty to protect you, and all Travellers. I'm the Ceannfort."

Scowling, I bit his lip. Not hard enough to hurt him, but enough to make my point. He gave me a crooked smile. "Fine. That isn't the only reason I want to protect you."

"I fought him off, Michael."

Michael touched his forehead against mine and gently caressed the bruises on my neck. "I should have been there. I guard what is mine."

Mine. I sort of liked that word, even though it was rather chauvinistic and normally would have annoyed the living heck out of me. I wrapped my arms around his neck, pulling his head down in order to kiss him thoroughly. I was glad to have something to hold onto when his tongue slid into my mouth like warm velvet, making me so hot and hungry for more that my knees began to buckle. Michael reached down and cupped my bottom, pulling me closer against him. I felt his erection, long and hard, through our clothing, and found it a little hard to breathe.

Michael pulled away, jumping back like I was a live wire and he'd been shocked. He ran a hand over his head, trying to catch his breath, but I didn't want him to stop. I moved closer, reaching for him, but he shook his head.

"Not here, Emerson."

I understood his concern when the door to the street opened suddenly, and Anthony and Quinn waltzed in. We were in a public area, and I'd almost forgotten.

"Did you just get back?" asked Quinn. He slapped Michael on the back, and then seemed to read something on Michael's face. "What is it?"

"Emerson was attacked." His voice was clipped. "Meet me at my caravan in an hour."

They nodded, and looked at me with concern. "I'm fine, boys."

It touched me that they cared. They'd been kind to me when they thought I was a Dweller, but things were different now. I'd become one of them. Word had spread quickly through the compound, and made me wonder if this acceptance would be shared by the women, too. It would probably make things with Nella a lot worse. She'd see me as an even bigger threat in her quest to have Michael.

We went to my grandparents' caravan. Matthew and Anselina sat outside, drinking tea and looking like the quintessential English couple. Anselina wore a floral skirt, and Matthew had on a wool sweater. If I'd seen them in another setting, I would have had no idea they were gypsies. They smiled at me in greeting, and when Anselina's eyes went to my neck she stood up slowly, her face grim.

"What happened?"

I reached to cover the marks with my hand. They had been faint red spots when I'd checked them in the mirror at my apartment, but I bruised easily. They must have looked like humdingers now.

Matthew gave Michael a nasty look and started toward him. I stepped between them, holding out my hands. "It wasn't Michael. Oh, my gracious. Someone else did this."

I explained what had happened, but couldn't make sense of Leo's behavior. "He was never like that before. I have to call Brooke and warn her."

Brooke's phone went immediately to voice mail, and then came a message that her mailbox was full. I groaned in frustration and texted her instead. I was brief, telling her Leo was dangerous and it would be wise to stay away from him. I also begged her to call me.

Matthew, Anselina, and Michael were having a very serious discussion. They stopped as soon as I approached. Michael's cheeks turned pink, a new look for him. He pulled me aside.

"Stay here with your grandparents. I have to talk to my men."

I narrowed my eyes at him. "Are you going after Leo?"

"No." His response, a little too quick, told me he lied. I folded my arms and tapped my toe. He knew I wasn't going anywhere until he gave me an honest answer. A muscle worked in his jaw, and then he let out a frustrated growl. "I won't do any permanent damage. I just have to make sure the bastard doesn't try anything like that again."

"Define permanent damage."

Michael glared at me. "I won't kill him, so he's getting off lucky." Then his voice got very quiet. "I need to get the journal from him, too."

I grabbed the lapels of his leather jacket and pulled him close. "Don't you dare put yourself in any danger, do you hear me?"

Michael raised one very arrogant brow. "He's a *Dweller*, Emerson."

I pursed my lips. "That doesn't mean he isn't dangerous. There was something different about him today."

"Drugs can make people aggressive and unpredictable."

I shivered. "It wasn't that. He was…strange."

I wondered if somehow I'd caused this by flirting with him and sending him mixed signals, then chastised myself mentally. Nothing I'd done warranted that kind of attack.

Michael slid his palm up my cheek, strong, and yet so gentle as his fingers twined in my hair. Leo had been completely different. I still felt the way his fingers had clenched my throat, cutting off my air supply.

Michael kissed my forehead. "I'm just going to scare him. I'll be back soon."

Anselina put her arm across my shoulders as I watched him walk away. "It's always hard to see them go."

"He shouldn't have to fight my battles."

"But he's the Ceannfort. It's his job."

I scowled. A lot of responsibility rested on Michael's broad shoulders. It wasn't fair. "What were the two of you talking about with him earlier? He looked fit to be tied."

Matthew coughed. "I think I have to go and…uh…well. Goodbye." He toddled off, and Anselina looked after him, shaking her head.

"Men."

"So you're stuck answering my question."

She sighed. "This will require a strong cup of tea and some biscuits."

"Uh, oh. That's never good. Grandma Sugar used to prepare me for bad news with sweet tea and cookies."

"I'm going to like Grandma Sugar."

Anselina poured the tea and handed me a plate of shortbread cookies. We sat in front of her caravan. The skies had cleared up significantly, and the sun peeked out from behind a cloud. A faint breeze fluttered through the compound, making tendrils of my hair tickle my face. I looked up at the dome Michael had constructed.

"Where does the wind come from?"

Anselina's eyes followed mine. "Ah. You've heard about our dome, Michael's design. The wind is part of a rather complex air circulation system. He designed an irrigation system, too. He really is a brilliant boy."

I sighed. "And yet he has to kill monsters instead of going to school."

"Has he quit school then?" Anselina didn't seem surprised.

"No, but he's on the verge."

"He's been under quite a bit of pressure, poor lad. Mavin especially has been insisting he quit. Matthew and I have always supported him, but we live in Guisborough. We're only here for meetings and such."

"Aren't you from Whitby? I went there a few times, trying to find…you." My mother had said they were both dead, and I'd actually just hoped to find cousins, but it seemed cruel to mention it.

"Guisborough is close to Whitby, just a bit inland."

I'd fallen in love with Whitby, and not just because I'd thought of it as my mother's hometown. A gorgeous little fishing village, nestled on the North Sea coast, with winding streets and buildings perched precariously on steep hillsides. I'd climbed hundreds of steps to reach the ruins of Whitby Abbey high on a cliff, and then watched the boats come in. It had been an amazing day.

"I liked Whitby. Bram Stoker wrote *Dracula* there. Isn't that amazing?"

Anselina shrugged. "I suppose, but we have real monsters to deal with. I don't pay attention to pretend ones."

"That makes sense." I sat back and sipped my tea.

Anselina cleared her throat and smoothed her skirt. Her discomfort piqued my curiosity. I had no idea what she wanted to talk with me about and waited patiently for her to get to it.

"Are you a virgin, Emerson?"

I nearly choked on my tea. She wanted to talk about sex. *Oh good gravy.*

"Ma'am?"

She pursed her lips. "You heard my question. It was difficult enough to ask it once. Don't make me do it again."

"I'm just a little flummoxed. Why are you asking?"

"We've already asked Michael. We need confirmation."

My jaw dropped. “You asked Michael about me? No wonder he looked so embarrassed. It is really none of your business.”

“I must disagree.” I opened my mouth again to protest, but Anselina held up a hand to stop me. “This is an important issue in our community, part of the reason our girls marry so young.”

“It’s *personal*.” My cheeks got so hot they felt like they might be on fire.

“Not to a Traveller. Michael is the Ceannfort. You are the granddaughter of a council member, and he is the son of one. Your actions and behavior will be noticed. It would be better for you in the long run if you knew the rules and followed them. If you aren’t a virgin, we’ll deal with it. If you are, that makes things much easier for everyone.”

I blew out a breath. This had to be one of the most uncomfortable discussions I had ever had with an older lady, and Grandma Sugar was the queen of uncomfortable conversations.

“I didn’t. I mean, I haven’t. Not yet,” I said and Anselina visibly relaxed. “But it’s no one’s business, but my own, you hear?”

“You are one of us now, Emerson. These sorts of things are not treated lightly. Years from now, when you and Michael are married and have children of your own, you’ll thank me.”

I almost fell off my chair. “Excuse me?”

She patted my leg. “I saw the way you two looked at each other, dearie. It’s written all over your faces.”

“Anselina. Grandmother. I really like Michael, but we met a week ago, and I’m going home in December.”

Anselina went back to playing with her skirt,

refusing to make eye contact. A little knot of worry formed in my chest. I didn't want to make things harder, but leaving her with false hope was unkind.

"You understand I'm leaving, right?"

She gave a little shrug, still refusing to look at me. I groaned inwardly. This was going to be tough.

"And as far as marrying Michael and having little Traveller babies, I'm only twenty years old."

I remembered my upcoming birthday and slapped myself on the head. Anselina looked up at me in surprise.

"What is it?"

"Crapity crap. Excuse my French. I need to ask you a favor."

"I'd do anything for you, Emerson." Her complete sincerity almost made me forgive her for the sexual Spanish Inquisition I'd just experienced.

"I'm turning twenty-one on Friday, and promised my friends I'd go out with them. I obviously can't do that now."

Anselina's face lit up. "It's your birthday? How lovely. Don't worry. I'll plan it all. And your friends are more than welcome to come here."

"Really?"

"Yes. Leave it to me." She pulled me into a big hug, smelling just like the lavender in my sheets.

"Thank you, Grandmother." The word still felt a bit funny on my tongue, but it grew easier each time I said it. I just hoped Michael reacted to the news about my birthday in the same way Anselina had. Somehow, I doubted it.

Chapter Twenty-One

Kiss my go-to-hell.

~Grandma Sugar

I managed to catch Michael before he left the compound. He dressed in full battle gear with knifes and other weapons. A leather strap crossed his body with a sword sheathed in the back.

"I hope you aren't going to an airport, because you will not get through a metal detector in that get up."

"What is it, Emerson?"

The other boys awaited him, armed to the hilt as well. Michael scowled, not in the mood to play. He was impatient and ready to rumble.

"Are you going to ask me not to hurt Leo again?" His voice was a growl.

I sighed in exasperation. "You can hurt him. In fact, please do hurt him. I just don't want you to *kill* him. But this isn't about Leo. It's about my birthday."

The look of complete confusion on his face was adorable. "Your birthday?"

"It's on Friday. I forgot about it, truth be told, with the Moktar, the Travellers, and the long lost grandparents and all. But Lucinda and Poppy reminded me. They insist we go out."

Watching Michael's face reminded me of watching the dark clouds roll over an English sky. "You aren't going out."

I tried to remain patient. It wasn't easy. "I'm not an idiot. I realize that, but I'm in a pickle. They've been talking about this for ages, since it's my twenty-first birthday and kind of important. They won't accept it if I brush them off this time. I talked to my grandmother, and she said they could come here. Would that be okay?"

"Yes. How many people?"

I blinked. That was easier than I thought. "Just four. Lucinda, Poppy, Nigel, and Sven."

Michael gave me a curt nod. "Not a problem. We have a section of the courtyard blocked off for outside visitors with a separate entrance. It's necessary on occasion. There are security measures in place so they can't access the main compound. Anselina knows this."

"Great. I wanted to check first with you, and also make sure you could come." Suddenly, I was a little shy. We'd been thrown together, but we never really had a date, and this kind of felt like one.

Michael gave me a puzzled smile. His friends called for him to hurry up, but he gave me a kiss so sweet I almost melted like stick of butter on a hot sidewalk.

He brushed his thumb against my cheek and laughed at the bemused expression on my face. "I'll be there."

After he left, I was at a loss. I hated this feeling, knowing he was going out to fight, and not being able to help him. I strolled around the compound until I found Audrey and her friends.

"Sorry I haven't returned your dress yet. I can get it for you now."

She waved off my apology. “No worries. If you’d like, you can wear it for your party.”

“My party?”

Audrey laughed. “Your grandmother spread the word. News travels fast.”

“I guess so. Can y’all come?”

“Anselina already invited everyone.”

“Everyone?”

I looked around the compound. A woman I didn’t know smiled and waved. “Many happy returns, Emerson,” she called from across the courtyard. Several other people did the same. I shook my head. Audrey was right. News traveled fast.

“You have to understand.” Audrey linked her arm through mine. “It’s boring around here. It was exciting enough to have a Dweller in the compound. Now you’re one of us. This kind of thing just doesn’t happen.”

“A few of my Dweller friends are coming to the party. Will that be okay with everyone?”

“Of course. And don’t worry. We’ll tone it down a bit.”

I gave her a skeptical look. She wore a silver lame spaghetti strap tank top with a white micro-mini skirt, and the other girls were dressed about the same. These were their casual clothes. I couldn’t wait to see what they wore for a party. I might have to tell Poppy and Lucinda it was a stripper themed birthday. Lucinda would love it.

“Could you teach us some more of that kung fu stuff?” Audrey struck a pose that wasn’t half bad, and the other girls nodded eagerly. She leaned forward. “In private, of course. If any of the men see it, they might get the wrong idea."

"Because you want to learn self-defense?"

Audrey blew on a strand of hair that had fallen across her face. "They might not see it as that, but what they don't know won't hurt them."

I studied her face. "Am I going to get into trouble for this?"

She thought about it. "It's possible, but the good outweighs the bad. The men have protected us so long they don't realize we might be strong enough to protect ourselves. The only way to make them understand is to show them. Are you willing to help us?"

I looked at their faces. They weren't asking for much, just for the right to defend themselves against monsters. I couldn't refuse them, but I saw a lot of potential problems on the horizon, most of them in the form of Michael Nightingale.

"I'd be happy to."

"Let's get some dinner first, and then we'll start."

Audrey and her friends took me to the dining hall. I'd never seen it before. Inside, it looked like just about every school cafeteria I'd ever known. We got our food and found a table in the corner. I pulled my hair back in a ponytail to keep it from falling in my face.

"What happened to you?" Audrey narrowed her eyes. The other girls, busy talking and eating, didn't hear her question. My hand went to my neck self-consciously.

Honesty was the best policy, even if the story was hard to talk about. "A Dweller attacked me. Someone I knew."

Audrey shook her head. "Michael will kill him."

I swallowed hard. The bit of bread I'd eaten almost

got stuck in my throat. “He promised he wouldn’t.”

Audrey shrugged. “You’re his now. Traveller men are very protective of their women. You’ll get used to it. It has its benefits.” She gave me a little wink.

I picked up my fork and played with my food. “I won’t be here long enough to find out. I have to go home soon.”

Audrey snorted. “That’s not going to happen.” Audrey acted the same way Anselina had, and it made me nervous.

“What do you mean?”

“She doesn’t know what she means. She never knows what the hell she’s talking about.” Nella and her posse of mean girls came up to our table. Audrey glared at her.

“Bugger off, Nella.”

Nella raised her hand as if to slap Audrey, but thought better of it. She leaned in and spoke to her through clenched teeth. “I’ll deal with you later, dirt lover.”

“Dirt lover? How creative. Whatever does she mean?”

I pushed back my plate and folded my hands together on top of the table. Bullies were the same everywhere. If you let them get away with it once, it only made them worse.

Nella leaned close to me. “Dirt lovers are Travellers who lower themselves to socialize with Dwellers, and we all know Dweller girls are a bunch of sluts and whores.”

I picked up my napkin and daintily dabbed the corners of my mouth. “Dwellers? There aren’t any Dwellers here, but there is some gypsy garbage. I think it's time we took out the trash. Ladies?"

Before Nella could even respond, I'd jumped up and twisted her arm behind her back with one hand, grabbing a handful of her hair with the other. She made a startled grunting noise, and I twisted her arm just a little farther. Not enough to break it, but far enough to hurt. As I led her out of the dining hall, Audrey and the other girls followed.

"Where does the trash go?" I asked, and Audrey grinned. She pointed to some large bins next to the door. One of them didn't have a lid on it, the natural choice. "It's always important to clean up when you see garbage lying around."

"Don't you dare." Nella spoke through gritted teeth. Her friends stood around, looking nervous. They weren't going to back her up. She tried one final strategy. "You're not even a true Traveller. You're a half-breed mutant. You shouldn't be allowed to stay here. You shouldn't be allowed anywhere near us."

Her words stung, but I leaned forward and whispered in Nella's ear, "Then why don't you just try to make me go away, you nasty bit of rubbish? Remember this the next time you try to bully someone. If I can fight off a Moktar, I can certainly handle you."

"You're a bitch."

"Maybe. But Michael is mine. Don't forget that, either."

I pushed Nella over until she went head first into the garbage. Her legs stuck up in the air, and she had on granny underpants. Audrey and her friends almost fell on the ground laughing. Several of the younger Traveller boys saw it, too, and starting making catcalls. Nella's friends had to push over the garbage can to get her out. She was filthy and mad, but with a healthy dose of fear in her eyes. Fear was good. And the fact her friends didn't even try to stand up for her was also a good sign. She wouldn't bother me again anytime soon.

Chapter Twenty-Two

They go together like moonshine and mason jars.
~Grandma Sugar

The next two days were as ordinary as days inside a gypsy compound could be. I taught self-defense to the ladies who wanted to learn and went to classes at the university during the day, usually accompanied by one of the younger Traveller boys if Michael was busy. No one had seen Leo, but they weren't taking any chances. Michael hunted at night. Nella kept her distance. No one else mentioned my half-Traveller mutant status. The two-week limit on my visit no longer applied, and I felt more and more like part of the community.

When Friday came, I couldn't wait for the party to begin. Michael would meet Lucinda and Poppy at the apartment and bring them to the compound. I'd planned to wear Audrey's gold dress, but my grandmother surprised me with a different one, a soft, white dress that shimmered with every step I took. Sexy and strapless, but more my style, it had a wide sash that tied around my waist, and a skirt that floated gently down to hit just at mid-thigh length.

"I love it," I said, spinning around in front of the mirror. Classy and elegant, but with enough sparkle to make it gypsy.

Anselina smiled. "It's custom for girls to get a new

dress on their sixteenth birthday. It's a little late, but it'll have to do."

She reached behind her and picked up a small box. "This is also for you. It belonged to your mother."

Inside the box rested a very simple silver necklace, a dove hanging on a delicate chain. The dove sparkled with one small diamond for an eye, but otherwise was bling-free.

"Doves are very lucky things in our culture. I hope this one brings you luck."

"Thank you."

"You look like her, you know." I glanced up at her in surprise, and she smiled. "Her hair was red, and her eyes were blue, but otherwise you could be carbon copies. You have her personality, too. As warm and as welcoming as a fire on a cool day."

Anselina's voice cracked, and I looked at myself in the mirror. I couldn't really see the resemblance, but I felt closer to my mother now than I ever had in my entire life.

Audrey and her crew came bounding into my grandparents' caravan. Audrey lugged a giant suitcase. "Time for hair and makeup."

"Uh, oh."

Audrey laughed and pulled out an assortment of bottles and creams. "I told you we'd tone it down. Stop looking so scared."

Surprisingly, it wasn't overdone. Audrey figured out exactly what would bring out my eye color and accentuate my skin tone without being gaudy.

"You should be a professional. You really know what you are doing. I was in the pageant circuit for years, and I've never seen anyone with your skills."

She blushed. "I wish I could."

I bit my lip and winced. "Sorry, Audrey."

She couldn't quite meet my eyes. "Oh, it's fine. I have enough to keep me busy around here. There's nothing a Traveller girl likes as much as makeup."

"Except sequins," said one of her friends.

"And men," said another.

We all laughed. When they finished, my hair shimmered and fell in a waterfall of curls against my bare shoulders. My makeup was perfect, the dress divine.

"Thank you," I whispered, and everyone smiled. I kissed Anselina on the cheek.

"Happy Birthday, dear child. Now go and have fun with the young people," she said. "Matthew and I will see you when you come back."

That was her not so subtle way of telling me to return to her caravan tonight. I'd been hoping to stay with Michael again, but being a Traveller made things trickier, not that things had been any easier under Grandma Sugar's eagle eye. This trip to England had been the first time I'd lived away from home, and I enjoyed every minute of it, but now my newfound independence had come to a grinding halt.

We walked together, and more young people joined us along the way. Soon quite a crowd had assembled. Nella was absent, fortunately, but a few of her friends came. When they gave me shy smiles, I smiled right back, not wanting to hold a grudge.

We passed through a gate in a stone wall and entered a smaller courtyard strewn with twinkle lights. Small tables surrounded a fire pit. Flowers in vases graced tables covered in pristine white tablecloths.

Music was being piped in from somewhere. Margaret and Leah stood next to Patrick and Ryan, proud of their handiwork. I looked around in wonder.

"It's amazing."

A door opened to the outside, and Michael came in with Lucinda, Poppy, Nigel, and a tall blond man who had to be Sven. Lucinda and Poppy carried bottles of champagne and wrapped parcels. They screamed when they saw me, pulling me into a group hug and handing me their gifts. Poppy had used her designing skills to make me a beautiful woolen cape, and Lucinda gave me a gorgeous pair of earrings. After I thanked them, Leah took them to a table for food and drinks, and Michael finally came to my side.

"You're beautiful," he said, his voice deep and rich. He wore a dark suit and tie, and looked completely yummy.

"So are you." My heart swelled at the sight of the festive courtyard, the lights, and the happy people. "Thank you for tonight."

He shrugged. "The women did it," he said, but he slipped his hand into mine and squeezed it.

Soon, we were all dancing and singing and drinking. A lot. I lost track of how many people asked me to do shots. Before long, I was completely toasted.

Michael supplied me with water and food, and also kept a watchful eye on me the whole night. He rescued me several times from people trying to make me drink more, and finally pulled me onto the dance floor for a slow dance. I reached up, twining my arms around his neck, and gave him a loopy smile.

"You said you couldn't dance."

He gave me a crooked smile. "I can make an

exception. For you."

"You're lovely, you know. Lovely, lovely, lovely man."

He touched his nose with mine. "And you're drunk."

"I'm supposed to be drunk. It's my birthday." I began to sing. "*Happy Birthday to me, I can drink legally, but not in Kentucky, I live in dry Warren County.*"

He laughed. "Beautiful and musically talented."

I sighed happily. "This has been the best night ever. Thank you for letting my friends come."

I looked over at Poppy and Nigel. They danced, completely in their own world. Lucinda and Sven made out in a corner, and judging by the intensity of it, it wouldn't be long before she finally conquered Antarctica. I was glad they were happy. I was happy. I wanted everyone to be happy. I was very drunk.

"I love this place." The twinkle lights were a blur as Michael twirled me around in his arms. The people were a blur, too, but they all looked so sparkly and pretty. "I love these people, too. But do you know what I love most of all?"

"Chocolate?" Michael's lips grazed my ear when he spoke, making me shiver.

"Yes. But do you know what else?"

I unlaced my hands from around his neck and ran them slowly down his body. No one could see what I was doing because he had his jacket on, and we stood very close. I caressed the hard muscles of his abdomen, enjoying the noise he made deep in his throat when I touched him. I got all the way to the waistline of his pants before he stopped me.

"Emerson." His voice was a deep, shaky plea. He shook his head and brought my hands up to his lips to kiss them.

Everything sort of shifted and swayed. "Oh, wow. I'm drunk as a skunk."

Michael swung me into his arms as easily as lifting a feather. I sighed and snuggled into his chest. "Don't take me home yet. I want to play with my friends."

After more food, water, and a bit of black coffee, I felt much better, still buzzed and happy, but not falling over drunk. The party was quieting down. Many of my gypsy friends had gone home. My Dweller friends remained. We sat around the fire with Michael's family and a few of the gypsies I'd grown closest to and talked and laughed until very late, then everyone stood to leave. Sven wobbled a little, and Lucinda wrapped an arm around his waist.

"I'd better get you home, my big tall Viking."

Sven nodded very seriously. "Yes, you should, my luscious Lucinda."

"The boys will see you back safely," said Michael. He nodded at Quinn, Anthony, and Sean. My friends tried to protest, but Michael insisted. I wanted to stay and help Leah and Margaret clean up, but they would have none of it.

"Most of it has been done already. We'll finish tomorrow." Leah yawned, and gave me a little peck on the cheek. "Many happy returns."

Margaret kissed me, too. "Happy Birthday," she said.

When we reached my grandparents' caravan, Michael pulled something from behind his back. "Happy Birthday, Emerson." He looked embarrassed as he handed me two carefully wrapped bundles.

"Michael. I don't know what to say."

He rubbed his head with his hand. "Just open them. They're only small, but I wanted to give you something."

The first package contained a beautifully bound, limited edition copy of *Self Reliance* by Ralph Waldo Emerson. The second package held a small box with a dainty ring inside. I looked up at him in surprise.

"It was my mother's." Michael's voice was gruff. "And her mother's before that. I wanted you to have it."

"Thank you." My voice was thick as I struggled not to cry. The ring was a simple, elegant Celtic knot. It slid easily onto my ring finger.

Michael pulled me into his arms and looked into my eyes. "You never finished what you were saying before. You were telling me what you loved most of all. I guessed it was chocolate."

I gave him a coy smile. "Chocolate is a close second."

Michael trailed kisses up my neck. I sighed and tilted my head back so he had better access. He worked his way to my mouth and began giving me soft little kisses that took my breath away. I tried to get the words out between kisses, but he could be very distracting when he set his mind to it.

"The thing I love most of all…is you, Mr. Nightingale."

Michael cupped my face in his hands and stared at me, his face inches away from mine. The stars twinkled brightly in the inky black sky above him. I felt like I was spinning and spinning, but not because of the alcohol. Michael himself was able to make me dizzy with a single glance.

“And I love you, Emerson Jane Shaw.”

Chapter Twenty-Three

The only place you'll find sympathy here is in the dictionary.

~Grandma Sugar

I slept with Michael's ring on my finger and the book he'd given me next to my pillow. It didn't matter that Leo had tried to strangle me or a Moktar wanted to kidnap me. I was miles away from my family, I'd lost my journal, and had to write a paper for my Shakespeare class, but I didn't care about any of it, because Michael loved me.

Daddy's telltale ringtone filled the air, waking me. I answered it immediately, a big, happy grin on my face.

"Hi, Daddy."

"Hi, pumpkin." Something wasn't right. I knew it as soon as he spoke.

"What happened?"

"Pappy George had a little spell. He's in the hospital. Sorry I didn't call on your birthday."

"Is he okay?"

Suddenly, I found it a little hard to breathe. I sat up straight in my bed. Pappy George was getting older, but he'd always been as strong as an ox, or so I'd thought.

"He just needs to rest, and stop eating so much fried food. Grandma Sugar said he is too stubborn to die, and too stupid to change."

"Should I come home?" I closed my eyes, dreading the answer.

"No, he's going to be just fine. Please don't worry your little head about it. I just felt bad I couldn't call you. I couldn't use my phone at the hospital. Did you have a nice birthday?"

I told him about my party and my friends. I wished with all my heart to tell him about Anselina and Matthew, but that wasn't the kind of thing you dumped on someone during a long distance telephone call.

"Well, I'd better go, sugar."

I clung to my phone, not wanting to hang up. "Daddy, if Pappy George gets worse and I need to come home, you'll tell me, right?"

He didn't hesitate. "You know I will, Emerson. Now you get back to those books. I love you."

"You, too."

I hung up the phone and just stared at it. Pappy George, with his giant frame and winning smile, was indestructible. I couldn't imagine him in a hospital bed attached to tubes and wires and a machine on the wall. I just couldn't do it.

Anselina came in carrying a breakfast tray. "Good morning. I heard your phone, so I knew you were awake. Did you have a nice time last night?"

I smiled, but it took some effort. "It was wonderful." A tear trickled down my cheek. "My daddy called. My grandfather is in the hospital."

Anselina patted my head. "There, there. I'm sure he'll be fine."

"That's what Daddy said." I wanted reassurance, but she'd already turned her back to me and started tidying the room.

"Eat your breakfast, love."

The tray was piled high with eggs and bacon, sweet rolls, and a pot of coffee. My stomach lurched at the sight of the bacon and eggs. I managed to nibble on a roll and drink a few cups of coffee, and felt a little better with something in my stomach. I showered and dressed in a pair of jeans and my Western Kentucky sweatshirt, needing comfort today. I didn't bother with makeup, and just let my hair air-dry.

I had to get my mind off Pappy George, and finish a paper for my Shakespeare class, so I pulled out my laptop and set to work. It didn't take long for me to realize I needed materials from the library. There were works to cite, and information I couldn't find online. I went out to search for Michael.

He sat in the middle of a meeting with several of the council members, including my grandparents. Apparently, they were having a serious discussion. Mavin was among them, and squawked on and on about something. Every time she paused to take a breath, her gaze went right to Sampson. He never once looked at her. I started to think the abrasive Mavin had a little thing for him. Anselina attempted to calm her down. Michael looked irritated. I interrupted them, but didn't know what else to do. They all went silent when I approached.

"What is it Emerson?" A muscle worked in Michael's jaw. Not a good sign.

I shoved my hair behind my ears. "Can I speak with you for a moment, or should I come back later?"

Michael and Anselina shared a look, and then he narrowed his eyes at me. "Now is fine."

We walked over to a quiet spot under a tree. Actually, I walked. Michael sort of stomped. He was in a delightful mood this morning. I felt bad asking him to take me to the library, but he wouldn't want me to go by myself.

I opened my mouth to speak, but Michael held up a hand to stop me. "I know what you are going to ask, and the answer is no."

I looked at him in shock. I knew it was a pain for someone to escort me around all the time, but it wasn't exactly my fault.

"Excuse me?"

Michael put his hands on his hips. He wore a tight black t-shirt and jeans, and he looked luscious as always, but he was making me angry enough to ignore his hotness for now.

"Anselina told me about your grandfather, and I'm sorry, but you can't go back to Kentucky. I will not permit you to leave."

I took a step back. "You will not *permit* me?"

He folded his arms across his chest. "I have your passport."

"What are you talking about?"

My passport had been safely tucked into an inside pocket of my backpack. I'd grabbed it the first time I went to my apartment with Michael and hadn't checked it since then, but assumed it was still there. Apparently, I'd assumed wrong. I swallowed hard.

"You stole my passport. That's why you looked so nervous when I searched through my backpack after Leo attacked me. You thought that was what I was looking for."

Michael's face was as hard as a stone. "It's in a

safe place, and I did it for your own good. If you leave, you'll die."

"Which is why I agreed to stay." My lips began to quiver and I brushed angry tears away with the back of my hand. "For your information, I wasn't planning to go back to Kentucky. My grandfather is doing fine, thank you for asking. I just came to tell you I have to go to the library and need an escort."

Michael winced, reaching for my arm. I backed away. "Em, I'm sorry. I'll take you to the library after this meeting."

"No, thanks."

I turned on my heel and walked away. Michael called out to me, but I ignored him. He didn't follow, which was wise. I found a quiet spot under a tree where no one could see me, and sat down to have a good cry.

I was homesick and missed my family. Pappy George had always been a huge part of my daily life, and now he'd had a "spell," southern-speak for a heart attack, and I hadn't even known about it. I'd been getting drunk and making out with Michael when the people I cared about most in the world were suffering.

The thought of Michael brought a fresh flood of tears. I loved him, but he was difficult and controlling and awfully hard to get along with. He just stepped in and took over, without ever asking what I wanted or how I felt. He did it to protect me, but he treated me like a mindless idiot.

"Are you okay, Emerson?" Margaret stood a few feet behind me, a worried frown on her face.

"I'm fine."

I tried to wipe my tears and hide my face, a hopeless endeavor. I looked like a swollen lobster when

I cried. I obviously wasn't fine.

Margaret sat down next to me on the grass, so close our arms brushed against each other. "We didn't start off well, but I really like you, Emerson. You can talk to me if you have a problem. I hope you know that."

I sniffed. "Thank you, Margaret. I just miss my family. My grandfather is in the hospital, and I wish I could be there with him."

Margaret put a comforting arm around my shoulders. "You'll get used to it, Emerson. It's not that bad here. We're your family now."

I leaned away from her and looked at her face. "Everyone keeps talking like I'm staying here, and I'm not."

Margaret gave me a sad little smile. "Do you really think he'll let you leave?"

"Michael? Of course, he will. He can't force me to stay."

Margaret bent her knees to her chest and wrapped her arms around them. Her dark hair fluttered in the artificial breeze of Michael's air circulators.

"When you were a Dweller, it was different. You were an outsider. Now that you're a Traveller, it changes everything. You are his, Emerson."

"I am not." My voice shook, and I had to wipe away more tears.

"Traveller women are like trinkets placed on a shelf. Pretty little baubles. Our men guard us with their lives, but they will never treat us as equals. If you expect more, or hope for more, you'll just be disappointed."

Margaret's voice sounded hollow and dull. She was so full of pain, the extent of which seemed impossible for me to understand.

"I'm sorry, Margaret. I'm not that girl."

"Neither am I," she said with a wry grin. "Not any more, at least."

I fell back on the soft grass and stared up at the sky. It was a beautiful sunny fall day. Big white fluffy clouds floated past like giant wads of cotton candy. Margaret lay down beside me.

"Patrick and I have started talking more. He's drinking less. We're getting to a happier place. But I don't have options, Emerson. A Traveller girl gets taken every single year. Because of the Moktar, I'm a prisoner, even if my cage is a shiny, new, state of the art caravan."

My laugh was completely devoid humor. "Michael took my passport. I wasn't even planning to leave, but now I'm trapped here."

Margaret reached for my hand. "We all are."

We lay there, hand in hand, just watching the sky. It felt nice. Margaret and Leah were like the sisters I'd never had. I told her about my paper, and how I couldn't get it done without going to the university, but didn't want to ask Michael.

"Patrick can take you. Let me get him."

Patrick suggested Margaret come, too, which made her very excited. Getting out of the compound was a big deal for her. "Do I look all right?"

She wore the standard gypsy gear of a micro mini and a tank shirt. I'd gotten used to seeing a lot of skin at the compound, but wasn't sure the outside world was ready for it.

"You might want to bring a cardigan. It's a little chilly today."

Margaret flashed me a brilliant smile, and ran back to get a sweater. I grabbed my backpack from my grandparents' caravan. They were still at their meeting. I checked the inside pocket just to be sure Michael spoke the truth. My passport was definitely gone.

As we walked through The Shambles, Margaret took everything in, her eyes aglow with excitement. When she begged to duck into a little shop, Patrick and I waited outside.

He folded his brawny arms across his chest, and squinted up at the sun trying to fight its way through the clouds. He looked so much like Michael, and yet they were very different. Michael hid his pain and controlled his emotions. Patrick wore his hurt, and his heart, on his sleeve. But both of them used tattoos to record what they'd lost. Michael had a tattoo for each friend who'd died, and even for the monsters he'd killed. On Patrick's right bicep was a Celtic cross with his mother's name and the words *Ar Dhies De' go Rabh a Hamen.*

"What does that mean?"

Patrick looked down at his bicep. "May she sit at God's right. I got it when I turned eighteen, and finally gave up on ever seeing her again. I guess a dozen years is the limit to keeping false hope alive."

"I'm sorry about your mother."

Patrick gave me the typical Nightingale shrug. "Thank you for being kind to Margaret. She's been going through a rough patch. She seems to be getting better, and you're helping."

"I think you're helping, too."

Patrick nodded. "We've had…problems. I didn't handle things well I'm afraid, and I'm sorry for that."

Patrick stood almost as tall as Michael, but with a bulkier build. If Michael looked like a lean panther, Patrick was a bull. He had the same shaved head as his brother, and his eyes were blue, too, but he had lines of worry on his face Michael didn't possess yet.

"I need to explain something about my little brother." I gave him a wary glance. He pulled on his leather jacket and tucked his hands into the pockets, his eyes scanning the street. "He takes his job very seriously. I wish I could help him, shoulder some of the burden for him, but he is the Ceannfort. I am not."

"I understand he has quite a bit on his plate right now…"

"You don't understand half of it." He shook his head. "I don't mean to sound harsh, but do you know what that meeting was about this morning? Mavin wants to stop you from going to university, from leaving the compound at all."

"Can she do that?" My throat was tight, and I felt a little sick. They didn't even know about my missing journal.

Patrick rubbed a hand over his head, a gesture so reminiscent of Michael it pulled at my heart. "She has a valid argument. You were attacked. It's put all of us on high alert."

"But Leo is just a Dweller."

"Dweller or not, it falls into Michael's lap. They've finally succeeded in making him stop going to university, and now they're going after you. Do you have any idea what university meant to him?"

"He deserves to go. They shouldn't be able to stop him."

Patrick gave me a hard look. "They didn't stop

him. You did. The minute that Moktar started tracking you, the decision was made for him."

I felt like I'd just been sucker punched in the gut. "That isn't fair."

Patrick turned to me, his expression grim. "Life isn't fair, but we make the most of it. We don't have a choice. Don't be so hard on my brother, lass. I know you care for him. Just try to understand. It'll make things easier for him."

"I will."

Margaret bounded out of the shop with a huge grin on her face. Her excitement was contagious as she ran on ahead of us, peeking in shop windows. Others noticed, too, but not in a good way. Men ogled her, and women glared at her, but she seemed oblivious. Patrick observed the furious expression on my face and chuckled.

"You get used to it, Emerson. There's something about us that sets Dwellers on edge, something deep inside us they recognize as a threat."

"But you work to protect them."

"We work to protect ourselves. The safety of the Dwellers is just a byproduct."

I wrinkled my nose. "That's cold."

"The truth usually is."

Patrick and Margaret left me at the library, after I assured them I was safe. They needed some time alone, and so did I. I set to work on my paper, but my thoughts kept going back to Patrick's words. I was the reason Michael had to quit school, and I needed to find a way to help him. I was ruining his life.

Suddenly, it became clear what I had to do. Stepping into a quiet alcove of the library, I called the

U.S. Consulate in York, explaining I'd lost my passport, and needed to visit my grandfather in the hospital. It was easier than I expected because I had my drivers' license with me. They said they could have a temporary passport for me by tomorrow.

I hung up, and called my father. He answered on the first ring.

"Daddy, I need an airplane ticket. I'm coming home."

Chapter Twenty-Four

Don't go off with your pistol half-cocked.
~Grandma Sugar

After I made my decision, it felt like a weight had been lifted from my shoulders. I'd leave quickly, and the Moktar would not be able to track me during the day. A risk, but one I had to take. I would not be a prisoner here.

I felt a little pang at the thought of Michael and my grandparents, but I had little choice, and it would be better for Michael in the long run. With me out of the picture, he could go back to school, and I wouldn't feel so guilty anymore.

Thoughts of my mom made a shiver pass over my heart. She'd operated under the assumption Kentucky was safe when she ran away. I knew the truth, but felt better prepared. I'd fight the Moktar if they found me and would not die like my mama. I refused.

Lucinda and Poppy's calls went straight to their voice mail accounts. I left the same message for both of them, telling them I had to go home for a few days and asking them not to say anything to Michael because goodbyes were so hard. That much was the truth, and I was satisfied they'd buy it.

I thought about going to the consulate immediately, but Patrick and Margaret waited for me outside.

Gathering together the materials needed for my paper, I set off, knowing I'd have to bide my time and leave early in morning while the Travellers slept.

That afternoon a strange calm descended on me. I finished my paper in record time, emailed to my professor, and had a nice dinner with my grandparents. Michael tried to talk to me, but I brushed him off without saying a word. He thought I was still mad at him, which was true, but I also didn't want him around in case he said or did something to make me change my mind.

That night, when the men went out to hunt, the ladies had their last lesson. I desperately tried to think of everything possible to help them. Judging by what they told me, the only person grabbed by a Moktar who'd lived to tell the tale was yours truly. I wanted to teach them what I knew, and they were grateful. They were also fast learners. The progress they'd made in only a few short days was impressive.

After the lesson finished, I pulled out my copy of *The Art of War* and read key points to them. The most important thing I emphasized was in chapter three, "The Plan of Attack."

Looking each of them in the eye, I spoke softly, but they hung on every word. "It doesn't matter if the Moktar are bigger than you, or stronger or faster. Sun Tzu said from unity comes strength, and you have to stick together. Even if I'm not with you, you have the skills you need. If you work together, you'll survive together."

I excused myself, knowing full well staying any longer would mean blubbering like a baby, which didn't often happen when one read *The Art of War*. Sun

Tzu would have punished me for my weakness, and he would have been right. My feelings weren't important here. The survival of my friends was all that mattered.

When I got back to my grandparents' caravan, a rather snarky little message from Brooke showed up on my phone. She planned on going out with Leo the next day, and was under the impression I wanted him for myself. The thought made me ill. I tried to explain to her via text exactly what had happened, but she wouldn't respond. She wouldn't take my calls either. Our animosity had gone on so much longer than our attempts at friendship. She thought she couldn't trust me.

I set down my phone, deciding this was a Dweller versus Dweller issue, even if Leo seemed unstable and dangerous. I'd done my best to warn her, and there was nothing else to do. I decided to tell myself that over and over again, until I actually believed it. Or at least until the sick and uneasy feeling in the pit of my stomach disappeared.

The night seemed never ending. I barely slept. When the guys came home from the hunt, I listened to the sounds of their hushed voices and soft footsteps, and then waited a few more hours. When the sky just began to lighten, it was time to go. Packing everything I needed into my backpack proved challenging, but it would be impractical to haul a suitcase around and might slow me down. I kept the silver dove necklace around my neck and Michael's ring on my finger, but left my beautiful white dress because I didn't want to crush the delicate fabric by shoving it into my backpack. The book Michael had given me was safely tucked inside, though. I needed little *Self Reliance* at the moment.

I wrote a long note to my grandparents, and cried the entire time. I put it on my pillow, wanting them to find it, but not too soon. Hopefully, they'd think I'd slept in, and wouldn't see it until late afternoon.

I'd written a long note to Michael, too, trying not to sound angry or bitter. He needed to understand I loved him, but he'd left me no choice. I wouldn't live as a prisoner, or as someone's possession. It was hard to write, and would be even harder to read. I decided to leave it in his caravan. If not, someone else might discover it first, and I didn't want that to happen.

Walking through the compound, it was completely silent and still. I smelled the smoke from the dying campfires and the dew on the grass made my tennis shoes wet. Michael's caravan was dark, his door unlocked, when I slipped inside. He had to be fast asleep by now.

At first, I couldn't see in the dim light of the caravan, but soon my eyes adjusted. Michael had been studying. His chemistry books lay on the table, and an open notebook on his desk was filled with chemical equations jotted down in his neat and precise handwriting. Seeing that just about broke my heart in two, and strengthened my resolve. He still studied, even after he'd dropped out of school, simply because he loved it so much. I was doing him a favor by getting out of his life.

Pulling out my copy of *The Art of War* from my backpack, with its wrinkled cover and notes in the margins of just about every single page, a wave of sadness came over me. This book had gotten me through some tough times, but Michael needed it more than me. He was the leader of a real army with an actual war to wage. Soon I'd be nothing more than an ordinary college student, with a former beauty title and a completely broken heart.

As I placed it next to my note on his kitchen table, I noticed a box I hadn't seen before. It looked like the sort of box a person might put important documents and other things in, like warranty information and stolen passports. Definitely worth a look, even if it meant riffling through Michael's personal belongings. Since no noise came from his bedroom, I gathered my courage and decided to be a little nosey.

My heart skipped a beat as I slowly opened it, surprised to find the box filled with photos. I sank to the couch, using my phone as a light. Photo after photo showed Michael as a young boy. There were shots of Michael with his brothers, and old and faded ones of his mother and father. But sitting on the very top, carefully tied up with a cream colored satin ribbon, was a pile that looked newer than the rest.

It took me a second to recognize the ribbon as the one used to tie back my hair the first time I'd worked up the courage to speak to Michael. It had blown away in the alley, and, evidently, Michael had found it and kept it. A little mud stained, it had been carefully cleaned and pressed, and now held together a stack of photos. They were all of me, and looking at them shook me to my core.

Michael must have been taking pictures of me long before we'd ever spoken. Some photos depicted me eating lunch with Poppy and Lucinda and laughing. Others showed me engrossed in a book, sitting in the teashop, and walking through The Shambles. And there was one of us dancing at my birthday party. We were staring into each other's eyes and smiling. I thought about taking that one home to Kentucky with me, even if it would be stealing.

I was about to shove it into my backpack when a light turned on. I blinked, startled. Michael stood in the doorway to his bedroom wearing nothing but a towel, his skin damp from the shower. My breath hitched at the sight of his body, all sinewy strength, sculpted abs, and rippling muscles. Glorious. The tattoos dancing on his skin only enhanced his beauty, as did the silver piercings. He was a god, a furious god at that. He folded his arms across his chest and leaned against the doorjamb.

"Going somewhere?" His eyes took in my coat and the backpack by my feet. He acted way too calm. He saw the letter and book I'd left on his kitchen table and sauntered over. "May I?"

He flipped through the book, noticing all the highlighting and notes scribbled in the margins. He raised a dark eyebrow. "An interesting choice. A little light reading, perhaps?"

He didn't wait for my answer. He reached for the envelope and ripped it open. His eyes scanned the page, and he grew angrier with every word. The color rushed into his cheeks and a muscle began working in his jaw. When he finished, his eyes blazed blue, full of fury.

"You're doing this for *me*?"

He walked toward me like a panther moving in for the kill. A predator, and I was an easy lunch, but I couldn't even move. I just watched and waited.

"I…I…thought it for the best. You could go back to school."

My voice sounded breathless and strange, and it may have had something to do with a nearly naked Michael only inches away from me. I felt the heat of his body, smelled the warm scent of his skin, and saw drops of water still drying on his shoulders, making me want to lean forward and lick one. I wanted to taste him on my tongue. He was mad at me, but I was more completely aroused than I'd ever been in my life. All I could think about were his hands on my body, and his mouth on mine. Nothing in my life had prepared me for this, and he hadn't even touched me. I was way out of my league.

He grabbed the lapels of my jacket and pulled me slowly into his dark bedroom. I didn't protest. I wanted to be there. His eyes never left mine as he took off my coat, letting it fall to the floor behind me with a soft thud. Quickly my blouse, jeans, undies, and bra joined it. I must have slipped out of my shoes and socks at some point, but had no memory of it. I was in the thrall of Michael Nightingale.

He still wore his towel, but I now stood in front of him, completely naked and panting like I'd run a race. He reached out a hand and cupped my cheek, gently stroking my face with his thumb. Closing my eyes and leaning into his palm, I knew I was lost.

"Emerson."

His voice, husky and low, sent shivers over my bare skin. He began kissing my forehead, my eyebrows, and the corners of my eyes. He rained soft gentle kisses across my cheeks and down my jawline. When I couldn't stand it anymore, his lips touched mine.

It felt like a lightning bolt had gone directly through my body. He must have felt it, too, because he groaned and pulled me closer. Suddenly, what had been heart stopping and slow became wild and hot. My arms went around his waist and I clung to him, wanting to touch all of him at once. My hands ran frantically over his body, caressing his back and arms and the strong muscles of his shoulders. I made funny little sounds in the back of my throat because I was on fire, and wanted Michael with an almost frightening intensity.

He seemed to feel the same way. His hands, rough and warm, stroked me and caressed me, making me even more insane with need. He held me so tightly against him it was no longer clear where I ended and he began. The feeling of his bare skin against mine was the most perfect and beautiful thing I'd ever experienced, but it wasn't enough. I wanted to be closer still.

My hands slid down his back until they found the towel still wrapped snugly around his waist. I yanked and pulled until it fell to the floor in a heap. Michael leaned back and stared at me, his eyes glowing in the faint light of early morning.

"Are you sure?"

I couldn't speak, but knew exactly what I wanted. I nodded, raising myself on to my tiptoes and kissing him with all that was inside me. In seconds, Michael used his exceptionally good Traveller reflexes to have me on the bed, pinned beneath his delicious body. He rested on his forearms, so as not to crush me, but I welcomed his weight. I wanted everything, every part of him.

I wiggled and squirmed until he rested in the cradle of my thighs, his erection hot and throbbing against my core. When he hesitated, I took control. Little virginal Emerson Jane from Bowling Green. I shifted my body and lifted my pelvis until the tip of him was finally inside me. Michael moaned. It wasn't just me. We were both lost.

He eased into me slowly, his breath warm on my ear. "Emerson, I don't want to hurt you…"

I answered with a sigh. "Don't stop, Michael. Please don't stop."

A brief spasm of pain made me gasp and grab his shoulders, but I forgot about it completely when I looked at his face.

"I love you, Emerson," he said, kissing me so gently and sweetly tears welled in my eyes. He froze when he saw them. "Did I hurt you?"

I shook my head. "I love you, too."

His eyes scanned my face to make sure it was the truth, and then he began to move slowly inside me. It felt strange at first, like I'd always imagined it would, but somehow different. I began to move with him, instinctively answering him thrust for thrust, like we danced to secret music that only the two of us heard.

Something strange and wonderful began to build inside me. It started at the tips of my toes and then grew and grew until I exploded with a series of gasping little noises. As soon as Michael heard me, he made a strange, strangled sound and he exploded, too.

Afterwards, he rolled to his side, took off the condom, and tossed it into the garbage can, pulling me into his arms. I said a little prayer of thanks to the saint who protected stupid virgins everywhere that he'd had the sense to use one. I hadn't even noticed he'd put it on, and had been too far gone to stop him if he hadn't.

"I guess I'm not a virgin anymore."

Michael kissed the top of my head. "No, you aren't."

"I do believe I just had my first orgasm as well."

He chuckled, a sound of pure masculine pride. "I'm fairly certain you did."

"Thank you, Michael."

He lifted his head and looked down at me in surprise. "Are you thanking me for deflowering you?"

"No. I'm thanking you for doing it so *well.* You really are a genius."

He gave me a grin. "We aim to please, ma'am."

I sighed. "I have so much to learn." Turning on my side, I ran a finger down his arm. He watched me, fascinated by the sight of my hands on his skin. Suddenly, I wanted to play, and Michael was my brand new toy. I pushed him onto his back. "This is lesson number two, I guess."

He swallowed hard. "Already?"

I grinned. "I want to learn about your body because I didn't really have a chance before. You were being so shy. I almost had to pry that towel off of you."

Michael lay back and folded his arms behind his head. "I am very shy," he said with a grin, his entire beautiful body naked and on display for my viewing pleasure.

I touched my chin with one finger. "Now let me see. Where shall I begin?" My gaze started at his head and trailed down his body until it reached the juncture of his thighs. As soon as my eyes rested there, he started to become erect again.

"Holy guacamole. That didn't take much." Michael reached for me, but I shook my head. "Can I touch it?"

He nodded, and I studied it carefully. It was huge.

"How on earth did that fit inside me?"

Michael almost beamed with pride. Reaching out a

tentative hand, and not sure what to expect, I touched him. The reality was far different from my imagination.

"It feels like velvet." I smiled at him in wonder. "Velvet with steel inside."

I gave it a gentle little squeeze and he gasped. I ran my fingers up and down the sides and he moaned. When I touched thc tip, a little bead of moisture pearled against my finger, and I grinned at him in delight. I'd never felt so sensual or powerful in my life.

Michael reached up, grabbed me by the waist, and tossed me onto my back. "My turn," he growled, and then the sweet torture began. He kissed and licked and touched and explored every single inch of my body until I begged and pleaded for him to be inside me once again. He complied, and, if possible, the second time was even better than the first.

Afterwards, we were both exhausted and curled up in each other's arms. Michael pulled me close, half asleep already, and whispered words into my ear that nearly broke my heart.

"Stay with me, Emerson. Please don't leave."

Chapter Twenty-Five

That made him crazier than a sprayed roach.
~Grandma Sugar

I fell asleep in heaven, and woke up in hell. I still lay in Michael's caravan, naked and curled up on his bed. The only problem was my grandparents, and his father, stood right outside, banging on the front door.

"Michael. You must wake. Emerson has run away."

Sampson sounded ready to barge in. I sat up with a start, but Michael, still fast asleep, didn't react at all. I nudged his shoulder frantically.

"Wake up," I hissed.

He turned and gave me a very knowing, very cat ate the cream sort of smile. That disappeared as soon as he heard his father's voice. He jumped up and pulled on his jeans, hopping to the front door as he buttoned them.

"Da, it's fine. She's here."

Michael went outside and shut the door behind him. I heard some angry murmurs from Anselina and Matthew, and I cringed and covered my face with my hands. My grandparents knew I'd been doing the horizontal mambo with Michael. Absolutely horrifying.

Michael didn't seem at all upset. In fact, he seemed rather pleased with himself. He walked back into the bedroom, and gave me a slow, sexy smile that turned my insides to mush. I threw a pillow at him.

"Don't you be doing that, Mr. Nightingale. That is exactly what got us into this predicament in the first place."

Michael put his hand on his chest. "*I* got us into this predicamcnt?"

I frowned. "I guess it wasn't all your fault."

Michael flopped down on the bottom of the bed. I was still naked, holding the blankets tightly against my chest as I hugged my knees close to my body. Michael just stared at me.

"I love you, Emerson."

I glared at him. "I love you, too."

He grinned. "You really aren't a morning person."

He was right, but it made me scowl. "Well, not when I'm woken up like that, with my grandparents outside and me naked as a jay bird in some man's bed."

He crawled toward me like a lion. "*Some* man's bed? Do you often wake up in *some* man's bed?"

I fell back onto the pillows. He climbed up my body, straddling me on his hands and knees. I bit my lip. I wanted him again. I'd turned into a nymphomaniac.

"Not usually." I slid my hands up his body, and then gently pulled on his nipple rings. He groaned, pressing his pelvis against mine. I answered with a thrust of my own. "Not ever, actually."

"That's good." He leaned down to kiss me. This time I nibbled on the little silver hoop in his lip like I'd always wanted to and ran my fingers up and down his back. Eventually, my hands found his jeans, and I began to push them off.

Michael nuzzled my neck. “We shouldn’t.” He dipped his head lower and began kissing my breasts. “We really shouldn’t.”

I disagreed. I pushed and pulled until his jeans were on the floor in a heap, and he lay completely naked against me. This time I grabbed the condom. He put it on in record time, and he was inside of me once again, moving with a rhythm as ancient as the waves in the ocean.

“Is it always *this* good?” I panted as he slid in and out of me, a fine sheen of sweat forming on his body. Even his sweat was erotic to me. I was a hopeless case.

“Never,” he rasped. “It’s never, ever this good.”

This time I came so hard and so fast, I almost screamed. He caught my cries with his mouth, and soon he came, too. Afterwards, he kissed my face reverently, like I was some priceless, delicate treasure.

“I could stay like this all day.” I loved having the weight of his body on me and wanted to hold him there, inside me, as long as possible.

Michael kissed my neck. “The gypsy council would have a thing or two to say about that.”

My eyes flew open. “Oh, crap. The gypsy council. Are we in trouble?”

Michael thought about it. “It depends on what you mean by trouble. I told your grandparents and my father you came to say goodbye last night. I talked you out of leaving and then fell asleep on the couch.”

“Did they buy it?” Michael winced, and I covered my face with my hands. “Oh, no. My grandparents know I had sex. Three times.”

Michael tilted his head to one side with little smile. “They don’t know it was three times, although I sort of wish they did." I smacked his arm, and he grinned. "It's impressive. I'm a beast."

I groaned, pushed him off me, and stomped to the shower. I looked at myself in the mirror, trying to see some sign written on my face that everything was different now. I still looked like myself, but would never be the same. I'd been changed forever.

When I finished with my shower, Michael showered, too. I called my father as soon as Michael got in to tell him I decided to stay and complete the semester. It wasn't just about the mind-blowing sex or because of the photos Michael had kept in that box with my ribbon. And it wasn't because he'd begged me not to leave when he was half asleep and had clung to me like I was a life preserver and he was adrift in a wild sea. I wanted to stay simply because leaving had been the wrong decision. I needed to finish what I started, at school, with the gypsies, with my newfound grandparents, and with Michael, but part of the reason I'd wanted to leave so badly had been just to prove to Michael and the others I could. It seemed a bit frivolous at the moment, since leaving could very likely get me killed. Even Sun Tzu would have agreed with the sound logic behind my decision this time.

"That's a relief, sweetie. It's better this way. You'll be home in a few weeks and all will be well."

He told me Pappy George would be released from the hospital the next morning. He and Grandma Sugar were both fine, so I had one item checked off my long list of worries. I texted Poppy and Lucinda to let them know I'd changed my plans, and called the consulate as well. I hung up the phone just as Michael finished, feeling much better about everything.

It didn't last long. Michael gave me a scowl, looking very serious and a little grim. "We need to talk."

He sat at the kitchen table, in front of a breakfast of coffee and chocolate croissants, which he must have picked up while I showered. I pulled out the chair next to him, and tried not to wince as I sat down. I was still a little sore from the night's activities. I'd dressed in a pair of jeans that made my bottom look exceptionally good and a tight white t-shirt. Michael wore his normal uniform of black with black.

"Okay, shoot." I took a long sip of coffee. I thought I might need it. I suspected I'd earned a lecture, and I was right.

"What you were about to do was very dangerous. That Moktar would have been on you instantly. You don't understand. You don't know him like I do. You have to promise you will never run away again."

I sat very still. "Then give back my passport."

Michael sat back, shoving his plate away. "What does that have to do with anything?"

I clenched my hands into little fists. "It's about trust, Michael."

Last night may have changed everything, but one thing remained the same. Michael didn't trust me, and continued to try to control me.

"It's about keeping you alive. Sorry to ruin your plans."

"Do you think I *wanted* to leave?"

"I don't know." Michael stared at my mouth. He wanted to kiss me again, but I wasn't going to let him until he was honest. His eyes went from my mouth up to my eyes and he frowned. "Yes. You wanted to leave."

I rewarded him with a brief kiss. The fact he showed any vulnerability at all was huge progress.

"Well, you're wrong, but I'll have to go back to Kentucky eventually. I don't have a choice." Michael opened his mouth to speak, but I stopped him with one finger on his lips. "My daddy needs me. My grandparents need me. I'm all they have."

I sat back in my chair again, my heart heavy. I felt stuck between a rock and a hard place, or, in the case of Michael Nightingale, a hard head.

"No." His voice was clipped.

I narrowed my eyes at him. "Excuse me?"

"You're a Traveller now. That changes everything."

"It changes nothing. I don't belong here. This isn't my home." Too angry and scared to cry, I folded my arms over my chest and glared at him.

He brushed a damp curl behind my ear, his face only inches from mine. Even when I was mad at him, my body still reacted to his nearness. I definitely had issues.

"If you leave before I kill Melo, he'll get you. It doesn't matter if you are in Kentucky or York or Kalamazoo. He'll find you. Please believe me."

"But you said I could go home."

He rubbed a hand over his head. "That was before I knew you were a Traveller, and before I knew Moktar could cross the bloody ocean. They got your mom, Emerson, and they weren't even tracking her. You wouldn't last a week."

"When you first brought me here, you had no idea there were Moktar in Kentucky." I frowned. "You could have sent me home right away, but you didn't. Why is that, Michael?"

He slammed a fist down onto the table, making me jump. He got up to his feet and leaned over me. "Selfishness. I wanted to protect you myself. I wanted you near me, even when I thought you were a Dweller. You should thank me. If I'd sent you home on the first plane as you wished, you'd be dead right now."

"Just because it all worked out doesn't change the fact that you lied to me. It's all words, like the way you tell me you love me and yet you don't even trust me. You stole my passport. What kind of love is that?"

Michael reached into a drawer and pulled out my passport. He tossed it to me across the table, his blue eyes blazing with fury. "You are the one who has to trust me. If you leave, you'll die. If you stay, I'll keep you safe. Just promise me right now you will be careful. Stop making idiotic decisions. Think before you act."

"I promise. I'm not stupid. Give me a little credit."

He came close to me, his cheeks flushed with anger. I swallowed hard. I wanted to reach up and shake him, but I wanted to kiss him, too. My feelings must have been glaringly apparent on my face because Michael swayed toward me, his eyes dark with passion.

"You'll be the death of me, Emerson, and I'm not lying about that." His voice was soft and husky. "I've wanted you since the first time I saw you. I want you all the time. Even when you make me crazy, I still want you. The only consolation is I know you feel the same way. It's almost like a sickness, but at least it's one we both share."

He was right. I was madder than I'd ever been in my whole life, but still wanted to rip his pants off.

"It's better than the stomach flu, I guess."

Michael growled as desire and anger flashed in his eyes. "Don't try to make me laugh. It will not work."

"Fine, Mr. Grumpy Pants. You were the one who started this argument in the first place."

He took a deep breath, trying to calm himself down. "For good or bad, you're a Traveller, and right now, in true Traveller fashion, we have a pair of irate grandparents to deal with. We'll have to continue this discussion at a later time."

He pulled on his boots, his hands yanking on the laces as he tied them up. I picked up my tennis shoes and sighed as I put them on.

"I'd rather go back to your bed."

"Me, too, but it's time to face the music. Or the firing squad, as the case may be."

I stood up grudgingly, shoved my passport into my backpack, and stomped to the door. "Not as much fun as your bed."

"Not by a long shot." He reached for my hand and pulled me back to him. He looked very serious again. "No matter what, I'll never regret a moment of what happened between us. I'm glad you're here, Emerson."

I gave him a quick peck on the check. "We'll see if you still feel that way after you talk to my grandparents."

As we walked hand in hand to their caravan, I was nervous. "Is Matthew going to freak out?"

"I'm more afraid of Anselina."

I winced. "Will they be able to tell?"

"All I have to do is look at you and they'll know."

I swatted his arm. "Then don't look at me."

He raised his hands in surrender. "I can't help

myself. I've been trying for months."

I gave him a loopy, lustful smile. I thought about the photos he'd tied so carefully with my ribbon, and the way his naked body felt against mine. Michael sighed.

"And if you look at me like that, we're doomed."

Matthew and Anselina waited for us with Sampson. I tried to release Michael's hand, but he held it firmly in his. He was right. There was no sense in pretending.

I was about to sit down, but Anselina took my arm. "I'd like to speak with Emerson alone." I shot Michael a panicked look, but there was nothing he could do. Anselina was a powerhouse.

She brought me into the neat and tidy sitting room of her caravan. She poured me a cup of tea, and then fixed her blue-eyed stare on me.

"How could you?" To my horror, her lip quivered, and she was close to tears. "After what happened to your mother when she ran away, how could you put yourself in that same sort of danger?"

"I'm sorry." I swallowed hard. "It had nothing to do with you and Matthew."

Anselina slammed down her cup. I was surprised it didn't break. "It had everything to do with us. We love you, and you're all we have left of our Jillie."

I knelt next to her and hugged her around the waist. "I'm sorry. It won't happen again."

She held me tightly, her body trembling. I felt so bad. I'd never considered how running away would make my grandparents feel. I'd only been thinking about myself.

Anselina let go and dabbed her eyes with a white

handkerchief. "Drink your tea. It's getting cold"

I sat down and took a sip, but before I could even swallow, she almost made me choke. "Now what are we to do about you sleeping with Michael Nightingale?"

I coughed into my napkin, feeling my cheeks redden under her steady gaze. Lying seemed pointless so I sucked it up.

"Is there anything that has to be done?"

"I only trust you'll be discreet until we can plan the wedding."

"Wedding?"

Anselina took a delicate sip of her tea. "Of course. Michael is the Ceannfort, and a very eligible male. Many girls have tried and failed to gain his attention. The fact that you swooped in and took him does not sit well with everyone. The sooner you're married, the better it will be."

"I'm not getting married. I'm twenty-one years old. And you can't force Michael into it either."

Anselina snorted. "Michael knew exactly what would happen when he welcomed you into his bed. You're a Traveller, part of a proud and ancient line, but there are those that think your Dweller upbringing has corrupted you. They will look for you to make mistakes. Sleeping with the Ceannfort without any intention to marry him would be one of those mistakes."

I bit my lip, trying to be gentle with her. "I love Michael, but I won't be forced into marriage. Not now. Not ever."

Anselina sighed. "I'm afraid you have no choice in the matter. He's already given you his ring, and you accepted it. That's the equivalent of a hand fasting."

"A hand fasting?" I gripped the chair, an ornate wooden affair with detailed carvings and embroidered cushions.

"You wear his mother's ring on your finger. You're already his."

I took a shaky breath, trying to be respectful of cultural differences. "I'm going back to Kentucky in December. You can't force me to do this."

Anselina shrugged. She didn't believe me. In her mind, the deed was done. "We should go and check on that young man of yours. I'm sure he needs rescuing. Matthew was furious."

Outside, no one was furious, and no one required a rescue. They lounged in the sunshine, drinking beer, and talking about soccer. Sampson stood up to give me a kiss on the cheek. "Welcome to the family, love."

"Thank you," I said through gritted teeth.

Matthew and Sampson toddled off to get more beer. Celebrating. I was not. When Michael saw the look on my face, he jumped to his feet.

"Emerson…" he began, but I wasn't in the mood to talk to him at the moment. I pointed my finger in the direction his father and my grandfather had just gone, and he ducked his head and followed them. It reminded me of the way my golden retriever, Bessie Sue, acted when I punished her. If he'd had a tail, it would have been between his legs right now.

My ring flashed in the sunlight, and I stared down at my finger. Michael had known what this meant, and he never told me

"Men," I said in disgust.

Anselina nodded. "You can't live with them, and

you can't live without them."

I pursed my lips. "I only agree with the first half of that statement."

Chapter Twenty-Six

She's busier than a moth in a mitten.

~Grandma Sugar

I had the very best of intentions, but broke my promise to be more careful and stop making idiotic decisions before a single day had passed. It wasn't really my fault. I did it to help a friend.

Michael had just left to go on his nightly search for Melo. I'd watched him leave from my grandparents' porch, his broad back encased in black leather. Part of me wanted to ignore him because he'd made me so mad, but when he looked over his shoulder and his eyes met mine, I couldn't help it. I ran after him.

He pulled me into his arms, holding me close, his face in my hair. "I'm sorry, Emerson."

I put my hand on his cheek. "I'll yell at you later. Be careful out there."

He kissed me, and I pressed against him, twining my arms around his neck. His kisses were sweet and soft, and he begged for my forgiveness with his lips and tongue. I sighed.

"It's awfully hard to stay mad at you, Michael Nightingale."

He grinned, kissing my forehead as his friends teased him and called for him to hurry up. "I'll be back soon. Promise me you'll stay out of trouble."

"I already did."

"Do it again."

I rolled my eyes. "What trouble can I possibly get into here? Go catch a Moktar, will you?"

He laughed, but we both knew he was becoming obsessed with it, working even on days he should have been off. He wanted me to be safe, but that wasn't the only reason he hunted Melo with such single-minded intensity. Whether he knew it or not, he thought killing his monstrous half-brother would somehow avenge his mother. I wasn't completely certain it would work out that way, but there was nothing I could say. I wanted Melo dead for my own reasons.

I called Grandma Sugar, tearing up when she gave the phone to Pappy George because he sounded normal and well. When she got back on the phone, she complained so much it reassured me he really was okay.

"He is more stubborn than a mule on Monday, but I'm taking charge now. Fried chicken is no longer a part of that man's life."

I smiled, knowing full well if she didn't fry it for him he would sneak into the KFC first chance he got. "How's Daddy?"

The pause that resulted spoke volumes. "He misses you something awful. He's counting the days until you come home, like we all are."

I said goodbye and hung up the phone, cradling it against my cheek for just a moment. I needed to go home, but it hung over my head like a dark cloud.

Later, I joined Margaret and some of the other girls for a martial arts lesson. Sun Tzu said to love your soldiers like your own children, but these ladies were more like sisters. Ten in all, and together we had some serious skills.

My phone rang just as we got started. It was Brooke. She'd been very snippy with me the last time she'd sent a message. I thought about ignoring her call, but then I remembered she was going out with Leo tonight.

"Hello?"

Her broken sobs echoed through the phone. "Emerson, you have to help me."

"What is it, Brooke? Did he hurt you?"

My heart thumped in my chest as I waited for an answer. Even though I'd tried to warn her, I still felt guilty. I'd introduced them in the first place and shouldered some of the responsibility.

"We're at The King's Head Pub. Do you know it? It's not far from the tea shop."

"Yes, I know it. What's going on, Brooke?"

Brooke's voice hitched. "He thought you'd be coming, and was furious when I showed up alone. I should have listened to you. There's something really wrong with him, and I'm scared. I'm hiding in the bathroom."

I winced. "You have to leave, Brooke. Walk out of there and go straight back to your dorm room. Or better yet, call the police."

"He said he would hurt me if I left, and I believe him."

"Is there anyone in the pub who could help you?"

Brooke sniffed. "It's just a bunch of old people. If one of them tried to help, he might hurt them, too."

"Tell him I'm coming." Margaret, who stood next to me, listening to our entire conversation, shook her head frantically. I held up my hand to stop her.

"He won't believe me." Brooke's voice was a whisper, and someone yelled in the background. It had to be Leo.

"Is that him?"

"Yes. He's knocking on the door."

I felt my temper rise. "Let me talk to him."

Brooke hiccupped. "Are you sure?"

"Yes. Put him on the phone."

I heard their conversation, Brooke's frightened pleading and Leo's angry cursing. Finally, he took the phone.

"Emerson? Is this really you?" Something in his voice frightened me. He sounded like a strung-out junkie, a person on the edge.

"It's me, Leo. What are you doing with Brooke?"

"You hurt me. You were supposed to come tonight and apologize."

I took a deep breath and exhaled slowly. I'd dealt with low-level crazy people before, but Leo ranked much higher. I had to handle this well, or things would turn out very poorly for Brooke.

"I was…jealous."

"You have a boyfriend. I read your journal."

I couldn't believe I'd been so stupid. I should never have written all that stuff down. I had to think fast. "You were in there, too, Leo."

That seemed to pacify him. "There's something between us, Emerson. You know that as much as I do. You shouldn't fight it."

"I thought you liked Brooke. If you don't, just send her home. I'll come and meet you in a few minutes."

Leo let out a harsh laugh. "I don't think so,

Emerson. This is the plan. You come here, alone, and I'll let this little bitch leave. If you don't show up in thirty minutes, I am not responsible for what might occur."

"Leo…" I began, but he hung up on me.

With wide eyes, Margaret asked, "What happened?"

I stared at my phone. "Crap. I have to go help Brooke."

"You can't," said Margaret. The other girls began crowding around us.

"He's just a Dweller, but he's crazy. If I don't go, he'll hurt her."

I tried to call Michael, but he didn't answer, so I left a message. Margaret called Patrick, and she left a message as well. The clock ticked as time ran out quickly for, Brooke.

"Are any of the boys off tonight?" Desperately, I tried to come up with a solution that wouldn't end up making Michael furious with me. I didn't think there was one. Right now, the idea of Leo hurting Brooke took precedence over the idea of a Moktar coming after me on my internal fear scale.

"Sean is off," said Audrey. "Everyone else went out."

I groaned. This would put Sean, the youngest of the warriors, in a mighty tough position, but I didn't have a choice. "Where is he?"

Sean was eager to help, and probably would have been eager to help with anything Audrey asked him to do, but he wanted to go out by himself. I refused.

"If Leo even sees you, he might hurt her. He can't even know you're there. I have to go into the pub alone."

"I'm coming, too." Margaret began strapping on one of Sean's weapons belts. She wore black yoga pants, a tight black t-shirt, and tennis shoes. She'd dressed that way for our martial arts lesson, otherwise she would have had on a short skirt and hoochie-mama shoes. I tried to take the weapons belt away from her.

"You can't. It's too dangerous."

Margaret gave me a stern look. "You know I can fight, Emerson, and you need my help. Remember what Sun Tzu said, 'Our strength is in our unity.' "

"Oh, God. You actually listened to me."

"Yes, I did, and you were right."

I thought about it for a second. She was an excellent fighter, and I had no idea what kind of stunt Leo might pull. With her long hair and curvy body, she could create enough of a diversion to buy me some time.

"Patrick will kill me."

Margaret handed me a belt. It held an assortment of knives, as well as some sticks, chains, and other fun things. I took a second to get familiar with it, and then strapped it over my jeans.

"Patrick will kill me. *Michael* will kill you." Margaret gave me a little grin.

Sean shook his head. "You're both wrong, ladies. Patrick and Michael will kill *me.* And it'll be a slow, painful, and terrible death. Let's go. We're running out of time."

I grabbed a black jacket from a hook on Sean's wall, and we took off, slipping through the door of the compound and walking quickly through the dark streets of York. My heart raced. Brooke didn't have much time left.

I traced my fingers nervously over the weapons on my belt. "Maybe I should take this off?"

Sean shook his head. "Dwellers can't see it. It's charmed. Keep it on, Emerson."

I zipped up my jacket just to be sure, not wanting to risk Brooke's life over a careless mistake. Then I took my phone out of my pocket and called the police, giving them a description of Brooke and Leo and timing it so I arrived at the pub just before they did. I also decided to describe Sean, Margaret, and myself to them. If the police saw Sean, he might get into trouble just because he looked like trouble. Safer to cover all the bases.

"That was clever," said Sean.

I gave him a nervous smile. "I have my moments."

The night was quiet. Most people had work or school the next day, so the King's Head was not hopping. I peeked through the window. Brooke and Leo sat at a table in the corner. Brooke cried softly, her shoulders shaking. Leo stared at his watch. I reached for the door handle, and Margaret grabbed my arm.

"Good luck, Emerson."

I took a deep breath, and opened the door. The inside of the pub was quaint and comfortable. I'd often come here for meat pies and beer with my friends. Tonight, only a few customers filled the booths. Most were eating. A few old men played darts. Some watched a television hanging over the bar. No one even looked at Brooke and Leo.

As soon as Brooke saw me, her face lit up. She tried to stand, but Leo pulled her back into her seat. When he saw me, he let go of her arm.

I approached the table slowly, trying to buy a bit of time. Leo seemed less like the handsome, charming guy I'd known and more like an addict. His hair was messy. He didn't look clean. He had dark circles under his eyes and hollows in his cheeks. Something was definitely wrong with him.

I maintained eye contact, trying to calm him.

"Hi, Leo."

He closed his eyes briefly at the sound of my voice, like it was the sweetest thing he'd ever heard. "Emerson." He gave me a shaky smile. "I didn't think you'd come."

I pulled Brooke's arm, never breaking eye contact with Leo. She stood up, and I sat down in her chair. "Of course I came. I wanted to see you."

Out of the corner of my eye, I saw Brooke slowly backing toward the door. Once she was outside, my body almost sagged with relief. Margaret and Sean would take care of her now.

Leo leaned forward, his hands grasping mine. "I needed to see you. I didn't mean to frighten you the other day. I would never hurt you." His grip tightened on my hands and I winced.

"You're hurting me now."

Immediately, he let go. "I'm sorry," he said, running a hand through his hair. "I had to talk with you. There is so much I need to explain."

"We have plenty of time."

I lied through my teeth. I already heard the faint whine of a police siren. Leo didn't seem to notice. His golden eyes narrowed as he stared at my face. "There's something different about you. What is it?"

I shrugged. I had no idea what he was talking

about. He leaned closer, almost like trying to smell me. He grabbed the sleeve of my leather jacket.

"Where did you get this?" His voice was a growl.

I looked at him in confusion. "It belongs to a friend. I didn't have a coat with me when Brooke called."

"A *friend*?" His fist clenched around my wrist. "Does it belong to *Michael Nightingale*?"

Thankfully, Leo held my left wrist. I used my right hand to slide a knife out of the weapons belt.

He came so close his nose was mere inches from mine. I almost gagged. His body reeked.

"I know what is different about you. You've been with *him*. You aren't a virgin anymore."

Spittle from his mouth hit my cheek, and I flinched. "How could you know that?"

Leo's eyes grew sad. He suddenly looked very old and tired. "It's written all over your pretty face. It was supposed to be me, Emerson. I should have been the first."

He stood up just as the police came through the door. He looked at them in surprise, letting go of my arm long enough to fling over the table and block their path. As soon as the table hit the floor with a crash, he reached for my arm again, but I'd already shot to the opposite side of the room, out of his grasp. His eyes met mine, full of pain, before he turned and ran toward the back of the pub, the police right behind him. I went out the front to find my friends.

As soon as my shoes hit the cobblestones outside, I heard something that sent shivers through my heart. The roar of a Moktar echoed through the empty streets. Sean heard it, too. His face paled in the light of the streetlamp. It came from the roof of one of the buildings across the street. The timing couldn't have been worse.

"Melo must have tracked you. Run, Emerson."

I shook my head. Margaret and I assumed a defensive posture with our backs to Sean. I pulled Brooke behind me, the safest spot for her at the moment.

In minutes, Moktar fell from the sky like a rain made of monsters. It hadn't been just one Moktar on the roof. It was an entire herd. They slid down gutter pipes and walls, the sound of their claws scraping against metal and stone filled the quiet night. I counted half a dozen at least, but didn't recognize Melo among them.

"What's going on?" Brooke breathed in short little gasps as her eyes darted around in alarm, on the verge of losing it.

"Just stay behind us, Brookie. It'll be fine." My voice was soft croon, as I tried to calm her. It didn't work.

"What are those things? Oh, my God. Oh, my God."

As Brooke worked herself into a panic, I had more important things to worry about. The Moktar approached us slowly, grinning, six of them in all. They were bigger, scarier, and smellier than I remembered, but I had no time to be frightened. Brooke apparently disagreed. She screamed and tried to run away wearing heels and a silly little dress. She wouldn't make it far.

"No, Brooke. Come back."

I shouted her name as a Moktar grabbed her, staring at me with his creepy yellow eyes, and laughing. Brooke screamed and flailed her arms, but it had no effect. He threw her over his shoulder, smacked her once on the bottom, and disappeared up a drain spout. My eyes scanned the rooftops, desperate to catch a glimpse of her, but she was gone.

I took a deep breath and stood a little taller. I couldn't do anything for Brooke, but I could save Margaret and Sean. There were only five Moktar left to fight. I pulled a knife from my belt and held it high. When the first Moktar attacked, I slashed him through the chest, as easy as slicing through soft butter. I grinned as he fell to the ground. I felt no remorse at all, only delight; one down, four to go.

The remaining four decided to attack at once. We were outnumbered, but only slightly. It didn't worry me. A surge of confidence spread throughout my entire body. I didn't know where it came from, but I knew we would win.

One of the Moktar struck, knocking Sean to the ground. Unconscious, he bled from a wound to his forehead. Margaret stood over his body protectively, and I jumped in front of her. Suddenly, two knives appeared in my hands. I didn't remember pulling a second knife out of the belt, but there it was. I slashed and kicked, and my body moved automatically, fighting to ward off blows and cause as much harm as possible.

Pretty soon, I was no longer on the defensive. I was the aggressor, killing each Moktar so effortlessly it was almost fun. When the last one tried to run away, I chased him down the street, jumped on his back as he shimmied up a drainpipe and stabbed him in the throat before he made it past the first floor. He fell to the ground with a thud. I landed gracefully on my feet, crouched and ready to fight, but my opponents were all dead or mortally wounded. I grinned. I'd never felt so happy or so alive in my entire life.

I heard a gurgling sound from the Moktar dying at my feet. He tried to speak. I leaned closer to hear him.

"It's too late. He'll kill you all."

I almost laughed. "Who?"

The Moktar's eyes were closing, but he forced out the words. "He who can walk in the sun."

A chill went through my body as the Moktar let out a rattling breath and died. I cleaned my bloody knife on my jeans, and turned back to the pub.

Margaret and Sean weren't the only ones waiting there for me. Michael, Sampson, Patrick, Ryan and several other Traveller men stood next to them, watching me in disbelief. I gave them a little wave. They didn't respond.

Michael, his hands clenched in fists and a muscle working in his jaw as he fought for control, was ten shades of furious. I'd have to deal with him later, but had more pressing concerns at the moment. We needed to move fast.

"I took care of five of them, but one got away with Brooke. We might be able to catch him if we're quick."

Sean shook his head. He looked woozy. "They have nests, and they're well hidden. There's no way we could find her. She's gone."

My shoulders sagged. I'd come here to save her from Leo, but failed miserably. The sad truth was she wouldn't have even been here if it weren't for me.

"Did you kill Melo?"

Michael's voice was tight. He stared at a spot just above me, unable to meet my eyes. I shook my head as I checked the other weapons on my belt. I'd used almost every one of them, judging by the blood, but didn't really have a memory of it. It had happened so fast.

Ryan jogged around from the back of the pub. "There are two dead policemen back there."

I closed my eyes, horrified. "It's my fault. I called them here."

Margaret patted my arm. "If it weren't for you, Sean and I would both be dead."

"Was Leo killed, too?" I asked.

Ryan shook his head. "I didn't see another body."

Michael took charge once again. "Ryan, call the authorities. Let them know what happened. We'll clean up the Moktar, but they'll need to take care of the policemen."

Sampson stared at the carnagc, shaking his head. "She killed five Moktar. I've never heard of such a thing."

"It shouldn't have happened. Neither one of them should have been here." Michael gave Sean an angry glare, and Sean got even paler.

I felt bad. "We forced him to take us. Leo was going to hurt Brooke."

Michael stomped over to me. "And now she's facing a fate far worse. You promised you'd be careful, but you behaved in the most reckless way imaginable."

The fury came off him in waves, an almost palpable thing.

"You've broken the law," he said softly. "This isn't a game, Emerson. You could have been killed. Margaret and Sean could have been killed. You're all lucky to be alive."

Chapter Twenty-Seven

Don't get your knickers in a knot.

~Grandma Sugar

The expression on Michael's face frightened me. I reached for him, but he backed away, rubbing his hand over his head the way he always did when stressed.

Sampson gripped Michael's shoulder. "You saw the truth with your own eyes, boy-o. She's a fighter the likes of which I've never seen, but it won't make a bit of difference to the council."

"We can't talk about this right now. We have other things to deal with. Sean, take the women back to the compound. Da, go with them. The rest of you stay here and help me clean up this mess."

I tried to meet Michael's eyes, but he refused to even look at me. A few hours ago, I'd been naked in his arms. I could still feel his hands on my skin and his breath in my ear. Now he seemed scared and distant, and I had no idea why.

We'd only been back a few minutes when the whispers started. I held my head high, and walked straight to my grandparents' caravan. Thankfully, they weren't there, so I showered and dressed in peace. I needed to wrap my head around what had just happened. I'd always been good at martial arts, but today had been very different. Today, I'd been unstoppable.

I wiped down Sean's jacket with a damp cloth and cleaned his weapons belt. Blood, gore, and Moktar parts clung to my clothing. My white shirt was blood stained and ruined, and my jeans were beyond repair. I tossed everything into the trash.

Opening the door, I was greeted by a crowd of gypsies holding white candles and waiting in complete silence, hoping to catch a glimpse of me. I found it completely creepy.

"Aw, Jiminy Christmas."

Michael pushed his way through the crowd, and came to stand next to me on my grandparents' porch. He looked at the crowd in irritation.

"Go home. The party is over."

He grabbed my hand and led me away, walking so fast I had to run to keep up with him. We headed straight to his caravan.

He pulled me inside and slammed the door without turning on the lights. In the dark silence, I heard only the sounds of his slow, measured breaths and the thumping of my heart. Michael had been pissed off at me before, but never like this. The anger radiated from his body.

Instead of yelling, though, he pulled me into his arms and kissed me with a furious hardness hinting at desperation. I kissed him back, happy that what I'd done hadn't caused a permanent rift between us. It didn't take long before we were both stark naked and back in Michael's bed.

There was nothing slow or gentle about our lovemaking this time. He slammed into me with the force of a wave hitting the shore during a hurricane, and

I answered him, thrust for thrust. We came in moments, crying out at the same time in voices that barely sounded human, and clung to each other afterwards like survivors of a shipwreck. He sighed and softly kissed my shoulder. The storm had passed.

I had so many questions to ask I didn't even know where to start. The crazy, hungry, angry sex had thrown me for a loop. I'd enjoyed every single minute of it, but the primal nature of it had shaken me.

"I've heard make-up sex is even better than angry sex, but I'm just not sure that is even possible," I said, trying to get my breathing back to its normal rhythm.

Michael kissed my cheek and rolled to his side, cradling me in his arms. "We'll find out if we ever make up." His voice was a growl, but I knew he wasn't mad anymore.

I stroked his face and stared at him, still finding it hard to believe this impossibly perfect man could be mine, even if only for a little while. I kissed him once on the lips, and then broke the spell by talking. I couldn't help it. There were things I had to know.

"Was there any sign of Brooke?"

Michael shook his head. "Another reason we don't mix with Dwellers. It's dangerous for them even to be around us."

I swallowed hard. "My father is a Dweller."

Michael cupped my cheek with his hand and stroked my lips with his thumb. "He's lucky he survived."

I frowned. "Not luck. My mom did what she had to do to keep him safe. When she drove off the cliff, she saved all of us. Don't dismiss her sacrifice by calling it luck."

"But you aren't safe, Em. You'll never be safe until Melo is dead." He spoke to me like a child, and it was getting a bit irritating.

I glared at him. "And it's up to you to keep me safe, right? Another thing on your long list of duties and responsibilities. Well, Michael, I have news for you. I can take care of myself."

Biting his lip, he turned away. "You demonstrated that quite nicely this evening. That's why they showed up with the candles. They do it to honor the warrior if a Moktar is killed without Traveller lives being lost. It's a sign of respect, and gratitude."

I sat up against Michael's pillows, and pulled him over so his head rested on my naked stomach. I didn't want to fight. He hugged me around my hips, and I stroked his back.

"But I still broke the law."

Michael sighed, his breath warm against my belly. "You did. Women cannot fight. It's been that way as long as there have been Travellers."

He had the decency to look embarrassed. He put his face into my stomach and kissed me. I rolled my eyes.

"You're a scientist, Michael. You work with facts. Do you seriously think that law is necessary?"

"No, but I can understand the reasoning behind it. What the Moktar do to women is crueler than death."

"And now they have Brooke." I slid out from under him and started getting dressed.

"Where are you going?" Beautiful and naked, he lay on his stomach gifting me with a great view of his bottom. I almost had to fan myself. I would never get tired of looking at his body.

"I want to talk to your father. There has to be a way to help her."

Michael stood up slowly, giving me a glimpse of his full frontal glory as well. He looked like Adonis with tattoos.

"And if there isn't?"

I tore my gaze away from him, although it required great effort on my part. "I don't know."

I should have just gone and hit my head against a brick wall. That would have been a more productive use of my time because nothing could convince Sampson Brooke might have a chance if we only tried to save her. To make matters worse, my own grandparents had jumped on the bandwagon. They agreed with him completely. I tried talking to them and reasoning with them. None of that worked. Finally, I threw up my hands in defeat and stomped out. Michael followed closely at my heels.

My phone buzzed, alerting me I had a text, and I yanked it out of my pocket. The number made me look at Michael in shock.

"It's from Brooke."

I fumbled, almost dropping the phone, as I opened the text. The message was short and sweet.

We have her. You want her. We offer a trade; you for her. Wait for more details, and don't try anything stupid. She is safe for now.

Even the Moktar monsters thought I had poor decision making skills. A really great idea formed in my mind. "This could work. Trade me for Brooke. I'll kick their Moktar butts, Brooke will be safe, and everyone will be happy. Except the Moktar. They'll be dead."

Michael shook his head. "They'll be prepared for you this time. It won't be so easy. I can't let you do it."

"I'll do whatever I please, Mr. Nightingale."

Sudden anger lit his eyes. "That's the last thing we need. They knew you were a Traveller before we did. They knew I was the Ceannfort. They knew Melo was my brother. Why are we always one step behind?"

He slammed his fist into a tree. It had to hurt. Blood trickled down his knuckles, but he didn't make a sound.

I took his hand and dabbed it with a tissue. "Now what did that poor tree ever do to you?"

At the sight of Michael's blood, I remembered the words of the dying Moktar. I'd completely forgotten to mention it.

Michael grew very still, the way he always did when receiving bad news. "He said, 'he who can walk in the sun'? Are you sure, Emerson?"

The expression on his face worried me. "Is it important?"

Michael paced back and forth. "It could mean a Moktar has finally overcome their genetic reaction to the sun and can go out in daylight."

I frowned. "Even if they weren't allergic to the sun, they couldn't go out in daylight. People would see them. A Moktar wouldn't go unnoticed."

Michael's expression was grim. "He could if he looked human. They've been taking Traveller women and mating with them for generations. Perhaps one of their offspring came out more human than Moktar. There have been tales of such a thing."

"Is that even possible?"

He frowned. "Possible, but not plausible."

My mind raced, imagining golden eyes, abnormal strength, and a powerful stench. My knees almost gave out. *Possible, but not plausible.*

"Leo is a Moktar."

My hands reflexively went to my neck. My bruises had almost healed, but I remembered exactly how his hands had felt. I'd really thought I was going to die.

"Why do you say that?"

"A lot of reasons, but mostly his eyes. Normally, they're a sort of golden color, but tonight they were different."

"Yellow?"

I nodded. "And he was a mess, both mentally and physically. He looked like he hadn't washed or eaten. He acted just like a drug addict. Wouldn't that be how a Moktar would act if he hadn't eaten any brains lately?"

"The Moktar go through something described as a thousand times worse than cocaine withdrawal. Most of them are born with the addiction, and many don't survive infancy because of it."

I almost felt bad for the Moktar, but not quite. "You know that Traveller sense you told me about? Well, I feel it now. He's a Moktar. I'm sure of it."

Michael sighed. He tilted his head up to look at the stars, his expression sad and resigned. "We must tell the council."

The last thing I wanted to do was to deal with Sampson and my grandparents again. "There's nothing we can do right now. Everyone is asleep, we have no idea where the nest is located, and we aren't going to go out looking for it in the middle of the night. Why don't we go back to your place, take off our clothes, and have make-up sex?"

Michael gave me naughty little smile. He tilted his head down until his forehead rested against mine and our noses touched. “Does that mean you’ve forgiven me for what happened earlier with your grandparents?”

I held up my hand. “Did you know they would see this ring and think we’re getting married?”

“Would it be so awful?” He needed reassurance, but I wanted to shake him.

“Answer my question.”

He let out a frustrated sigh. “I understood how it might be perceived. I gave it to you anyway because I knew you’d leave, eventually, and I just wanted some part of me to go with you.”

The anger building inside of me came out in a whoosh. “I think I’m ready for the make-up sex now.”

He gave me a small kiss. “I’d never force you into marriage. Can you be patient until I come up with a diplomatic solution to our problem that will appease your grandparents? Although it may not even matter.”

“Why?”

He stroked my cheek with his thumb. “What you did tonight was very brave, but also idiotic.”

“I know I broke that stupid, old law, but I was defending myself. And Margaret and Sean, too.”

“Is that what you call it?” He shook his head. “When that Moktar ran away and you chased him, everyone saw you. The law is very clear, as is the punishment.”

I trembled and it wasn’t because of the cool night air. “What is the punishment?”

His blue eyes were dark with sadness. “Exile.”

Chapter Twenty-Eight

A friend in need is a friend indeed.

~Grandma Sugar

The next morning, Michael got a text saying the council was ready and waiting for us. We dressed quickly and met them in the center of the compound. They weren't wearing robes. They sat in a circle looking like a bunch of elderly English people enjoying a spot of sunshine. Judging from their conversation, they didn't seem to notice our approach.

"She's a menace," said Mavin with a sneer. "She put my Nella in a garbage can. She needs to go."

I made a face at Michael, and he shook his head in disgust. I hadn't realized Nella was Mavin's daughter. It explained a lot.

Sampson glared at her. "Nella probably deserved it, and this is far more important than a petty squabble. I saw Emerson fight, Mavin. We need her."

"She's just a girl," she said, almost spitting out the words. "Nothing more."

Sampson gave her a long, steady look. "I'm beginning to think she might be a great deal more, Mavin, and I think you understand my meaning."

Mavin flinched, like she'd been struck, and then she shook her head vehemently. "That's a myth."

She looked up at that instant, and her eyes met

mine. They were as black as onyx and so cold they seemed almost reptilian. She knew exactly what was about to happen, what punishment I faced for my actions, and she found pleasure in it.

"Here she is now," she said.

I kissed my grandmother and sat next to her. She took my hand in hers. Her hand was soft and warm and she smelled like lavender, but her face was pale and frightened. I wanted to ask Sampson what he'd been talking about when he said I was something more, but the look on his face told me now was not the right time to ask.

Michael took a deep breath, trying to compose himself. "All of you are aware of what happened yesterday. A Dweller girl was taken."

The council nodded in unison. Thcy listened to him, but most of them snuck little glances at me, trying to see if I would suddenly turn into a crazed Moktar killing machine. It annoyed me.

"And whose idea was it for Margaret and Sean to go out alone to help a Dweller?" Mavin's lips twisted in disgust when she spat out the word "Dweller."

"It was my idea, but we thought Leo was just a Dweller, too. Like Brooke." I glanced at Michael. "Now we are fairly certain he's actually a Moktar."

"The man who attacked you?" My grandmother's voice rose an octave higher than usual. "How can that be?"

Several members of the council gasped. One old lady clutched a hand to her heart. Even Mavin looked shocked. Her bony hands fluttered to her throat.

Michael nodded. "One of the creatures told Emerson, in his dying breath, about a Moktar who can walk in the sun. I think one of them now has enough Traveller blood that he looks human. It might be Leo."

One of the older council members put his head in his hands, like he might weep. Several of them acted shell shocked. So much happened at once, they couldn't quite process it. I understood how they felt.

The head councilman, Monroe, spoke. "Moktar cannot take human form. It isn't possible." He shook his head. "I understand what you're trying to do, but it comes down to one thing. The lass has broken our laws, Michael."

Every member of the council turned and looked at me, and my cheeks grew hot. Michael's body tensed next to mine.

"You think I'd make up a lie to protect her?"

He gave Michael a sad little smile. "I think you'd do anything to protect her. It's obvious how you feel about her."

Michael's jaw clenched, displaying his fury. "It's irrelevant. She fought in self-defense. That's not forbidden."

Monroe's face turned cold. "She chased a Moktar down the street and climbed a wall to catch him. That's not self-defense. It's madness. And if we let her stay, her madness may infect other girls. She's not even a real Traveller anyway. There is really no need for such a fuss."

My grandmother's hand tightened on mine, like she would hold me there by sheer will alone. "She's our granddaughter, Monroe. All we have left. If you exile her, you send her to certain death."

"She's given us no choice."

It ended very quickly. The council voted and only

my grandmother and Sampson thought I should be allowed to stay. There was no hope.

Monroe stood, and I saw something odd flash through his eyes. If I hadn't known better, I would have said he looked pleased. A second later, his expression turned somber, like he'd suddenly remembered to act like he felt bad about his actions, but I knew the truth. He wanted me gone.

"Pack your things, Emerson. The Ceannfort will escort you back to your home."

Further protests would not change their minds, so Michael and my grandmother walked me back to her caravan. Anselina helped me pack, her face tense with the effort it took not to cry.

"I wish Matthew were here. He'd want to see you. He's away for the morning on Traveller business, of all the terrible luck. I'm so sorry, child…" she began, but I stopped her by gently squeezing her arm.

"It isn't your fault. I'll call you, okay?"

She shook her head, her lips trembling. "It's forbidden, dearest. Once you're exiled, we have to pretend you never existed."

I sank down onto the bed. My knees had given out on me. "Even Michael?"

She nodded, putting her arms around my shoulders. "But I shan't forget you. Ever." Her words were a soft whisper in my ear. "And he won't, either."

I walked back to my apartment in a daze. Michael was inches away from me, but neither of us spoke until we reached the door of my building. He turned to me, his face tense and pale.

"You'll have to talk to Lucinda and Poppy. They need to know the truth. It's the only way to keep them safe."

"What should I tell them?"

"Everything. I give you my permission to tell them everything." His voice cracked, and he pulled me into his arms. I realized it might be my last memory of Michael Nightingale, and I clung to him. "I'll figure this out, Emerson. I'll find a way to fix it."

I shook my head. "Some things just can't be fixed."

He leaned forward, touching his forehead against mine. "Stay safe. Don't be foolish. Don't take any chances. Please, Emerson. For my sake, promise me you'll be careful."

"I'm always careful, Michael," I said, and gave him one last kiss before slipping out of his arms and into my building. The door closed behind me with a thud, but I didn't look back. If I had, I never would have been able to keep going.

Poppy and Lucinda were upstairs. When they saw my face and the suitcases in my hands, they knew something was very wrong. After setting me up with a cup of warm tea on the couch, Poppy started the inquisition.

"Tell us what is going on."

When I didn't answer immediately, she let out an impressively long string of curse words. Normally, I loved to hear Poppy swear. She even said the "f" word in a cute way, making it sound more like *fooook.* I didn't find it so cute today, although her outfit was adorable. She wore tiny shorts, black lacy tights, and Doc Marten's. She'd added a hot pink cardigan with feathered fringe that nearly reached her knees to further enhance the look.

I swallowed hard. "I don't know where to start."

The fact I refrained from weeping was pretty amazing. I really deserved a medal for holding back the tears. Eventually, it would to hit me, and I'd cry like never before, but for now I was too numb. In shock.

"The beginning," said Lucinda.

"You'll think I'm crazy."

"We *know* you're crazy, and we love you for it, but something is terribly wrong. You need to tell us what's going on. Now."

Poppy was as stubborn as a mule when she set her mind to something. I sighed.

"I guess I'll start with the day I saw Michael outside the library and followed him through York."

I told them about seeing Tad's body and the Moktar and everything else that happened that night. It felt good to get it off my chest. I'd hated lying to Lucinda and Poppy.

Their expressions went from shock to disbelief to confusion and finally something that looked a whole lot like acceptance. When I got to the part about how the Travellers had unusual abilities, my cheeks got a little hot. I was sure they wouldn't believe me. I was wrong.

"I knew it." Poppy slammed her hand down on our kitchen table. "I just knew it."

Lucinda raised one dark eyebrow at her. "You knew Emerson was part of a secret race of gypsies with special powers?"

Poppy shook her head so hard the blue spikes in her hair wiggled. "Of course not, but I knew there was something strange about her. Her reflexes were too fast, and she always seemed to sense when something was about to happen."

Lucinda huffed, and I held up a hand to stop them

because I knew they would go on forever. "Look, ladies. I had to tell you everything because I wanted to keep you safe. I'm putting both of you in terrible danger just by being here. I'll move into a hotel tonight."

Lucinda rolled her eyes. "Nonsense. We'll lock the door, and we won't go out at night until this is all over. We'll be fine."

"If anything ever happened to either of you…" The tears I'd held in threatened to fall. I kept them in check by sheer willpower alone. "And because of me, Brooke is in very serious trouble, too. She'll die if I don't help her. She might be dead already."

"None of this is your fault," said Lucinda. "But I think I can help you."

"How?"

"You know I studied computer science as my undergrad major, right?" I nodded, confused. "Well, in all honesty, I had some skill as a hacker. I was being recruited to find new ways to track people using their cell phones and laptops, but I preferred sex to spying, and got away from it."

"Really?" I asked. A tiny glimmer of hope bloomed in my chest.

Lucinda nodded. "If they used Brooke's phone to contact you, I just might be able to track it."

I pulled my phone out of my backpack and handed it to her. "Thank you, Luce. I owe you one."

She didn't look up, intent on finding Brooke's number, but I heard the smile in her voice when she spoke. "I happen to be in an exceptionally good mood. I got laid last night. At last." She glanced up from the phone and gave me a saucy grin.

"You conquered Antarctica," I said, and Lucinda grinned.

Poppy squealed. "*Finally*."

Lucinda winked at us, and then grabbed her laptop to work on finding Brooke's location. I curled up next to her on the couch. "Can you do it, Lucinda?"

She put on her glasses, black and sexy with rhinestones dotting the edges, and started typing. "This is child's play."

A few minutes later, she gave me an address. I wrote it down quickly, committing it to memory. "I can't believe I have an actual physical address for a Moktar nest. I want to go and kill them all right now."

"But you promised Michael you'd be careful," said Poppy. "Shouldn't you call the police instead?"

"And tell them what? My friend was kidnapped by a bunch of brain-eating monsters? I'm sure that would go over well."

"Then what exactly do you plan to do?" asked Lucinda.

I opened my mouth to answer her when I heard a knock at the door. I grabbed a knife from the kitchen and made Poppy and Lucinda stand back while I opened it. The sun remained above the horizon, but I wasn't taking any chances. I looked through the peephole and stepped back in surprise before opening the door. Margaret and Audrey stood there, grinning at me, obviously very pleased with themselves.

"What are you doing here?" I pulled them into my apartment, giving each of them a big hug. "You shouldn't have come."

Lucinda and Poppy decided to leave to pick up groceries and supplies. It looked like we were going to spend a lot of time locked in the apartment. I sat down with Margaret and Audrey and poured them some tea.

"What's going on? You'll be in so much trouble if the council finds out you came here," I said.

"We had to come. Right after the council meeting, Mavin disappeared," said Margaret. "She's not in the compound."

I frowned. "So?"

"She left this behind." Margaret handed me a small leather journal. Inside were dates and names.

"What is this?"

"A list of all the Travellers who've been taken. Look at the first name on the list," said Margaret. "It's Roseanne."

"Michael's mother?"

She nodded. "And look at the last name."

I flipped through the pages, and my eyes widened in shock. "Me?"

Margaret nodded. "I told you one girl is taken every year, but now it seems like it was planned, like those girls are chosen as some sort of sacrifice. And you're next."

"Someone is betraying you," I said.

"Us, Emerson. They are betraying *us*." Margaret reached out and squeezed my arm. I swallowed hard.

"I think you're right. The Moktar are too aware of everything going on inside the compound. They knew I was a Traveller before we did."

"They did that by smell."

"But how did they know so much about Michael? They called him the Ceannfort. And how did they know Tad would be alone the night he was killed? He was set up. I'm sure of it."

Audrey flinched when I said Tad's name. "They may have just wandered across him…"

I shook my head. "It felt wrong, like it had been planned."

"You think Mavin is a traitor?" asked Audrey.

I flipped through the book until I found something that made my heart drop in my chest. Written in the back was an address I'd seen before. I compared it to the one given to me by Lucinda only minutes before.

"Well, this is pretty incriminating."

"What is it?" asked Audrey.

"This is the address of the Moktar nest. Mavin knew where they were, and yet she did nothing."

Margaret put her head in her hands. "What should we do?"

I gave them a sad little smile. "Both of you need to go back to the compound and tell Michael what you've discovered."

"We couldn't. He wasn't there."

He probably couldn't face going back there right away, but Michael would never desert his people. He was a leader, through and through. "He'll be back, and it isn't safe here for you. I can't believe you came on your own."

Audrey giggled. "We didn't. Sean is downstairs standing guard. If anyone asks, he'll say he never saw you and it'll be the truth."

"You really do have him wrapped around your little finger, don't you?"

She grinned. "Yes, I do, but this isn't about me. You saved his life, and he owes you a debt."

Margaret patted my hand. "I know the council members didn't stand up for you. They do whatever

Monroe Skinner wants. But many of us were absolutely outraged about what happened, and we plan to fight it."

They got up to leave. "Just stay safe, okay?"

Margaret gave me a steady look. "I finally understand what my dream meant, Emerson."

"The dream you had when you first met me?"

"Yes." She took a deep slow breath. "It wasn't about a funeral. When I saw those candles in my dream, it came true the night you killed those Moktar and saved Sean and I. You aren't here to hurt us. You're going to save us all."

I swallowed hard. "I'm a former Junior Miss Kentucky who picked up a few martial arts skills. Please don't make me out to be more than I actually am, Margaret."

"You don't know what you are yet, dear little Emerson, but eventually you'll figure it out." She leaned forward and kissed my cheek. "Can you promise me you won't go to that nest and save Brooke on your own?"

"I can't do that. I'd be lying. But I do have a plan."

"What kind of plan?" asked Margaret.

I bit my lip. "Let me just begin by saying, 'All warfare is based on deception.' It's a fundamental truth."

She narrowed her eyes at me. "Says whom?"

"Sun Tzu, of course. I think it's time to practice a little deception of my own."

Chapter Twenty-Nine

Ain't nobody going to mess on me and call it apple butter.

~Grandma Sugar

Margaret and Audrey returned to the compound, but not before giving me a precious gift. A belt loaded with knifes, and a large duffle filled to the brim with other weapons. After they left, I opened the bag and went through the weapons one by one. Better than Christmas.

Lucinda and Poppy came home with Indian take-out, and we ate dinner together. Poppy planned to stay with us until the danger had passed. They told Nigel and Sven we were having a much-needed girls' night, and I wished that really were the truth. I had something completely different planned, however. I told them everything Margaret and Audrey shared with me. The time had come to take care of this myself, and I knew what to do.

"I'm going to get Brooke back."

Poppy froze, a forkful of chicken tikka masala halfway to her mouth. "Are you mad?"

Lucinda shook her head very slowly, her lips pinched. "You cannot go on your own. You're the next name on that list. That means the Moktar plan to capture you."

"I'm not sure if the Moktar even know about that list. I think someone inside the compound arranges a yearly sacrifice, and they've chosen me as the newest prize."

"Aren't virgins usually chosen for these sorts of things?" asked Lucinda, giving me a knowing look.

I blushed scarlet. "I guess not. How did you figure out I'm no longer a virgin?"

She snorted. "It's so obvious."

Poppy gave me a worried frown. "Why would someone from inside the compound do this?"

"Maybe Mavin figures one girl a year is better than ten. She must have made some kind of deal with the Moktar, but I have no idea how she chooses her victims. The first woman recorded in the journal was Michael's mom, and she was Mavin's friend."

"So sick and wrong," said Poppy.

"Another reason you shouldn't do this, Emerson," said Lucinda, her dark eyes sad. "Have you thought about how this will affect Michael if something happens to you? He lost his mother to them when he was a baby. He can't lose you, too. It'll destroy him."

I swallowed a lump the size of Texas in my throat. "I have to do this. Can't you understand? It's all my fault, and I'm the only one who can stop it."

They tried arguing, yelling, and even bargaining with me, but I knew I was doing the right thing. Poppy cried, which was an unfair tactic, but I refused to budge. I didn't have a choice.

I dressed in black, like Michael, and pulled my hair into a tight bun. I borrowed Lucinda's leather jacket. She didn't know I needed it for protection against Moktar claws. I doubted it would do much good, but every little bit helped.

I called my daddy before I left. I needed to hear his voice one more time. I kept my voice neutral and complained about the English weather. He laughed and said I'd be home soon. That was almost my undoing, but I stayed strong, told him I loved him, and hung up the phone.

I strapped the weapons belt around my waist, and put the duffle over my shoulder. Poppy, still teary-eyed, giggled when she saw me.

"You look like *Tomb Raider*. It's very badass. I may have to steal that outfit for my final project."

I hugged her, which was tricky with a row of knives strapped to my waist. "I've always been badass. I just disguised it under wool skirts and cardigans."

Lucinda turned very businesslike and serious, how she always dealt with stress. "Right-o. If we don't hear from you in an hour, we're calling the police."

"Three hours."

"Two," she said, folding her arms across her chest.

I rolled my eyes and gave her Michael's number. "Call him…if anything happens. Not the police."

She pursed her lips. "*Nothing* will happen," she said, but took his number anyway, tears filling her eyes.

I slipped out the door before she started crying in earnest. If Lucinda cried, I'd lose it for sure. I hung on by a thread.

As soon as I stepped outside, I called Leo. I didn't have a choice. The address was useless unless I had someone on the inside willing to assist me. Only Travellers could open the door to the Traveller compound, and I was certain only Moktar could open the door to their nest. Fortunately, Leo answered on the first ring. “Emerson?”

I decided not to mince words. “I know what you are, Leo. I want to save Brooke, but the Ceannfort won’t let me negotiate. I need your help.”

I didn’t have to wait long for an answer. We arranged to meet in front of the teashop. “Come alone this time.”

I took a deep breath. “I’m on my way.”

Closed for business, the windows of Mrs. Burke’s teashop were dark and empty. Leo already waited for me. He appeared to be alone.

“Emerson.” His face lit up the same way it did every time he saw me. I tried to control the bile that rose in my throat.

“You look well. Better than the last time at least. You must have eaten recently.”

Leo’s golden eyes darkened. “How did you figure it out, Emerson?”

“Your eyes. Your strength. Your stench.”

Leo sighed. “It gets harder to control those things if I am low on HT, but, as you can see, I’m fine now. I’m me again.”

“Because you murdered someone and chowed down on their brains.” I couldn’t keep the bitterness out of my voice. He was a monster.

Leo gave me a crooked smile. “I thought you were here for my help. Shouldn’t you play nice?”

“Like you did with Brooke?” I looked around. “Where is she?”

Leo moved closer. I remember thinking Michael looked like a predatory beast, but I was wrong. Leo was the beast.

“She’s safe. She’s in our nest.”

Somehow, I managed to keep my voice calm and steady. "Did you hurt her?"

Leo shook his head, but he seemed nervous. His gaze kept darting to the buildings surrounding us as the shadows from the dim light of the street lamps danced across his face. "You're the one who's in danger, Emerson. I need to get you as far away from here as possible."

He tried to pull my arm, but I planted my feet and stood firm. "I want to go to the nest. I know where it is. If you don't help me, I'll go on my own."

Leo ran a hand through his dark hair. It reminded me so much of Michael it made my heart squeeze in my chest. But Leo and Michael were nothing alike. Leo might look human, but inside he was just as much a beast as the other Moktar.

"And what do you plan on doing when you get there?"

I straightened my shoulders. "Trade myself for Brooke."

"Of all the idiotic plans..." He began, and then folded his arms across his broad chest. "I could force you to come with me, Emerson."

I raised an eyebrow at him. "And how did that work out for you last time?"

He had the decency to look embarrassed. "The addiction...it's a nightmare. It turns me into a stranger, someone I don't even recognize. I honestly didn't mean to hurt you. I'd never hurt you."

"Oh. You're the victim here? I feel so bad for you."

He stared at me, his golden eyes furious and yet resigned. "You're going to be stubborn about this, aren't you?"

I sighed. "I was born that way."

It only took him a few moments to make his decision. "I'll take you, but only on one condition."

I didn't like that very much, and scowled at him. "What?"

He stepped closer, close enough I felt the warmth of his body. It took everything in me to remain still and not move away from him. He brushed a lock of hair behind my ear, and I shut my eyes to hide my disgust. When I opened them, he watched me with a sad, little smile.

"You have to trust me. Can you do that?"

"Of course," I said, and he laughed.

"You're a terrible liar."

"And you're a terrible person. Can we go now?"

We walked in silence through the dark streets of York. I checked my GPS several times, and we were definitely heading in the right direction. Leo kept glancing at me, his face a worried mask. When we were only a block away from the nest, he stopped.

"Emerson, before we go any farther, there is something I need to tell you."

A noise from the rooftops startled me. Leo grabbed my hand and pulled me behind him just as Melo jumped down onto the cobblestone street in front of us. Several other Moktar leapt down as well. The road was still damp from an early evening rain, and the sky so dark with clouds I couldn't see the moon or the stars. Pitch black, except for one streetlight shining down on Melo. He drew himself up to his full height, well over seven feet, and lifted his head to howl at the sky. He was even more terrifying than I remembered, much larger, stronger, and scarier than any of the Moktar I'd killed, and he was hunting me. I'd just made things rather easy for him, sort of like a rabbit crawling into a trap and begging to be eaten. But this bunny had a few tricks up her sleeve.

He walked toward us, and nodding once at Leo. "Well done, brother," he said, his voice somewhere between a hiss and a growl.

"Brother?" I asked.

Leo pulled me around to his side, his hand still gripping my arm. "That's what I wanted to tell you. Melo isn't just our alpha. He's my brother. My twin."

"Twins?" I looked back and forth between then, one so beautiful and one so terrifying.

"One human, one Moktar," said Melo.

"What happened to Roseanne?"

Melo gave me a cruel smile, and moved closer to catch a whiff of my scent, his nose rubbing against my skin. "She was the first human I ever killed," he said, and I shuddered.

"She died giving birth to us," Leo said, clearing his throat and pulling me closer. This time I didn't protest. I wanted to be as far away from Melo as possible.

Melo towered over both of us. "Why did you come, little Traveller?"

Leo answered for me, which was good. I wasn't sure if I could speak. "She's here to negotiate for the Dweller's release," he said. "She asked me to bring her to the nest to meet with you."

Melo bowed to me formally, a gesture that struck me as comical, but I bottled up the hysterical laughter rising in my throat. "Follow me," he said.

The door to the Moktar nest opened in much the

same way as the door to the Traveller compound. Instead of a finger, however, Melo inserted a single claw. I watched in fascination as the door slid open.

"That's quite the party trick."

Leo put his hand on my shoulder, leading me through the door. No handle existed on the other side, and no doorknob. When it closed with a loud click, I was trapped. I wanted to reach for a knife and kill Melo on the spot, but I forced myself to think of Brooke. If there was any chance she was still alive, I had to try to save her.

"Rid her of weapons, brother," said Melo.

Leo turned me around to face him. He took my duffle bag from my shoulder and tossed it onto the concrete floor. We stood at the top of a high metal staircase. I glanced over the side to see where it led, but found nothing below but darkness. Leo slid his hands around my waist, his gaze never leaving mine.

"What are you doing?" I asked, trying to control the rapid hammering of my heart.

"Checking you for weapons."

His hands slid over my belt, loaded with knives and even a nice, shiny *sai.* His eyes met mine, and I knew he'd felt them. I held my breath as I waited for him to expose me to Melo, but oddly enough he didn't say anything. After he finished, he zipped up my jacket, covering the belt completely.

He raised one eyebrow; a gesture so much like Michael's it felt like a stab in my chest. "You look like your brother," I said.

He looked surprised. "Melo?"

I shook my head. "Michael. I can't believe I never noticed it before."

Leo acknowledged it with a little bow of his dark head, and his lips curved up into the barest hint of a smile. “At least I look like someone in my family.”

I glanced at the Moktar standing next to him, with his saggy skin and menacing eyes. “Just be happy you take after your mama and not your daddy.”

“Looks can be deceiving. What was it you wrote in your journal about me, ‘like someone on the cover of an erotic novel’? You thought I was desirable.”

I felt my cheeks get warm. “That was before I knew you.”

He shook his head. “That was before you knew Michael.”

“I want my journal back.”

He laughed. “Too bad. It’s mine.”

Leo led me down a narrow hallway. I kept looking over my shoulder, hoping to find an escape route. There wasn’t one. I’d gone into this knowing it was probably a one-way trip, but I still had to try. I touched my cell phone in my pocket. Lucinda tracked it at this very moment, my only safeguard, but useless because, as suspected, only a Moktar could open the door to the nest.

We exited the dark, narrow hallway and walked through an ornately carved wooden door and straight into what looked like a prison. I searched the room until my eyes found Brooke. She was naked and chained up in a cell, her body filthy. She looked barely conscious, but at least she was alive. For now.

I don’t know what I’d expected to find in the Moktar’s nest, but this wasn’t it. Leo led me past the other cells, and I looked around in shock. Naked women were chained in each of the cells, some of them pregnant, most half starving.

"They're all Travellers," he said. "Except for Brooke."

"The stories about what you do to Traveller women are true," I said, trying to swallow the bile rising in my throat. "You really are beasts."

Leo didn't respond, and I stepped away from him. I couldn't stand even being close to him. We passed through the prison and entered a cavernous room, full of Moktar, a long wooden table in the center. The Moktar sat around the table, as if feasting, but the only thing on the table was a woman with her spindly legs spread eagle and her body very still. She wore a black robe. I couldn't see her face, but I knew who she was.

"Mavin."

I marched over, prepared to give her a piece of my mind, but as soon as I reached the table, I realized the awful truth. The top of her skull was missing, and the Moktar had eaten her brain.

I stumbled backwards. Leo pulled me away from the body. "I'm sorry you had to see that, but she was a nasty old thing."

"You *ate* her."

"She served no other purpose. She was too old to breed, and we do what we must to survive."

I shook from head to toe. "You might look like a person, but you are a monster, Leo."

Melo sat at the head of the table, and he laughed. "A monster? My brother? He is as weak and human as any Traveller. He is not Moktar, Emerson Shaw. He is a burden. We keep him alive because he can walk in the sun. In that capacity, he serves us well."

Melo lifted a heavy silver chalice to Leo, and then

took a long, deep sip. I hoped it wasn't blood, but judging by the color of what ran down his face, I was pretty certain it wasn't Kool-Aid. I felt like vomiting.

The other Moktar around the table laughed at Melo's comments, and Leo's cheeks turned red. He turned to me, his golden eyes sad. "I cannot adequately describe to you what the withdrawal feels like, Emerson, but just imagine your entire body on fire, and as it burned, someone began pulling off your skin. That is the closest I can come to making you understand."

I gave him a level look, trying to keep my cool. I had to find a way to help all these women. I'd come in hoping to trade myself for Brooke, but I hadn't expected to find a bunch of Traveller women locked in the Moktar dungeon.

"You're a bunch of drug addicts, rapists, and murderers."

Leo closed his eyes for just a second and shook his head slowly. "It's not drug addiction. There's no detox or rehab or hope of recovery. Without it we die."

"I'm sorry for you, but it's better to die than to kill innocent people."

Leo's lips curved into a smile, but it lacked humor. "Is that why you came here tonight? Is that why the Ceannfort is at our gate at this moment searching desperately for a way to get in? Because it's better to die than to kill?"

I swallowed hard. The idea Michael might be outside terrified me. Lucinda and Poppy must have panicked and called him.

"I came here to save Brooke. If I kill a few Moktar in the process, it isn't the same as killing a human. You are monsters. You deserve it."

Chapter Thirty

Your ass is grass, and I'm the lawnmower.

~Grandma Sugar

"Would you like a tour of our nest?" asked Melo. "Before we assign you a cell of your own?"

I nodded, not trusting myself to speak. This was the chance I'd been waiting for. If I could get Melo somewhere alone, I'd have a better chance of killing him. My blood hummed with excitement. Something odd had been unleashed when I'd fought back and killed all of those Moktar. A thirst, a desire, to do it again, and again, and again.

Maybe the Moktar weren't the only monsters. Maybe I'd become one myself.

Melo led me through the nest, his hands behind his back, looking every inch the respectable host, except, of course, for the yellow eyes, saggy skin, and nasty teeth. He still had a bit of blood and what looked like part of Mavin's brain on his chin. Leo followed a few feet behind us.

"I heard you had a rather eventful evening yesterday," said Melo.

"Are you making conversation with me?"

He shrugged, the effect odd with his gray, loose skin. "I am trying to be polite. You should do the same.

There are those among us who would like to kill you immediately after what you did."

"Are you one of them, Melo?"

He shook his gigantic head. "No. I'd like to enjoy you first, and a strong woman like you would make fine sons for me."

My disgust must have been apparent on my face, but I couldn't hold my tongue. "The only way you can have women is if you rape them. Do you think that makes you strong? I think it makes you a sick, smelly, weakling."

Melo turned toward me, raising his hand. Sure he was going to hit me, I closed my eyes, but the smack never came. I opened my eyes to see Melo staring down at me.

"You have no idea what you are, do you?"

I clenched my jaw. "I know I'm a Traveller. Or at least half Traveller."

Melo moved a step closer to me, and Leo's entire body tensed. I still hadn't figured Leo out. He seemed devoted to his nasty brother, but he'd let me keep my weapons belt. Either he didn't think it was important, or he wanted his brother dead as much as I did. I lifted my chin, refusing to cower, and Melo laughed.

"You are so much more than that, little golden one. It is why you are such a danger, and also such a gift."

Melo continued his tour, taking me down to see where the newborn Moktar were kept. Babies are always cute, even animal babies, but baby Moktar were just as ugly as their parents. There were several females with the children or pups or whatever they were. They fell to their knees and touched their foreheads to the ground as soon as they saw Melo.

"I didn't know girl Moktars existed," I said.

"They are worthless," he said. "Unable to breed, and with remarkably short life spans. We don't bother giving them much HT anymore. It's better if they just die in infancy."

"You are just all kinds of lovely, aren't you, Melo?"

He shrugged, and for just a second I saw a glimpse of Michael beneath the monster form. It vanished almost immediately.

"I am practical. I do what I must for our race to survive."

He took me into a room with maps and computers. "This is our command center. Right now, we only communicate with the nests in England, but soon it will be global. We are not going to stay here much longer. We will begin setting up shop in your home country. Perhaps our first nest will be in Bowling Green, in honor of your poor, dead mother."

I reached up to slap his face, but Leo stopped me. "Don't," he said softly in my ear. I let my hand fall back to my side.

Melo's eyes grew dark. "If you keep it up, our first meal in Kentucky will be your father. The esteemed professor and historian, Dr. George Shaw."

"How do you know so much about me?" I could barely speak. The idea of my father being a target made a cold, horrible fear sweep through my body.

"We have our sources," he said with a nasty smile. "And here he is now."

His eyes went to the door, and automatically, I turned to look to see who'd come in. My knees buckled beneath me when I realized the terrible truth.

"Monroe Skinner."

If he was surprised to see me in the nest, he certainly didn't show it. "Ah, Emerson. They caught you rather quickly. I must say I'm a bit disappointed. I thought you would have put up more of a fight."

"She came here of her own accord. She wants to bargain for the life of the Dweller," said Leo.

Melo tilted his head to one side. "And what will you bargain with?"

"Myself," I said, and Melo and Monroe burst out laughing.

"But, my dear," said Melo. "You are already mine."

We walked back through the cells together. Melo was ahead of us and Monroe by my side. Several of the women looked up when they saw Monroe. He didn't even glance at them.

"How could you do this to your own people?"

He shrugged. "What you must understand is by giving the Moktar one girl a year to play with I avoid other girls being taken. It's for the good of the entire community. I pick the girls, get rid of a few bad apples, and everyone is happy."

"These girls don't seem very happy."

He frowned at me, looking every inch the white-haired, grandfatherly English gentleman. Leo was right. Looks could be deceiving.

"Their happiness really is of no consequence."

"Why did you pick Roseanne?"

"Ah. That was a bit different. She chose Sampson over me, you see. My wife was worthless. She couldn't produce a child. Giving the Moktar Roseanne was simply an act of youthful vengeance on my part, but it worked out well for me. I made the original agreement with Melo and Leo's father. He was so pleased with the results he allowed it to continue for over twenty years. Think of all the lives I saved."

I stopped walking. "You're actually proud of yourself."

He nodded very seriously. "Of course, I am. But my plans far exceed what I've accomplished already. I can tell you this since you'll never again see the light of day. We're changing our strategy. Rather than working for the Dwellers and their idiotic alliance, we're joining forces with the Moktar."

I tripped over my own feet, but caught myself before I fell. "You're forming an alliance with the monsters who want to eat you?"

"Yes. It's brilliant, actually. Rather than being kept as virtual prisoners in our dirty little compounds, the Travellers will be free to roam the earth once more."

"Michael won't let that happen."

He chuckled. "The Ceannfort will no longer be an issue, my dear. As soon as we have you locked up and secure, I plan to hand him over the Moktar. He's become such a pain. It'll be nice to be rid of him once and for all, just like I got rid of the other one. Only sixteen years old, but he'd gotten too close to the truth, you see. He left me no choice."

"Tad," I said softly, and Monroe flinched at the fact I'd said his name aloud. "What about Mavin?"

He rolled his eyes. "That nosy bitch. She was about to ruin everything. She snuck into my caravan and stole my journal. Can you believe the nerve?"

"How awful for you."

Apparently, he missed the sarcasm in my words.

"It was. But at least her little act of thievery did have one positive result. It got you here, and this is where you will stay."

He opened the door to an empty cell, ever so politely, like a gentleman opening the door for a lady. I had few options at this point. Being a lady was not one of them. Leo stood a few feet behind us, Melo a few feet ahead. I did what any respectable southern girl would do in this situation and went bat crazy, kicking Monroe as hard as I could right in his private parts. When he doubled over in pain I kneed him in the face and shoved him into the cell, slamming the door and locking him inside. He curled up on the floor, holding his crotch, with blood flowing out of a broken nose.

Melo turned and gave me an evil grin. "Emerson wants to play."

He lifted his head and howled, a horrific sound that echoed off the stone walls of the dungeon, making the women cover their ears and cry. I wasn't crying. I unzipped my jacket, pulled out two knives, and enjoyed the sight of the bright silver in the dim light of the prison. Melo backed away. He must have sensed I planned to save these girls, or die trying.

As Moktar streamed into the narrow hallway, Leo stood next to me, his back to mine. He had a knife in his hand as well.

"What are you doing?" I asked.

"I will not permit you to die here, Emerson Shaw."

I rolled my eyes. "So bossy. Just like your brother."

He scowled. "Perhaps we wouldn't have to be so bossy if you simply made better decisions. We really must work on your impulse control."

I wanted to argue with him about it, but the swarm of Moktar approaching us proved a bit of a distraction. Due to the narrowness of the hallway, they could only attack a few at a time. It really wasn't even a very fair fight. I slashed and lunged and killed them without much effort at all. I found it almost boring. Every so often, I'd turn and help Leo out. He was sweating and breathing hard. I was covered in blood, but completely calm. An odd Zen-like experience for me. It felt like I was doing what I'd been born to do. There was something very right about it, like my whole life had built up to this moment.

Melo had disappeared as soon as the fighting started. I searched for him as I fought, but he hid somewhere, probably waiting for me to tire so he could finish me off. He would be sadly disappointed. I wasn't tired at all, but Leo was dragging, and he looked like he'd been injured. I wanted to shove him in a cell for his own protection, but instead I tried to cover him as much as I could.

Another long howl erupted and the Moktar froze, backing off a few feet. I was breathing hard, but not as much from exertion as from excitement. This had been enjoyable for me, which was sort of scary on so many levels. My enjoyment ended as soon as I saw Melo. He held a barely conscious Brooke in his arms, one sharp claw poised just above her exposed neck.

"You have fought well, Emerson, but this will stop now or your friend dies."

Leo, doubled over next to me, gasped for breath as he bled profusely from a wound on his side. "He'll kill her anyway."

Melo growled. "You are worthless, and now you

have betrayed your own race. I will no longer call you my brother."

Leo looked up at him and smiled. "Good," he said. "That makes this so much easier."

He stood and tossed a knife directly at Melo's head. A great throw, but Melo was just a little too quick. He jumped out of the way, dropping Brooke in the process. She curled up on the floor in a crumpled heap, looking nothing like a southern belle and a former beauty queen. Her eyes, glassy and unfocused, gave me hope she'd remember very little from this night.

Melo straightened to his full height, an army of Moktar behind him. A terrifying thing to behold.

"You have made this easier for me, Leo, no-brother-of-mine. I will kill the girl first and make you watch. Afterwards, I'll take my time with you," he said, and then shouted at the Moktar behind him. "We shall dine well tonight."

The Moktar roared. Leo pulled himself back up to a standing position. He leaned heavily against the bars of one of the cells, determination and resignation shining in his golden eyes. I handed him one of my knives.

"Thank you," he said. "You're going to owe me a coffee when this is all over."

We both knew we weren't getting out of here alive. No matter how many Moktar I killed, more kept coming, and Melo might prove to be too powerful. Even for me.

I gave him a crooked smile. "You never give up, do you? I'm dating your big brother, remember?"

"A minor detail," he said softly. He was pale and sweating. He'd lost a lot of blood, but he'd made his choice. Sun Tzu would have been proud of him. He would have been proud of both of us. We would die with honor.

Melo snarled, stepping closer. I held up my knives. He didn't need any weapons. He had his teeth, and his claws. A killing machine.

A loud noise came from the door leading to the great room. Several Moktar began howling, but it sounded different this time. The cries coming from their throats seemed like howls of pain.

Melo kept his yellow eyes on me, so he didn't notice his army deserting him. They'd turned and fled. The look on his face when he glanced over his shoulder and realized no one stood behind him was almost comical, but it didn't last long. He was even more pissed off than ever. He'd already decided to kill me, but now as I saw the evil gleam in his eyes, I knew he wanted to make it as painful a death as possible.

He wouldn't get his chance. Michael appeared in the door way like an avenging angel. "Emerson," he said, his eyes on Melo. "Have you been hurt?"

"I'm fine and dandy, darlin'. But I was just about to kill your little brother Melo here."

He shot me a signature Nightingale look that was so irritated it almost made me giggle. "Didn't I tell you earlier you aren't to kill Melo? He's mine."

Leo could no longer stand by himself, so I held him up. "You were right," he said, his voice barely a whisper. "He *is* bossy."

"Don't I know it."

Leo's skin had taken on a deathly pallor. I helped him sit, his back to the bars of one of the cells. He closed his eyes. I lifted his shirt and saw several puncture wounds as well as a long slash right across his chest. I found a dirty old blanket in one of the cells and applied pressure as Leo faded in and out of consciousness. Not sanitary, but it worked. His pulse waned, but his heart kept beating. The only way to save him was to stop the bleeding, but doing that meant I couldn't help Michael.

Michael and Melo circled each other. Brooke had crawled into a corner and huddled there, shivering. I couldn't get to her. I couldn't get to Michael either. All I could do was watch, wait, and pray.

The battle between the Ceannfort and the Alpha was a mighty thing to witness. They proved to be rather evenly matched. If it weren't for the fact I was madly in love with one of the opponents and my life was on the line, I might have actually enjoyed watching. As it was, every time Melo's sharp claws sliced Michael's skin, I felt like I'd been hurt myself. As the battle progressed, I realized one very important thing, something I'd learned from Sun Tzu a long time ago, but I'd never experienced firsthand.

Every battle is won before it's even fought.

Michael didn't fight for himself. He fought for me. He fought for the women imprisoned in the cages. He fought for his people. He was the Ceannfort, and he was glorious. Melo, on the other hand, fought only for himself, and soon it became very clear who would be the victor. Melo backed away, on the defensive, as Michael took control.

Watching him as he lunged and stabbed, dodging Melo's bloody claws and knocking him off his feet, I realized exactly why he'd earned the title of Ceannfort. He was magnificent, a warrior like no other. When he jumped on top of Melo and pressed a knife against his throat, my heart skipped a beat. Soon it would all end, and Melo knew it, too. I saw the truth is his ugly yellow eyes. He could barely breathe, but he managed to rasp out a few words.

"But you are my brother."

Michael slashed him across the neck, and Melo made a gurgling sound as blood pumped out of his body and onto the stone floor of the dungeon.

"You are no brother of mine," he said softly, echoing the words Melo had said only moments earlier to Leo before cleaning his knife and slipping it back into his belt.

Chapter Thirty-One

Why, I'll swaney.

~Grandma Sugar

The Traveller warriors poured into the room. At first, they looked around in shock at the Moktar bodies lying in piles and the women chained inside the cells, then they sprang into action. One of them took care of Leo. Others began to gently see to the women, including Brooke.

Michael turned to me, and when his eyes meant mine, relief mixed with fury on his face. A typical Michael Nightingale reaction to stress. He reached me in two long strides, pulled me into his arms, and buried his face in my neck.

"I thought I'd lost you. We couldn't get in."

I pulled back and looked at him. Exhausted and splattered with blood, but still the most beautiful thing I'd ever seen.

"How did you manage it?"

"We found the entrance, and the hole in the wall, but we couldn't open the door. I sent some of my men back to the compound to get a hand from one of the Moktar corpses. It worked like a dream."

"I'm glad. We were in trouble."

I took Michael's hand and led him over to Leo. He was barely conscious.

"Michael. I'd like you to meet your little brother."

Michael sank down on one knee. "Wasn't Melo my brother?"

"Twins," I said softly. "One human and one…not. Leo fought with me tonight. We thought we were going to die, but he wouldn't leave my side."

Michael's jaw was set in a hard line as conflicting emotions warred on his face. Patrick came to stand next to him, breathing hard and covered in blood.

I saw the moment Michael made his decision. "We need to call our emergency services unit, Pat," he said, looking over his shoulder at his older brother. "For the women…and for Leo."

"We're calling an ambulance for a Moktar?" asked Patrick.

Michael nodded very slowly. "He fought with Emerson. And we are…we share a mother."

"He's still a monster. Does none of this matter now?" Patrick grabbed Michael's shoulder, but Michael shrugged him off. I saw the pain in his eyes. Patrick might have been right, but Michael knew there was more to it.

Leo's eyes slowly opened. As soon as he saw me, his face lit up, like always, but his skin was ashen, and he had trouble breathing. His gaze went to Michael.

"Keep her safe," he said his voice barely a rasp.

Michael nodded. "Like you did."

Leo gave Michael the barest hint of a smile. "I could not allow her to die here. She's too important. To both of us."

Michael swallowed hard. "I know. I'm sorry. I didn't understand. I didn't understand any of it until now."

Patrick ran a hand over his head, trying to decide what to do. Then he knelt beside Leo, and patted his uninjured shoulder a little awkwardly. When I smiled at him, he rolled his eyes.

"I can't believe we're doing this," he muttered softly.

Leo's breathing sounded shallow and faint. "I wanted so much to know you, to be human like my brothers. I tried, but couldn't quite do it. None of that matters now. It's over."

Leo started to close his eyes again, but I wouldn't let him. I heard the sound of the ambulances approaching. "Don't you dare shut your eyes, Leo, or I'll make you regret it. I promise you that."

Leo chuckled, his eyes, still closed. "What are you going to do? Kill me? It's too late."

"Don't be an idiot. It's barely a flesh wound."

Michael raised one dark eyebrow at me. More than a flesh wound, but I wasn't about to let Leo know. He managed to open his eyes again, just as Ryan approached.

"All of my brothers," Leo said softly. "My family."

The ambulance arrived, and the men loaded Leo onto a stretcher. They hooked him to an IV drip and he rested more comfortably.

Michael pulled Patrick aside, and they had a quick and heated discussion. Patrick protested, but finally gave in. He followed the EMTs as they pushed the stretcher outside, and climbed into the ambulance after Leo. He reached out and straightened Leo's blanket, looking decidedly uncomfortable about the whole situation. When he caught me watching, he frowned.

"I've never babysat a Moktar before."

"Don't kill him." My voice was stern.

Patrick looked shocked. "Of course not."

"Don't hurt him, either."

Patrick grinned, but didn't answer. I scowled as the EMT closed the door, and went back inside to join Michael.

"I never thought I'd see the day." He looked at Monroe, still locked in a cage.

"He betrayed you," I said. "He gave all those girls to the Moktar."

Michael nodded; his face a study in hard planes and clenched muscles. "Aye. We followed him here tonight and watched a Moktar escort him right through the door like an honored guest."

"What are you going to do with him?"

He shrugged. "I'd like to leave him here to rot, but that's for the Gypsy High Council to decide when they meet early next spring. It's the worldwide governing body of our people. I'm sure they'll think of a better punishment for him than I ever could."

Monroe turned suddenly pale. "Everything I did, I did for my people."

Michael lost it. "These *are* your people. My mother was one of your people, too. My *mother.*"

His voice was a booming roar amplified by the narrow confines of the dungeon. Monroe covered his ears with his hands and wept. Not for Roseanne. Not for the other women. He wept only for himself.

Michael turned away in disgust and left the room. I followed him, but not before taking one last look at Monroe. Crumbled on the floor, a broken man, I felt no pity for him. All I felt was deep, simmering anger.

As we walked out into the great room, Michael

took my hand in his. He must have seen something on my face that gave him a clue about the turmoil inside me. I had just killed a legion of Moktar, but I still wanted more. I wanted vengeance. I wanted to keep fighting.

"A warrior's blood runs hot right after a battle. You fought and you won. Enjoy it, but let it go."

"How?"

He put his hand on my neck and pulled me close. "You'll find a way," he said, and then he kissed me, and my blood began to boil in a completely different way.

Sampson interrupted us by clearing his throat very loudly behind us. My cheeks turned bright red when I noticed my grandparents standing behind him.

"Lass," he said. "We owe you a great debt. You saved our girls tonight. We thought they were lost forever. And you saved your friend, Brooke, too. They are all on the way to hospital. But, once again, you have broken our laws."

I couldn't believe what I heard. "Those laws are the reason your girls ended up in cages."

Sampson was sympathetic, but it didn't change a single thing. "It's not in our power to change a law that has been in place since the first Travellers walked the earth. Nor is it up to us to alter it in any way. This is a matter for the Gypsy High Council. They will have to decide when they meet next year in Edinburgh. Until then, my hands are tied. I'm sorry, Emerson."

I blinked away tears, my hand gripping Michael's. "So I have to walk away and never see or talk to any of you ever again? I have to pretend none of you ever existed?"

My gaze went to my grandparents. Anselina remained stoic, but Matthew looked ready to weep.

"That's why I brought your grandparents here. I felt you earned the right to see them one last time."

"How kind of you." I shot him a hostile look, but it really wasn't his fault. He only knew one way to do things. The gypsy way. He was trapped inside their laws the same way the girls had been trapped in the cages.

I hugged my grandparents, and kissed them goodbye. I was covered in blood and Moktar gore, not how I wanted them to remember me, but I had no other options. When they turned and walked away, they looked older and smaller than before.

"I didn't have much of a choice, you know. If I'd obeyed your idiotic laws, Sampson, I'd be dead right now, too."

He looked around at the dark, grim walls of the Moktar nest. "To think my Roseanne spent her last days in this terrible place. She suffered here, and died here. I want to tear it down, stone by stone with my own bare hands. I don't ever want anyone to go through what she went through. I'll do what I can, Emerson."

"Can Michael walk me back to my apartment?"

"Of course," he said. "I'll finish up with everything here. Take the time you need. Just let the paramedics see to your wounds before you go, Michael."

Michael did as he asked. I didn't have any wounds. I escaped completely unscathed. When Sampson noticed, he gave me a long look.

"You're more than you seem, lass."

"What do you mean by that?"

He sighed. "You'll understand, eventually. And

I'm sorry it has to be this way. You don't deserve it, and neither does Michael."

I called Lucinda just as the paramedics finished with Michael's wounds to let her know everything was fine, and we would be back at the apartment soon. She cried on the phone, and so did Poppy.

"I was so frightened."

I cradled the phone against my cheek. "Everything is okay. Love you guys."

Michael and I walked through the streets of York in silence. When we got back to my apartment, it was dark and quiet. A note on the fridge told me Lucinda had decided to stay at Poppy's place for the night. I said a silent prayer of gratitude.

"How long do we have?" I asked, my whole body still.

"Until sunrise, I think."

I took a deep, shaking breath. Our last moments together. When I turned around, from the look in his eyes, his thoughts were the same as mine.

"I'm going to take a shower, get the Moktar guts out of my hair, and then I'm going to rock your world. Are you okay with that plan?"

He gave me a sexy, crooked grin. "Aye. That's sounds quite agreeable to me as well."

I showered, letting the hot water wash away the blood, gore, and everything else that had happened in the Moktar nest. My body still hummed with energy, but the blood lust had dissipated. It had been replaced by a completely different kind of lust altogether.

While Michael showered, I dressed in the tiny black teddy Lucinda had given me, and slipped a silk robe on over it. I pulled my damp hair up into a messy bun, and sat down on my bed to wait.

It didn't take long. Michael came to me wearing only a white towel wrapped tightly around his waist, the water from the shower still drying on his skin. As soon as I saw him, I rose to my feet.

"Are you going to make me wrestle you to get that towel off again?"

"No." His eyes were locked on mine as he took the towel off and let it drop to the floor.

"Holy guacamole."

He opened his arms to me, and I flew into them. His kisses were desperate, hungry, and sad. I wanted to remember every single moment, every touch, every caress, every kiss. These precious memories were all I would have in the long and lonely days ahead.

I backed away and let the robe slide off my shoulders. Michael growled, taking a moment just to stare. Like the first time I saw him, I looked into his eyes and was lost. I reached up, tracing the lines of his face, his arrogant nose, his stubborn chin, his strong jaw. He took my hand and kissed my palm, his eyes closed.

"I love you, Emerson."

"I love you, too, Michael Nightingale. With all my heart."

With that, the floodgates opened, and the time for gentleness ended. He was the Ceannfort, and he worshipped me in the way only a warrior could, completely.

Michael pulled me against him, kissing me with unbridled passion. Our tongues warred, dancing against each other. Michael put his hands on my bottom, holding me close so I could feel his hardness pressing against me. My entire body reacted, and suddenly I was warm, wet and wanting.

He lifted me onto the bed, and his hands slid up to my breasts. He kissed me through the black lace, using his tongue until my nipples became hard little peaks, but still I wanted more. I pushed the teddy aside and arched so my naked breasts could reach his mouth. He made a sound deep in his throat and kissed and sucked and teased my nipples until I was breathing hard and clutching his head against my chest.

But the sweet torture wasn't quite over yet. Michael kissed his way down my stomach and knelt between my legs, giving me a very naughty look. I had my suspicions about what he was about to do, but nothing had prepared me for the way it felt when he kissed me through the black lace covering the most sensitive part of my body. I had to stifle a scream. It was so intense. And when he pulled my teddy off and began licking me, kissing me, and worshipping me with his mouth, I did scream. A few times, in fact.

When I couldn't stand another minute of it, he rose in front of me like an ancient pagan god. I quivered, his eager human sacrifice, the bed beneath me my altar.

His eyes never left mine as he thrust into me again and again. Every time it became too much, and I shut my eyes even for a second, he stroked my cheek and pleaded with me.

"Look at me, Emerson. See me. Please?"

I did what he asked. I kept my eyes open as I climaxed, calling out his name, and watched his face as he did the same. He was amazing. And leaving him would be the hardest thing I'd ever had to do.

We were quiet afterwards, unsure how to act, our

sadness weighing on us like a heavy cloud. He held me close, stroking my hair and raining soft, sweet kisses on my face until we both fell asleep from complete and utter exhaustion.

In the early hours of the morning, his phone rang, and I knew our time was up. He spoke a few minutes in hushed tones and then turned off the phone. He sat on my edge of my bed, his head bowed. I slid up behind him, putting my legs on either side of his body and resting my cheek against his broad back as I wrapped my arms around his waist.

"You have to go."

"Yes."

I sighed. I'd promised myself I wouldn't cry, but I did anyway. They were soft, silent tears, though. I planned to save the serious weeping and wailing for after Michael left.

He pulled me around so I sat on his lap and held me gently in his arms. "Hear me now, Emerson. I will find a way to be with you. If you can't be a Traveller, I'll become a Dweller."

I almost laughed. The idea of Michael, a Traveller through and through, living as a Dweller was ridiculous. The thought of him deserting his people seemed impossible to even contemplate.

"You'd make a terrible Dweller," I said, giving him a little smile. "But I love you even more for suggesting it."

His blue eyes were steady. "I will find a way, Emerson. I promise you."

I nodded, but couldn't speak. If I did, I would cry, and I didn't want Michael's last memory to be of me with a red nose and swollen eyes.

We dressed in silence. I found some of Sven's clothes in Lucinda's room and lent them to Michael. His clothes were soaked with blood and beyond repair. He had scratches all over his forearms and some serious bruises on his face. He looked a little funny in the "Greenpeace" hoodie and sweats, but he was glorious no matter what he wore.

He pulled me into his arms and kissed the top of my head. "My Da went to the hospital. Brooke is doing well and her parents are on their way from America to get her. He checked on Leo, too, and it looks like he's going to be fine. Patrick donated his blood, if you can believe it. They had to give him quite a lot, but he's responding well."

"I'm glad," I said, giving him a tremulous smile. "I hope you'll get to know him. He's a lot more like you than I realized."

He raised a dark eyebrow at that. "Well, we both seem to find ourselves oddly attracted to spunky wee Americans with curly hair and very poor judgment."

I was about to protest, but he covered my lips with his fingers to silence me. "Hush," he said softly. "I will visit my brother. I promise."

He removed his fingers and I gave him a grateful smile. "Thank you. Leo needs you."

He rolled his eyes and muttered something about a "bloody Moktar," but I ignored him. I put my hands on his waist and stared directly at a spot in the center of his chest.

"I'm going to do you a huge favor and be very, very brave right now. I'm going to kiss you goodbye with a smile on my face, just like the women do when all the Traveller men go off to battle. I'm going to pretend you're coming home to me. I'm going to pretend this goodbye won't last forever."

"It's not forever, Emerson. I swear…"

This time I silenced him by resting my fingers against his lips. "Don't make promises you can't keep, my love. Just kiss me goodbye and pretend with me."

I kissed him, pouring all of my love and pain into it. Wanting to hold onto him forever, but knowing I had to let him go. When I released him, I still hadn't cried, but the brave, brawny, leader of the Traveller warriors turned out not to be quite as strong as a skinny little beauty queen from Kentucky.

I'd made the Ceannfort weep.

Chapter Thirty-Two

Home is where the heart is.

~Grandma Sugar

The day was warm for early spring in Bowling Green. It had been months since I heard any word from Michael and once again I tried to act like everything was just fine and dandy for the sake of everyone around me and for my own sanity.

I wore a short yellow sundress and let my hair hang loose. It nearly reached my waist now. I loved the weight of it, the way it felt on my back. As I enjoyed that sensation, I remembered how Michael used to stare at it, how he'd once said I looked like an angel when I wore it down, and my heart slammed to a stop in my chest.

This happened to me all the time. Something triggered a memory, and at first I'd be filled with joy, but then spiral downward in a sea of bittersweet moments. I clung to them, but they caused me pain.

I'd come home at the end of the semester in a daze. It didn't take long for my daddy to pull me into his study, plop me onto one of the leather chairs near the fireplace, and insist I tell him what the Sam Hill was going on. At first, I didn't know where to start, but once I started talking, the floodgates opened and I told him about Michael and the Travellers and the Moktar.

Everything. Maybe even more than he needed to know, but as soon as I told him why my mother had sacrificed herself, it looked as if a heavy weight had been lifted from his shoulders.

“Dear lord,” he said softly. “She didn’t desert us. She died protecting us.”

I patted his hand. “The best way she knew how.”

After that, things changed at home. He talked about her more. Long hidden photographs appeared on the walls and the mantel. The stern lines around his mouth softened, and a new light glimmered in his eyes.

I got through each day as best I could, but the not knowing was the hard part. I had well and truly been exiled by the gypsies. My calls went unanswered. They didn’t respond to my texts. I had no idea when the Gypsy High Council planned to meet, or when my fate would be decided. The only thing that kept me going was Michael’s promise he would find a way to be with me. That was all I had to hold onto.

My phone rang just as I walked onto campus. I pulled it out of my backpack, my pulse quickening when I saw the number.

“Michael.”

“Hello, beautiful girl.”

I hadn’t heard his voice in months. I closed my eyes for just a second, letting the sound slide over me like a soothing balm.

“I have missed you,” I said. “So much.”

“I missed you every moment of every day since we’ve been apart. I love you, Emerson.”

I made a sound halfway between a laugh and a sob. “I love you, too, Michael. More than anything.”

“You look lovely in that little dress.”

My sundress *was* pretty cute. I glanced down to admire it and then froze. "How do you know what my dress looks like?"

"Because I'm standing right behind you."

I turned around so fast I nearly lost my balance and fell over, my backpack sliding off my shoulder. My eyes scanned the brick sidewalk, and the lawn with its shady trees, and the students milling about, but I couldn't see him. I started to think this was some kind of terrible joke when Michael stepped out from behind one of the trees.

I utilized a Traveller skill I didn't know I had and leaped to him without even thinking about it. I saw him and wanted to be next to him more than I'd ever wanted anything in my whole life. When I jumped into his arms, I nearly knocked him over.

We clung to each other, holding on for dear life. His face was in my neck, and when he spoke, his words were muffled.

"I thought I was dying. Nothing was right without you. I couldn't even seem to breathe properly without you."

"Me, too, Michael. Me, too." For the first time in months, I felt alive again.

I put my hands on his face and kissed him. I kissed his cheeks and his eyelids with their long, sooty eyelashes. When my mouth found his, once again the magic happened, like we were the only people in the whole world.

Michael pulled away gently, resting his forehead against mine. I knew he felt it, too. The completeness of it. The rightness. Then he scowled.

"Did you just leap in a public place?"

I nodded, looking around. No one seemed particularly interested, so I could only assume they hadn't noticed. "I think I did. Walking was too slow."

"Women cannot leap," he said very sternly. "It's too dangerous."

"Shut up and kiss me some more."

Michael smiled a slow sexy smile that made everything inside of me clench and tighten before he complied. By the time he was done, I could barely stand.

"How long can you stay?"

He pulled me over to a bench to sit down, and I climbed onto his lap. Even sitting next to him on the bench felt too far away. He wrapped his arms around my waist and pulled me close.

"Thanks to a little intervention on the part of your father, I've been accepted into the doctorate program here."

"My father?"

Michael nodded. "He contacted me. We had a very nice long chat in which I assured him I had only the best of intentions as far as you were concerned, and he set the wheels in motion."

I suffered what I can only assume was a case of temporary paralysis brought on by shock and absolute joy. It took a few minutes before I could form a coherent sentence.

"But what about my exile?"

A shadow passed over his eyes, but vanished before I could figure out what it meant. "The Gypsy High Council met last week. They voted unanimously to reinstate you as an upstanding member of the Traveller community, and they changed the law as well.

Women can fight whomever and whenever they damned well please."

"Really?"

"My father is convinced…he's certain, actually…" He paused and cleared his throat. "He thinks you are more than just an ordinary Traveller."

I stared at him, nonplussed. "What?"

He rubbed a hand over his head. It took him a few minutes to respond, and when he did his cheeks reddened with embarrassment. "My father and several members of the council believe you are the reincarnation of the Scáthach, a legendary warrior goddess who will rid the world of the Moktar scourge forever."

"Oh, golly."

"Yes. It's ludicrous, but it was enough to convince the high council you were well worth protecting. My father used it as the bargaining chip to allow me to come here. A stroke of brilliance, actually."

"I always thought I was a goddess." He rolled his eyes, and I laughed. "No. Really. I'm very good at giving commands."

"Well, we know *that* to be true."

"What of the other Travellers? What happened to Monroe?"

"He was given a punishment perfect for his crime. He'll spend the rest of his days locked in one of those cells in the Moktar dungeon. He'll never again see the light of day, and he'll die in the worst way possible for any gypsy. Trapped inside a cage."

"He deserves it."

"That he does." His voice carried the weight of sadness in it. Being betrayed by Monroe had cut him deep.

"And Leo?"

He chuckled. "Well, getting Patrick's blood turned out to be a good thing. The transfusion cured his addiction."

I looked up at him in surprise. "It did?"

He nodded. "He's fine now, and basically just another average, run-of-the-mill, half Traveller, half Moktar hybrid."

"I'm happy for him."

"As am I. He isn't such a bad bloke once you get to know him."

I snuggled even closer. "I can't believe you're actually here."

"I would have come eventually no matter what the high council decided, but I didn't want to muddle things up. I was afraid if I did you'd never see your grandparents or any of the other Travellers again."

He kissed me, and the sweet intensity of it made me burst into tears once again. He brushed my tears away softly.

"Emerson, my love, you've done nothing but blubber since the moment you saw me."

I sniffed. "You cried, too. In York. When you said goodbye."

"That I did."

I sighed against his chest. "I know you're sick of hearing about him, but Sun Tzu was right once again. He said, 'Victory is reserved for those who are willing to pay its price.' "

"The price I paid was great indeed. I spent months without you. It hurt so much it was almost unbearable, and I realized something. We Travellers say we journey all our lives to find the missing halves of our hearts. Well, you aren't just the missing half of my heart. You're the whole bloody thing."

I blinked. That was possibly the most romantic thing I'd ever heard in my entire life. "Your whole heart?"

He looked straight at me, and I saw the truth in his eyes. "You're all I've ever hoped for, all I've ever dreamed of, and you have to know that, Emerson."

"I love you, Michael Nightingale."

He brushed a lock of hair behind my ear with one of his big, gentle hands. "As long as I live and breathe, I'll never leave your side again. I love you, too, Emerson Jane Shaw."

I kissed his sweet lips, his strong chin, and his perfectly arrogant nose. I kissed him until his breathing was unsteady and then giggled at the expression on his face. I was holding the Ceannfort, the legendary warrior, the leader of the Traveller people, in my arms, and I had just kissed him senseless. And no matter what I was, Traveller or Dweller or beauty queen, I knew one thing for certain.

I was his.

A word about the author…

Abigail Drake writes paranormal and contemporary romances with humorous and magical elements. Abigail lives in Beaver, PA with her husband, three sons, a puppy named Capone, and a very well used espresso machine.

www.abigaildrake.com

https://www.facebook.com/abigaildrakewriter.